THE BANKER'S BOX

**BY
B. R. BENTLEY**

 FriesenPress

Suite 300 - 990 Fort St
Victoria, BC, V8V 3K2
Canada

www.friesenpress.com

Copyright © 2019 by B.R. Bentley
First Edition — 2019

All rights reserved.

This book is a work of fiction. Any references to historical events, real people, real objects or real places are used fictitiously. Other names, characters, places, objects and events are products of the author's imagination, and any resemblance to actual objects, events, places or persons, living or dead, is entirely coincidental.

All rights reserved, including the right to reproduce this book or portions thereof in any form whatsoever.

Editor – Katie Heffring

ISBN
978-1-5255-4859-8 (Hardcover)
978-1-5255-4860-4 (Paperback)
978-1-5255-4861-1 (eBook)

1. FICTION, MYSTERY & DETECTIVE, INTERNATIONAL MYSTERY & CRIME

Distributed to the trade by The Ingram Book Company

OTHER NOVELS BY B.R. BENTLEY

The Cross

"The true story is so extraordinary it hardly needs much additional dramatization. A fast-paced thriller that's difficult to put down."
—*Kirkus Reviews*

"*The Cross* is a skillfully crafted enjoyable novel. Based on real events in Bermuda and written in the form of a growing literary jigsaw puzzle..."
—*The Cape Times*

The Bermuda Key

"A suspenseful thriller that weaves together journalistic research and fictional embellishments in a tale of a stolen religious artifact."
—*Kirkus Reviews*

"A perfect holiday read..."
—*The Cape Times*

www.brbentley.com

IN MEMORIAM

Mark Conrad Spires
June 8, 1952 – December 25, 2018

ACKNOWLEDGEMENTS

Midge, as always.
Dylan, our most valuable player.
Phoenix, on his arrival—July 5, 2017.
Friends and family for their endless support and encouragement.
Panda, without whom this novel would
have been written in half the time.

B.R. Bentley
Nanoose Bay, 2019

CHARACTERS

(In Alphabetical Order)

Andre Malherbe, captain of MV *Ubekamanzi*, Connie's son

Bo "Bobbie" Ng, John Ng's wife

Charles Crofut QC, solicitor general of British Columbia

Christopher "Chris" Broughton, security department manager of East Coast Bank

Connie Malherbe, Neil Mohle's sister

Damian Slater, president and CEO of Woodstock Marine

Dana Holmes, premier of British Columbia

Daniel "Dan" Fortin, VP and corporate secretary of Woodstock Marine

David Gibson, investment banker

DG, director general of CSIS

Dong Lai, personal assistant to Quon Jin Hu

Donna Gray, executive assistant to Hayden Jones

Drew Jamieson, biker gang member and RCMP undercover agent

Garrett and Griffin Evans, identical twins, biker gang members

Hayden Jones, intelligence officer, Canadian Security Intelligence Service (CSIS)

Hugh Ruff, chief fundraiser and strategist

Jack Bowie, RCMP inspector, Serious Crime Unit

James Lee, SVP Business Development of Woodstock Marine

Jannie Malherbe, Connie's husband, Stellenbosch farmer

Josh Small, RCMP corporal and dog handler

Jun "John" Ng, president of Monger Capital

Kate Harrington, RCMP sergeant, Serious Crime Unit

Kobus Koch, chief officer of MV *Ubekamanzi*

Larry "Scrubber" Barker, biker gang member

Liam Riley, Chris Broughton's hacker contact

Lian "Kitty" Lee, James Lee's wife

Liz Elliot, credit officer at East Coast Bank

Lori Chan, Vivian Mohle's sister

Malcolm O'Malley, senior vice-president of East Coast Bank

Mark van Aswegan, provider of Neil's fake passport

Marie Bergeron, member of the B.C. legislative assembly

Michael Burt, investment banker

Neil Mohle, vice-president of East Coast Bank

Nolan Kulla, retired RCMP officer and field contact for Drew Jamieson

Oscar Bott, defense lawyer

Quon Jin Hu, "Komodo", billionaire gang boss and Kitty Lee's father

Philip Mohle, Neil's brother

P.K. Chin, John Ng's replacement at Monger Capital

Rachel Burton, legislative assistant to the premier of British Columbia

Rick "Vegas" Kolnick, biker gang leader

Sonja Gous, Neil Mohle's daughter

Vivian Mohle, Neil Mohle's wife

Willy Sands, drug dealer

PROLOGUE

Hayden

They were both a little drunk. The lunch had lasted until three, and after the rest of the staff had left for an early start to the long weekend, they had stayed behind and enjoyed a couple more leisurely drinks sitting on the sun-drenched outside patio of the restaurant. When they finally shared a cab back to the legislature buildings and walked somewhat unsteadily through the long silent corridors to her office, they found it empty.

"Looks like the help has all gone," he said, pointing to the vacant desks outside her office as he turned to leave. "Make sure you get a ride home; driving is probably not a good option."

"Thanks, Jones," she replied. "You're a good friend. Enjoy the rest of the evening." She leaned forward as if to kiss his cheek, but twisting her neck at the last second, delivered a slow, soft, wet kiss full on his mouth.

As romantic movie kisses went, it would probably have ended on the cutting room floor. In reality, the kiss pushed every button he had, his response exacerbated by the heat radiating through her clothes as she squeezed him tightly before stepping back, the faint glimmer of a smile curling the edges of her mouth.

"Oh . . . oh. Looks like someone woke up," she said, the wide smile now fully in evidence.

Hayden stepped back, his arousal clearly on display through the thin fabric of his pants.

"Sorry," he said embarrassed.

"It's okay," she said, moving forward again, and reaching down, she rubbed him gently through the soft material of his suit.

Lust overriding every instinct to the contrary, he pulled her tightly against him. "I'd better go," he said.

"If you must," she whispered, her face buried in his neck. Then, with a final long squeeze, she stepped away. He stumbled backwards toward the door while she stood motionless and smiling. "Come again anytime," she said.

Hayden hurried down the corridor toward the restrooms. He couldn't walk around the building like this. Every nerve in his body was vibrating like a tuning fork.

"Hayden?" A woman's distant voice echoed from the far end of an intersecting corridor as he pushed open the restroom door.

Ignoring the call, he looked at the row of empty cubicles. Thank God, the place was empty. Walking awkwardly to the stall furthest from the entrance, he closed and locked the door with relief.

CHAPTER 1

Rachel

The "what" was easy. Hayden Jones, the newly appointed special advisor to the premier of British Columbia, was definitely screwing someone on staff. It was who, when and where that was proving difficult to uncover.

Rachel Burton, legislative assistant to the premier of B.C., glared at her computer monitor, her knees pressed tightly together. Years of pent-up frustration surged through her fingers as she pounded the keyboard, her anger rising with each brief twitch of the cursor across the screen. Why not her? Just once, why not her? She could barely remember her last relationship. Well, this time, it would be different; this time, he wasn't going to get away with it. She was determined to find out who, and when she did, watch out. She'd find a way to leak it out, and then the crap would really hit the fan.

Her unrequited fixation with Hayden Jones had been simmering ever since they both worked for the ECB, or the East Coast Bank as it was known back then, and flared up again several months earlier when he walked into the office for his interview with Premier Dana Holmes. Hayden had barely noticed her at ECB, seemingly totally preoccupied with one of her more outgoing colleagues, and left abruptly about a year after she joined. Now, without warning, here he was again, and she was a mess.

This time though he'd also have to contend with the premier, she of brilliant smile and sky-blue eyes. Little were her unsuspecting constituents aware of the razor-sharp teeth and iron-will hidden behind that sparkling exterior. Charming to a fault, she'd flay you alive if crossed, and that was what she'd do to whoever was involved with Hayden. She'd never allow an office relationship to jeopardize her political agenda, however slight the possibility, and Rachel planned to keep her fully informed.

Forcing herself to focus, Rachel re-read her e-mail to the head of security. She couldn't afford a misstep at this stage. There was no upside in alerting the whole administration until she was sure of her ground. Asking to see the security records for the previous several weeks was the easy part. Having a plausible reason that wouldn't come back to haunt her was proving far more challenging.

"Everything okay, Rachel? You're pounding that keyboard like an old typewriter."

Startled, Rachel looked up from her screen to see the premier emerge from her office. "Sorry, Premier Holmes. Frustrating constituent call." Rachel pointed to the telephone and simultaneously closed her e-mail. "Taking it out on my computer."

Dana smiled. "How about we stick to Dana in private, or just Premier, if you must. You've been here for quite a while now and the formality really isn't necessary when we're not in public. Speaking of which, can you track down Jones for me? I need to go over some announcements with him. Besides he's good eye candy, and if nothing else, that should cheer you up." As she finished speaking, Dana immediately turned and walked back to her office.

Blushing, Rachel stared at the premier's receding figure. *At least she didn't look back and see me like this*, Rachel thought. *I need to get out of here.* Pushing back her chair, she rose and hurried from the room in search of Hayden Jones.

#

"Morning, Rachel."

"Hi, Donna. Is Hayden around? The premier's looking for him."

"Afraid not. He left early this morning for Kitimat. He wanted to check the place out before Dana and the rest of the gang arrive tomorrow. He'll probably call in sometime later today. Want me to contact him? Or wait until he calls and then give him the message?"

As she considered her reply, Rachel marvelled at Donna's easy familiarity, right down to the use of the premier's first name. Why couldn't she be more like that? Perhaps that was it. If she were more casual maybe, just maybe, Hayden would pay more attention to her. Well, it was worth a try, but in the meantime, she would contact him herself. No point in missing an opportunity.

"Don't worry about it," Rachel said. "I'll check with the premier and follow up after that. Maybe she can just e-mail him with whatever it is she wants."

"Works for me," Donna replied. "I've got plenty to do. By the way, I like your blouse. Dark blue suits you, goes well with your hair and really makes your eyes stand out. I never even realized they were blue. You should wear it more often."

Flustered by the unexpected compliment, Rachel barely managed to mutter "thanks" before walking quickly away.

Heading back to her office, Rachel reflected on Donna's comments. Perhaps she needed a makeover, something to make Hayden sit up and take notice? Red and blue. She'd better remember to wear it more often. Red hair could be such a pain. *Except naked*, she thought smiling. Then, as any of her few but infatuated former lovers could attest, its relative rarity was a decided plus.

#

"You look happy. Looks like the eye candy worked."

Surprised to find Dana Holmes standing alongside her desk on her return, Rachel blurted out, "Oh, no, Premier. Hayden wasn't in."

Then, fearing that the reply left her true feelings exposed, she quickly added, "His assistant said he left early this morning for Kitimat. I was just about to try to contact him there for you."

"Okay, let me know when you track him down. I'd like to talk to him sooner rather than later. Oh, and two other things: I've left some documents on your desk for shredding, and get me Hugh Ruff on the phone, will you? Apparently, he has a donor request he needs to discuss. I only hope it's not another dinner; my hips can't take it."

Who does she think she's fooling? Mid-forties and she looks like that. Rachel thought as she watched Dana's near-perfect figure move gracefully away. She reached for the telephone, her natural efficiency quickly displacing her earlier drifting thoughts. Dana was the third woman to hold the province's most prominent position, and Rachel wasn't going to let her down, not even for an instant. There were issues at stake here beyond politics. Irrespective of the subject, the premier's gender, like all her female predecessors, remained an easy target for any critic of the provincial policy. While publically Dana brushed off the attacks, Rachel knew that in private, she seethed. In any subsequent meetings with her staff, she rarely left any doubt that through their collective behaviour, she expected them to behave in a manner that would forever change the assumption that women and leadership didn't mix.

#

The premier's hastily scribbled note from her call with Hugh Ruff, the party's strategist and chief fundraiser, still bore the dried circular brown stain marks where her coffee cup had rested.

As the yellow notepaper fluttered to the floor, Rachel turned over the small pile of papers waiting to be shredded. As expected, there were matching stains on the back of the bottom document where the two papers had previously stuck together. Bending down, she picked up the yellow notepaper and looked at the premier's scribbles.

Significant party donor. LNG investment. Ng. Can we help? Nineteen possible projects. Kitimat preferred. HR will call bank. Toronto head office, not local.

Rachel wondered what "Ng" stood for—no good? She thought she understood the rest, and with nineteen liquefied natural gas export proposals currently underway in British Columbia, it wouldn't be hard to find a suitable investment for this donor, even if whatever they had discussed so far was no good. She looked at the note for several more seconds, then, assuming it too needed shredding, slid it along with the remaining pile into the waiting teeth of the sleek silver and black high-speed machine alongside her desk.

CHAPTER 2

Hayden

Kitimat. Hayden Jones wasn't entirely sure what image came to mind when he first heard the name, but it wasn't this. *Why the hell were these projects always in some remote outpost?* The bear they had seen alongside the road as they drove from the Terrace airport was both rare and an unexpected bonus, but, in reality, he could see bears as he travelled from Vancouver to Whistler for a weekend of skiing. Not Kermode bears admittedly, but bears nonetheless. Moreover, Whistler had skiing, nightlife, women and booze, and if first impressions were anything to go by, it was only the last that would be of any comfort while he was here.

"You must be lucky, mister," his driver said. "Don't usually see spirit bears at this time of year and sometimes not at all. I didn't see any last year, and I drive this road all the time. Maybe it's an omen."

"An omen?" Hayden asked.

"Legend says, they're here to remind us of the ice age. You're not one of those people messing with the climate, are you, mister?"

"No." Hayden's unintentionally terse reply immediately discouraged any further conversation on the topic.

They continued in uncomfortable silence, the large black Cadillac Escalade easily handling the fifty-four-kilometre journey into town along Highway 37. Hayden realized he wasn't dressed for the place either. His fifteen-hundred-dollar suit and Italian hand-made shoes just wouldn't cut it. He looked at the driver; add a couple of days stubble to his face and, together with his various items of mismatched clothing, the man could easily be mistaken for yet another homeless inhabitant of Vancouver's city streets.

It wasn't that Hayden was vain, and there was nothing special about his own appearance. Although his clothes were expensive, they were stylish without being trendy. Thirty-eight years old, well-groomed and reasonably good looking, he had no specifically dominant features. It was the sort of face that people had trouble describing only hours after first meeting him. Women found him attractive, he knew that, and with his athletic build and quiet manner, his appearance was non-threatening to most men. Intuitive and tenacious, it was his appearance, coupled with an easily-recognized intelligence that made him the perfect choice for his current role—a fact that had not gone unnoticed by his Canadian Security Intelligence Service supervisors.

Hayden knew he had better give the premier a heads-up before she arrived tomorrow. No point in the entire contingent looking out of place, and she could be a real bitch if things weren't perfect. All smiles for the cameras and crowds, but when the public was gone . . . look out. Not that he couldn't handle the outbursts; he'd known her for far too long to let those worry him. Anyway, he understood. For a woman to expose a softer side while holding down a major political position was almost always perceived as a weakness, same old double standard.

Settling back in the rich leather seat of the SUV, he reached inside his jacket for his mobile phone, his thoughts drifting back to how this had all started.

#

"Got another assignment for you, Jones. Time to dust off that résumé."

It was almost six months to the day since the director general of CSIS responsible for British Columbia had dropped a large brown file on his desk.

"Should be right up your alley. All about ships and money, and I think you'll enjoy your new boss." Smirking at Hayden, who hadn't moved or spoken, the DG continued, "Don't get used to it. Remember, ultimately, you still report to me. You'll be undercover except to her. It's the provincial government, so politics dictate that she has to know. For everyone else, it's critical you remain undercover. Your résumé will have to fit the role, though. We need you as close to her inner circle as you can get. Read the file and then make any modifications to your résumé you feel are necessary. We'll cover off any background gaps as needed. Your 'interview' is on Tuesday." With a blatantly fake smile, the DG turned and left the room.

As instructed, Hayden read the file. The DG was correct; it was right up his alley. Working for CSIS ever since his last year of undergraduate studies in finance, he had flourished in a variety of minor surveillance assignments while simultaneously completing his post-graduate law degree. Later, as a fully-fledged intelligence officer, he successfully conducted business-related assignments in both Canada and abroad, the majority of these in banking or energy transportation-related fields. Absent a few gap years, his non-CSIS résumé could almost stand on its own merits.

Hayden knew that most Canadians remained blissfully unaware of the powers of their intelligence service and that there was no restriction on where CSIS could collect information relating to possible threats to the security of Canada, domestically or internationally. The agency also drew a clear distinction between security intelligence and foreign intelligence. While the former covered national security threats, like terrorism or espionage, the latter involved the collection of information relating to the political or economic activities of foreign entities or states. Most of this foreign intelligence was collected by people like himself working undercover within a wide variety of Canadian companies while reporting regularly to their supervisors in Ottawa.

This was, however, the first time Hayden had been placed within a Canadian government office, a posting that unlike most others, required at least the premier of B.C.'s knowledge of his CSIS association. To all others, he was just another opportunistic political appointee. Even then, while knowing whom he worked for and what he was engaged in, even the premier was unaware that his activities in this particular instance specifically targeted illegal Chinese monetary operations throughout Canada.

As expected, the "interview" had gone smoothly. Hayden smiled remembering the premier's first words after agreeing to his new position.

"Promise me," she had said when they were alone, "not a word to anyone about my knowing you while you were at university. This place is rife with paranoia, and although we both know it doesn't make any difference now, anytime I side with you on any issue, tongues will start wagging. Far better that you remain just another member of staff, okay? Besides," she had added before he could say anything, "they're probably not going to like you much anyway. No political background, seemingly loose LNG responsibilities and direct access to the ear of the premier—think you can handle that?"

Nodding, Hayden had reached over the desk to shake her outstretched hand. Most of his assignments started the same way. Neither had mentioned it since.

#

Relaxing at last, Hayden scrolled through the directory on his mobile until he saw his assistant's name and pressed the call button. After two short rings, she answered.

"You have reached the office of Donna Gray, executive assistant to the premier's special advisor, Hayden Jones Esquire. How may I help you?"

"Jeez, Donna, you don't really answer the phone like that, do you?"

Attractive, efficient and, although only in her mid-twenties, confident and frequently irreverent, Donna's reply continued in the same vein. "Of course not, dummy. I saw it was you on the display. What's up? I thought you were going to Kitimat."

"I was. I mean, I am. I'm in the car heading into town as we speak, but I need you to give the premier a message."

"Sure, she hasn't left her office yet. Her prissy assistant was just here looking for you. What do you want me to tell her?"

"Tell her to dress down. The more local she can look, the better."

"That bad, huh?"

"Worse."

"Ok, consider it done. Anything else?"

"Yeah, give Rachel a break. She's actually quite pleasant once you get to know her. I worked with her briefly years ago at ECB. She's just sometimes a bit starchy."

"Not today, she's not. You'd eat your heart out if you saw her now, but okay, I'll lighten up. I'd never say anything directly to her anyway."

"I know, but thanks. Just looking out for the underdog." Hayden laughed aloud as he heard Donna snort in disbelief while hanging up the phone. Hierarchical niceties were not high on her list of priorities—even if he was her boss.

Settling back once again in the rich, black leather seat of the rented SUV, he reflected on the DG's choice of this particular location for his investigation. The hotbed for Chinese immigration ever since the removal of the Canadian government's restrictive immigration policies, British Columbia's Chinese population had grown to over four hundred thousand and now comprised more than ten percent of the province's total population. With this growth, fuelled by China's enormous, wealthy but restrictive communist economy, came money—great globs of money, legal and illegal alike. Little demonstrated the sudden influx, or the source, better than Vancouver's skyrocketing real estate prices over the past several years, an event that ultimately resulted in the implementation of an offshore buyer's tax to curb what was perceived as predominantly non-resident Asian financial speculation.

Dana Holmes and her colleagues were now stuck in a difficult situation. Desperate for any means to stimulate the economy and provide well-paying jobs for B.C.'s residents, they were also well aware of the resultant dangers encountered by their predecessors when an inflow of funds went unchecked. LNG development provided a means of satisfying both objectives and allowing them to succeed where their predecessors had failed.

From the DG's perspective, the "dirty" money routes established during Vancouver's real estate boom were unlikely to come to a sudden stop. More probable was the deviation of this illegal money supply into other avenues as the property opportunities dwindled under increased tax and regulatory reporting. Hayden's stated assignment was simple: watch for opportunities and follow the money. Doing it without alerting suspicion was another matter entirely. His cover relied in part on using his legitimate financial background in helping to deal with the nineteen LNG applications pending various government approvals already on the table. He had his work cut out for him in fulfilling his undercover identity responsibilities even without his CSIS assignment.

Despite the number of pending proposals, the LNG outlook had become increasingly bleak, with a global supply glut and tumbling prices for the commodity. From Hayden's perspective, there were now only four serious contenders to export liquefied natural gas from B.C.: one small project near Squamish and three major projects, two at separate locations near Prince Rupert and another at the site of tomorrow's visit, just outside Kitimat. Progress on each of these had fluctuated along with their changing views of the global LNG market and delays by the federal government's environmental agency. In the meantime, Dana's provincial government continued to cling to the hope that any one of the major LNG export projects, each of which carried a budget of several billion dollars, would go ahead.

As Dana had noted in a recent speech, "these delays are not peculiar to B.C. The collapse of oil and gas prices, coupled with a LNG supply glut and resistance from various local interest groups have paralyzed new liquefaction projects everywhere."

Enough contemplation, Hayden decided. He could only do so much. He would start with the most likely four and drill down on those. While he was here, he'd also call the banker for the Kitimat deal and see how this one was coming along, and who was funding it.

What had Donna said the banker's name was again? Oh, yes, Mohle. Like the burrowing kind, but with an "h".

CHAPTER 3

Neil

Neil Mohle had worked for ECB for thirty years after arriving in Canada from his native South Africa. Fifty-five years old and the son of an English mother and German father, he was fluent in English, German and Afrikaans, with a passable knowledge of Dutch. Unlike his forebears, who almost always seemed to be well over six-feet tall and blunt to a fault, he was an engaging, dapper man, who, at five feet nine inches, couldn't have weighed more than one hundred and fifty pounds soaking wet. Always impeccably attired, his eclectically stylish clothing was highlighted by his bright blue eyes and frequently permed blond hair, the latter expertly maintained by his hairstylist and glamorous wife, Vivian. Fifteen years Neil's junior, at five foot six and a similar slight build to her husband, they made an attractive couple, with Vivian's straight jet-black hair and brown eyes providing a stark contrast to Neil's blond good looks. Born in mainland China, Vivian spoke both English and Mandarin. There were very few multicultural social functions they attended where their linguistic skills failed to impress.

Stepping from the elevator on the twenty-first floor of the ECB's downtown Vancouver office, Neil walked directly through the sterile rows of dark wood and fabric-partitioned cubicles of the bank's credit department. Carefully arranged, with the most senior members along the windows and the most junior in the middle, the department occupied almost an entire floor of the thirty-two-story office tower on Burrard Street. Inside each cubicle were identical long, low dark-burnished wooden filing cabinets set behind large matching dark-polished wooden desks. At each desk sat a single occupant, either male or female, in front of them a computer screen and keyboard flanked, in most cases, by a stack of brightly coloured files. In those few cubicles without files on the desk, a similar stack usually rested behind the occupant on top of the filing cabinet. Hardly a single item of a personal nature adorned the various workspaces. These were men and women with little need for frivolous adornments. These were precise, detailed employees who had already proven their decision-making abilities in a variety of lending positions within the bank and whose daily conversations now usually culminated with words like declined or approved. These employees made the final credit decisions of the British Columbia region of the bank.

Visitors were rare in the credit department, and Neil could sense the eyes staring at his back as he passed each cubicle heading directly for the corner occupant, whose cubicle boasted windows on two sides. It was home to the most senior credit officer, and a senior vice-president of the bank, Malcolm O'Malley.

"Morning, Mal."

Malcolm O'Malley looked up at the interruption. "Hi, Neil, what brings you downtown?"

"I wondered if my LNG application had reached you as yet, or whether it was still languishing in one of those colour-coded piles outside."

"You could have called."

Neil accepted the mild rebuke without rancour. Longevity in the bank had its privileges, and despite their differing levels of seniority, they were both part of the "old boy" network and enjoyed a cordial, if not close, relationship.

"I know, but I was downtown anyway and thought I'd brighten your day."

Malcolm smiled. "Good of you," he replied. "Actually your timing's not bad. It goes to the credit committee today. Bit beyond any of our local limits."

"Does that mean you've added your recommendation to the deal? Or do you have to send it forward even if you think it should be declined?"

"Given the size of the deal, we have to send it forward either way, with our recommendation either to approve or decline. Just between us, we've recommended approval but have a couple of caveats. I'll let you know as soon as its back."

"What sort of caveats? Anything I can tell my client now?"

"Afraid not. I've probably said more than I should have anyway. Keep it to yourself until you hear something formally."

"Okay, but what do you think? Will it fly?"

"Give me a break, will you. We shouldn't even be discussing it at this stage. Let me get the committee's response, and then I'll call you."

Knowing the credit department's well-publicized aversion to discussing applications that were "in progress" and recognizing from Malcolm's tone that he had pressed his questions as much as he could, Neil quickly switched tracks. "Okay, thanks. You going to the Canucks hockey game tonight?"

"I wish. You?"

"Yeah. Taking a couple of clients. We have club seats. So dinner and the game."

"Nice. Tough life in the trenches, isn't it?"

Neil smiled and stood. "I'll get out of your hair . . . what's left of it that is," he said.

"Bye, Neil," Malcolm replied, grinning. "Nice seeing you too."

Laughing, Neil turned and headed back to the elevators. Once again, he could sense several pairs of eyes following him as he walked.

#

"Who was that?"

Liz Elliot looked up from the document on her desk at the face of the newest member of the ECB credit department peering, like Kilroy, over the wall of her cubicle.

"Neil Mohle," she replied. "He's a VP in commercial banking. Different, isn't he?"

"I'll say. Did you see what he was wearing?"

"You mean, the dark green shoes to match his suit and the 'murse'? Nope, didn't notice." Liz smiled. "Don't let his clothes fool you. He's quite the ladies man."

"You've got to be kidding me."

"Not at all. Have you heard the rumour about the VP who tried to date the doctor after she had completed his last corporate medical exam?"

"You mean the one who got over-excited during his exam and then asked the poor locum doctor for a date? The rumour is that she was so intrigued by the size of whatever was under the towel he was wearing that she almost agreed."

"Right," Liz replied. "Well, that's him."

"Really? But he's quite small. Do you think the story's true?"

"Yes."

"Which part?"

"Both," Liz replied, remembering the awkward conversation with her very embarrassed and concerned physician friend when the rumour first surfaced before she looked back down at the pending credit application on her desk.

With a stuttered "oh", the face disappeared below the top of the partition.

#

Leaving the building, Neil headed for the offices of Woodstock Marine. *Better to get this over with now,* he thought. They had been pressing him all week for an answer to their Woodstock LNG credit request, and Damian Slater could be a real pain if things weren't going his way. Hopefully, he wouldn't have to see Damian and could deal directly with the finance team or James Lee. Despite James's primary responsibility being business development, he drifted between assisting Damian and coordinating interaction on any finance deal. From Neil's vantage point, it appeared that James was being groomed for an even more senior role in the parent company than the one he currently held. But, he enjoyed James, not that the pressure to deliver wasn't still there. James was just so much more civilized about the whole process.

Pulling out his mobile as he walked and realizing he had neither a direct line nor mobile number for James, he called the company's general number and asked to be put through to James Lee. After several rings, the disembodied voice of the Woodstock Marine voicemail service advised that James was away from the office and he would answer any message on his return.

There was a pause while Neil waited for the proverbial "beep" before he spoke. "James, Neil Mohle here. I've received an update on the Woodstock LNG credit application and thought I'd bring you up to speed. Can you give me a call when convenient for you? Office or mobile." Neil rattled off both numbers before terminating the call and walking back toward his own office.

CHAPTER 4

Damian

"Why is it that I always feel such a huge sense of relief when Damian leaves the room?" Michael Burt asked. "It's not as if we don't have other difficult clients."

"I think it's a release of the pent up anxiety that nothing went sideways during the meeting," David Gibson replied. "Much like balancing on the lip of a volcano and not falling in."

"You're probably right. If someone met him for the first time, his reputation alone would be enough to keep them on edge. What do you think of him, David? You meet with him as much as I do."

"I think he's arrogant, but the thing that really unsettles me, is how fast he can turn. You saw his reaction to your comment about Monger Capital. Charming and laughing one minute and then, when he disagrees with something as he did about Monger, the charm turns to menace. Actually, on second thought, I, like many others, think he's a prick. Highly intelligent, well-connected and successful, but a prick nonetheless."

"Tell me how you really feel," said Michael, bursting into laughter. "You've just confirmed my belief that the people in our business are rarely neutral on any topic. Dollars to doughnuts, I bet that because Damian can be so abrasive, he's probably got as many detractors as fans."

"Why did we meet in our offices?" David asked. "I thought he had some unwritten rule about making investment bankers come to his office just to keep them waiting and show them who's boss."

"He said he has a board meeting later this morning at some nearby hotel, although I'm sure that's not the real reason. As you heard, apparently none of his finance people were available due to other priorities, but that's probably all bullshit. For some reason or other, he didn't want anyone else in the company to know about this meeting. Playing things very close to the chest on this one is Damian."

"I think you're right. What's the real story on Monger Capital, though? I don't know anything about them other than what you told Damian this morning, and you sounded guarded."

"I wasn't trying to be cagey; I just don't know that much about them. I don't mean all the local guys, most of those I know, except John Ng, who heads up the office, that is." Michael smiled. "I do know he's got a pretty slutty wife though. They were at the fundraiser last Friday, and she looked like a cross between a hooker and one of those 'real housewives' on TV. It's the money behind Monger that puzzles me. Usually, we have a fair idea who the major investors are behind most of the firms in the city, but not Monger. That shop is a clam when it comes to their investors."

"So who approached whom? I missed that part of your discussion," said David.

"According to Damian, Monger's name had come up as a potential investor in LNG, and he wanted to know more about them even though he doesn't think Woodstock LNG needs more equity at this time. Because we're his regular investment banking advisors, he thought he'd see what, if anything, we knew about them."

"Want me to do some digging?" David asked.

"No, let's leave it for now. Damian said he'd let us know if he wanted to know more. No point in possibly stirring up a hornet's nest for no reason at all."

#

Hurrying to the elegant Vancouver hotel for his early morning breakfast with the board, Damian Slater, president and chief executive officer of Woodstock Marine, was still stewing over Michael Burt's unfavourable opinion of Monger Capital. Armed with a carefully cultivated network of contacts, Damian rarely missed an opportunity, and it came as no surprise to him when, several days earlier, through a mutual well-placed contact, he had received a request for a quiet drink with Hugh Ruff, the premier's chief fundraiser. Much to Damian's delight, Ruff was blunt to a fault. He left the meeting with a clear understanding that not only would the provincial government be seeking a local equity component of at least ten percent in any LNG deal they approved, Ruff also just happened to be aware of an investment group to whom the government was favourably disposed and who were interested in investing in LNG. Given the status of Woodstock's LNG deal as part of the Kitimat bid, which the government badly wanted to succeed, Hugh wanted to give Damian an early warning and perhaps an edge in getting their ducks in a row.

Not willing to reveal his source and sensing yet another opportunity to be ahead of the game, even among his own colleagues, Damian had decided to make some enquiries himself. That Michael did not know much about Monger Capital was somewhat troubling, but at the end of the day, if Monger's investment swung the deal, he wasn't going to let nerves stand between him and a bag of money.

Damian was still waiting for the traffic lights to change at the busy corner of Dunsmuir and Burrard streets when Neil Mohle exited the ECB building from the opposite side of the intersection. He couldn't make up his mind about the banker. What was it with the poncy clothing? What kind of banker dressed like that anyway? In his experience, bankers, besides the odd bow-tied intellectual, were generally a conservative lot, at least in their business attire. He should know; he'd been one himself.

In a rare moment of self-reflection, Damian recalled how, for a brief time after graduating with an MBA from one of the most prestigious

Ivy League universities in the United States, he had sported a bow tie. A habit he had maintained as he commenced his career as an investment banker in London. However, that was it as far as eccentric clothing went, his one and only attempt at deviating from the business norm. But, all that was history now. After several years in the UK, he'd left banking to claw his way up the corporate ladder back in the States. A decision that ultimately culminated in his current role although still only in his forties, as head of one of the world's largest shipping companies—Woodstock Marine.

His childhood had been difficult. His American mother and English father divorced just before his tenth birthday, and his mother left the house only a matter of days later. Within a year, his father enrolled him in boarding school because, apparently, full-time parenthood was too difficult after the divorce. Although Damian remained in contact with his mother, it proved to be no substitute for her regular presence.

Forced to fend for himself at his prestigious private school, Damian matured quickly, becoming something of a loner and often unpopular because of his intolerance of what he considered his peers' immature behaviour. Along with the unpopular streak, he also developed a contemptuous attitude to women; something his father put down to his mother having left home while he was still young.

A newspaper report, published as Damian rapidly ascended the corporate ladder, quoted his father as once saying, "I always thought when he was young, he was distinctly anti-women although his wife now tells me he has more female friends than male. Perhaps women see a different side to him than men do. He's an abrasive leader, which most people don't like, and makes it clear when he thinks they are perfect fools. That's certainly not how I taught him to make friends and influence people."

Damian initially defended himself. Then, after a while and almost if by so doing he would demean himself, provided the one and only response he subsequently ever made when asked to comment on his father's remarks: "humility is for saints."

CHAPTER 5

James

Breakfast. One of the few benefits of board meetings, thought James Lee, Woodstock Marine's senior vice-president of business development, as he walked into the opulent hotel dining area. Ahead of him, one other prospective diner waited to be seated. Stopping directly behind the waiting figure, he spoke. "Bonjour, Dan. Comment ça va? Okay if I join you?"

Daniel Fortin, Woodstock Marine's aging vice-president and corporate secretary, turned and looked at James. "Ça va, James. Sure, not eating with the big boys this morning?" Dan's smile took any sting out of his words.

James knew Dan usually ate alone at these events, his position insufficient to render him a fully-fledged member of either the senior executive team or the board. All of the other attendees, even contracted professional advisors, here by specific invitation, were treated, albeit temporarily, as equals, but not Dan. Damian's dismissive attitude ensured Dan remained in his place, and everyone else, to a greater or lesser degree, simply followed suit. It was also clear to James, who knew Dan better than most others in the company, that it wouldn't take much for him to pack up and head back to his native Montreal. After many years in his current role, the process operated like a well-oiled machine; but James knew they'd miss him if he left. For a while anyway, until some other poor soul took over Dan's underappreciated niche. He and Dan had worked together on various projects, ever since James joined the company almost eight years earlier. These shared experiences, along with a mutual respect for each other's abilities, had fostered a comfortable friendship despite their divergent corporate paths. Undeniably bright and politically astute, James had been fast-tracked to his current position, while Dan, stubborn and independent, remained fixed in the same role he had held when James first joined. As the youngest member of the senior executive team, James was also widely acknowledged as the company's most likely future president.

"I need a break," James replied. "We had a board dinner last night, and it went late. I'd rather catch up on what's new in your world instead."

Dan expression soured briefly at the mention of the dinner. He was about to speak when the maître d' interrupted.

"Table for two, gentlemen?" he said and, without waiting for a reply, continued, "Follow me, please."

#

James followed behind Dan through the dining area to their designated table at a window with a spectacular view across the harbour to the North Shore Mountains. He'd seen Dan's expression change at the mention of yet another dinner he'd missed. Attempting to raise the issue with Damian several months earlier, James had been brushed aside with, "No, let's keep it to senior executives and board members only. I'm sure Dan understands we can't start making exceptions." Petty, of course, but that was business in the big leagues under Damian Slater.

Despite James's regard for his colleague, he wouldn't rock the boat again. One didn't push Damian into a corner and escape unscathed, even over something as innocuous as a dinner invitation. No, as far as that item was concerned, Dan was on his own. He would cope; he was both intelligent and resilient as hell, quietly marching to his own drummer. James wondered what really went on in Dan's head. Not that they didn't share confidences; deal details, corporate rumours, even personal information were all shared without fear of repercussion. Dan's real motivation was just hard to read.

Dan's next question interrupted James's musings. "How's Kitty?"

"Great, thanks."

"Still working in her family's business? I can't quite get used to the idea of her as an employee."

James laughed. "I wouldn't really call her an employee. It's a somewhat pampered position. With her parents living overseas, the local staff actually run the business, and Kitty has as much freedom as she wants to indulge her passion for the design side. I don't think she spends much time on the mechanics of importing and distribution. She even takes that scruffy little dog to work with her every day. Although, to be fair, I'm not sure what we'd do with it otherwise. It's the Asian princess thing, you know. Her parents don't seem at all concerned by how the business is really doing, as long as she's happy. I knew they were wealthy when I married her, but I think I underestimated quite how wealthy they must be. Her father's a bit older, in his early seventies, I think, and very traditional. Certainly not the kind of person you can sit down with and ask how much he's worth. Even Kitty doesn't seem sure when on the odd time I've pressed the question."

"Tough problem," said Dan, who looked as if he were trying hard not to laugh. "No offence meant," he said, "but sometimes it's hard to picture the two of you together. Despite your outward appearance, you're more Anglo-Canadian than me."

"Just don't tell my parents, will you. I'm meant to be the perfect Chinese child; at least when compared to my wing-nut sister that is. She's totally westernized."

Pausing briefly to order breakfast from the menus on the table, the two men continued their conversation while enjoying their morning coffee. Dan was busy extolling the virtues of Montreal's annual International Jazz Festival when Damian arrived at the table, still breathless after his brisk walk.

"Has the bank approved the deal?" he asked, interrupting without apology and looking directly at Dan.

"Morning, Damian," Dan replied. "Haven't heard yet."

Damian ignored the greeting. "What's the delay?" he asked.

"We don't know that there is any specific reason. The finance guys are just waiting for the bank to respond."

"How soon will we know? I need to tell the board."

"Probably not before the close of business tomorrow. Do you want to sit down?" Dan gestured to the empty chair.

"Let me know as soon as you find out," Damian said, turning and walking away without acknowledging the offered chair.

James watched the byplay without saying a word. The tense relationship between the two men continuing to intrigue him. Whether this was due to an unspoken mutual dislike or Dan's outwardly apparent indifference in not being "one of Damian's boys", James couldn't tell, but whatever it was, neither one seemed interested in bettering the relationship. Damian could be as abrasive as anyone and usually was when it came to Dan. Dan, for his part, seemed oblivious to Damian's moods and appeared to take a perverse delight in questioning any of Damian's missed social niceties, just like his morning greeting minutes earlier.

As Damian moved away, James spoke. "Has the finance group really not heard from the bank yet? Or are you just twisting his tail?"

"No, it's too early."

"Do they think we'll get the approval?"

"They're not sure. To make matters worse, the deal team says that there are weird noises coming from the government."

"Weird noises?"

"Some change in bid parameters. No details as yet."

"Do they have any idea who's behind it?"

"No, and that's the strange part. There's usually some indication of the major player behind that kind of pressure."

James looked across to where Damian had now joined the other members of the board. Jovial and charming, it seemed like he could throw that switch anytime he needed it. James knew that had he been alone, or with other members of Damian's inner circle, the reception at his breakfast table would have been significantly different. He had nothing to fear though, he was Damian's "blue-eyed boy", and if he chose to have breakfast with the corporate secretary rather than the rest of the group, that wouldn't upset Damian. If anything were mentioned, James would pass it off as being necessary to obtain information. That was something Damian would understand and appreciate. He looked back at Dan and changed the topic. "Perhaps you shouldn't take a stand every time you two interact."

"It's not every time," Dan replied. "It's just that he's so damned rude. I know that you think I purposely try to drive him crazy, and perhaps I sometimes do, but frankly, I'm too old and jaded to waste time trying to satisfy his ego. Plus, I'm not sure anyone can truly satisfy an ego that big."

James smiled. Dan was probably right. Damian didn't revise his position very often, and once he'd made up his mind, that was it. If he didn't see any benefit from fostering a relationship, he could be as mean and ugly as hell. In fact, if he had to guess, it was probably Dan's seamless relationships with almost everyone else up or down the corporate ladder that drove Damian crazy. It was a quirk of independence that Damian didn't like, particularly from people who worked for him.

The buzz of a mobile phone broke the brief silence.

"Need to get that?" Dan asked.

Removing his mobile from his pocket, James looked at the screen. "No," he replied. "I forwarded the office voicemail to my mobile and can't see who it's from. Anyway, breakfast first; I'll check it later. If it's important, they'll call my mobile direct."

CHAPTER 6

Neil

Neil Mohle looked around the Woodstock Marine conference room at the twelve empty large leather chairs, one at each end of the long table and five evenly spaced along each of the sides. Choosing the first seat was always tricky, particularly when he wasn't sure who, or how many, would be attending. Deciding that the senior Woodstock executive in attendance would probably take the head of the table, Neil chose the second seat along the side facing the door. His coffee, brought in by the same receptionist who had greeted him in the lobby, arrived several moments later and was placed on the small, circular black leather pad on the table in front of him.

He was not looking forward to the meeting. Unsuccessful in his efforts to reach James and provide the company with an early indication of how the application was unfolding before receiving the bank's formal response, he was about to deliver it "cold".

In reality, the approval that now lay in the folder alongside his coffee was substantially in line with his original proposal. The curveball carefully, albeit almost casually, buried in the wording of the final paragraph. Not only did the equity level in the deal have to be above a certain amount, but it also had to include a minimum of ten percent local ownership. This latter requirement arising from an, unannounced, pending government edict to support domestic Canadian investment in LNG. To avoid entering into a deal with a customer that would fail later, as not meeting the government bid parameters, the bank was making the local equity provision an up-front condition.

Neil had never seen or heard anything of this nature before. There was obviously plenty of government pressure here, even if he didn't yet understand the quid pro quo. He had pressed Malcolm O'Malley for more detail and argued the necessity of the requirement at some length, all to no avail. Well, he was here now and would deliver the news. He just hoped they wouldn't kill the messenger.

Neil was on his third sip of coffee when the Woodstock team entered the room. He had expected the usual finance team, but not both Damian Slater and James Lee. This was not going to be fun.

#

The painstaking review of the details in the bank's credit approval by the Woodstock finance team had been going on for almost an hour when Damian rose from his chair and all conversation stopped.

"Okay," he said, starting to pace around the room without taking his eyes off his VP Finance, "let's cut through the crap. You people can work out the rest of the fine points later. Do we have a deal or not?"

James interjected, "I don't like this additional equity aspect."

"Nor do I," Damian replied. "But that aside, how does the rest of the deal look?"

"It's fine," Woodstock Marine's VP Finance replied. "It's substantially in line with what we expected and put forward in our board memorandum."

Damian switched his attention to Neil. "So where did this change come from? The government, the bank or was this your idea?"

"Not from me, and while I can't be sure, I don't believe our regional group had any say in the matter either. It seems to have come from back east. I assume this must be some form of new government strategy to stimulate local industry."

"That's bull and you know it," Damian replied. Ignoring Neil's rapidly colouring face, he continued. "Politicians are not that charitable. This smacks of political graft. I wouldn't be at all surprised if it's some funding deal cooked up between the B.C. government and their federal counterparts. Somebody's getting rich off this. That's what happens when you have a bloody woman running things out here."

No one spoke. Then, in a typical Damian moment, he switched gears, the ugly aggressor becoming the charming co-conspirator.

"Look, Neil, I know it's not your fault, but this equity thing puts us in a bind, and we'll have to revert to the board. You and I both want our deal with ECB to go ahead, but we'll need a bit of time before we can sign the agreement. How long can you give us?"

The release of tension in the room was palpable, and Neil, who had worked his proverbial butt off putting the deal together in the first place, was as susceptible to the mood as everyone else.

"How about a week," he replied, knowing full well he'd have to face the wrath of his own credit department for leaving the deal open longer than the anticipated forty-eight hours, but he was not willing to lose the business over some last minute head office demand unless it was absolutely unavoidable.

"Fine. I'll leave you all to it then," Damian said before walking out of the room without another word.

Neil looked at James Lee for guidance, who leaned over and, with one hand on the table supporting his weight, shook Neil's hand with the other.

"Thanks, Neil," he said. "I'll let you and the finance team to sort out the details." With that, James too left the room.

When Neil left the offices of Woodstock Marine some forty minutes later, an e-mail notification of an urgent board teleconference was already in the secure board portal inbox of every member of Woodstock's board. There were only two agenda items: vessel financing for the Woodstock LNG project and Monger Capital's interest in investing in the deal. The e-mail closed with a brief sentence indicating that the material covering the items under discussion would be available on the board portal within twenty-four hours.

#

Sprawled across the corner of the dark green leather sofa in the living room of his Kitsilano home later that evening, his wife curled up alongside him, Neil Mohle chewed on a slice of pepperoni pizza while watching the early CBC evening news.

Muting the television during each of the ever-increasing batches of mindless advertisements, he recounted, in installments, his meeting with Damian Slater and James Lee earlier that day. Just before restoring the volume at the end of yet another advertisement, he concluded, "Quite frankly, I think Damian's overbearing and unnecessarily aggressive. James thinks this is how he gets results. I think it's way too confrontational; and while he may get away with it in his current role, at some point he'll run into someone with more power, or who just doesn't give a shit, and then all hell will break loose."

Vivian Mohle stared mindlessly at the television, saying nothing, her thoughts elsewhere. She'd heard similar frustrated ramblings from her husband before. As Neil finished speaking and restored the volume, she sighed and squeezed the inside of his thigh reassuringly. She was well aware of the surest way to restore Neil's bruised ego from yet another fractious client meeting.

CHAPTER 7

Damian

The three-pronged speakerphone, a bright orange logo at its centre, sat in the middle of Woodstock Marine's dark brown conference room table like some alien craft about to launch. Around the well-polished table, several members of the senior executive team sat quietly, either thumbing through the papers they had brought or staring expressionlessly into space. No conversation disturbed the awful "stand-by" music emanating from the phone.

Board conference calls always started the same way, as the group, seemingly oblivious to the music, prepared themselves for their respective presentations or any question that might arise. No one wanted to be the only executive without immediate access to the information the board needed. No one wanted to reply to a question with the dreaded, "I'll need to get back to you on that." As a result, the board was rarely faced with rendering an important decision in the absence of all the pertinent information. Today, though, was going to be one of those days.

#

Many of the attendees had been present in this same room the previous day at the meeting with Neil Mohle, the company's banker from ECB. Only Damian Slater and James Lee, however, had partaken in the subsequent telephone conversation with John Ng of Monger Capital.

Despite a momentary flash of guilt at keeping how he discovered Monger's possible interest in the deal from his protégé, Damian had successfully feigned both surprise and delight when John confirmed that the investors of private fund that he represented were interested in participating in Woodstock LNG's Kitimat project. While the ensuing discussion covered the majority of details on consummating the deal, the two Woodstock executives made little progress in their efforts to determine the identities of Monger Capital's major investors. Despite this, the discussions concluded with both parties agreeing to seek approval from their respective boards for the investment to go ahead. According to John, the signing needed to take place as quickly as possible, as Monger had several other deals under consideration.

"How were you so sure they'd be interested in investing?" James asked as he and Damian ended the call.

"I wasn't really," Damian lied, "just played it that way to sound confident about the deal."

The answer appeared to have worked, and James had not pressed the issue any further.

Now let's see how that works with the board, Damian thought.

#

"It's three o'clock. Shall we get started?" Dan Fortin asked, looking directly at Damian as he spoke.

"Go ahead," replied Damian.

"Good afternoon and welcome to the Woodstock Marine conference call. I need to do a quick roll call to make sure everyone is here." Hearing no objections, Dan read though the list of invited board members and received positive responses as he announced each name. He then looked around and named all of those present in the Woodstock conference room before turning the meeting over to Damian.

"Thanks, Dan, and thank you all for making yourselves available at such short notice. Although you are all familiar with the LNG process, for completeness, we need the board minutes to reflect a full discussion of the background to the current request. I'll try to keep it brief, and Dan will sanitize it as appropriate for the minutes.

"As you well know, shipping forms an integral part of the LNG supply chain. The pipeline companies deliver the natural gas to liquefaction plants located at, or near, an LNG terminal. There, they convert the gas into a liquid form, at roughly one six-hundredth of its gaseous volume, by cooling it to minus one hundred and sixty degrees Celsius. This renders it safe and economically efficient to transport in our LNG tankers, which, to put it crudely, essentially become very large floating thermos flasks. As far as we are concerned, the predominant environmental risk at that stage of the process is more likely to be from a leak of the ship's fuel supply rather than its cargo. Absent a catastrophic fire, any LNG leak would evaporate without damage to the surrounding area. Once delivered to the destination terminal, the liquefied gas is transported via pipelines to a regasification plant where it is converted back to its gaseous form before being distributed to the final customers.

"Okay, with that out of the way, and assuming no one has any objections, this brings me to a quick overview of the LNG climate in British Columbia before we discuss the specific agenda items."

Hearing no dissenting voice, Damian continued, "By way of deep background, the LNG industry has been around since 1912, with the world's first LNG vessel carrying cargo from Louisiana to the United Kingdom, in 1959. Since then, an exponential increase in the global LNG trade, coupled with a worldwide focus on climate change, has resulted in many countries seeking to secure new supplies of a clean-burning fossil fuel, as well as finding ways to diversify their energy supply. China, for example, plans to double the role of natural gas in its energy portfolio while simultaneously displacing its coal usage by 2020.

"British Columbia's natural gas industry currently supports thousands of jobs, bolsters economic activity in many rural communities and enables the province to use the revenues collected for other services. The problem is that while historically B.C.'s natural gas has been exported throughout North America, in recent years the market shifted as new sources of gas were discovered in the United States. For B.C.'s industry to remain viable, new markets and customers are essential. Under the leadership of the last liberal government, the province embarked on an aggressive strategy to expand the natural gas sector and create opportunities to export to other markets. Several international groups, our consortium included, came forward with a variety of LNG proposals, all of which are now at various stages of development.

"By far the most substantial capital outlay in this process is for construction of the liquefaction and regasification plants. That said, while the shipping costs are a relatively small component of the final gas price, sea-borne transportation often attracts a significant level of concern from environmentalists and aboriginal parties alike, each group adding their voices to any real, or perceived, issues raised by the other.

"As you are aware, Woodstock LNG, in which Woodstock Marine has a controlling interest, is bidding, in conjunction with our Chinese state-owned offshore energy group partners, on a proposed liquefaction facility to be constructed near Kitimat, British Columbia. Our role is to supply and manage the vessels required to transport the LNG output, which is destined to service export opportunities in Asia. To do this, we need to purchase four LNG vessels at a cost of two hundred and fifty million dollars apiece. One billion dollars is our total commitment.

"While many different LNG projects are being considered by the B.C. government, only a few, ours included, are receiving priority assessment. Of these, only two near the port city of Prince Rupert directly affect our bid. All of the projects, though, are hampered by the same global supply issues and, in varying degrees, by the two major local issues—aboriginal rights and environmental concerns."

"Who's our toughest competition?"

Taken aback by the interruption, and unsure which board member had asked the question, Damian paused briefly to gather his thoughts and then answered, "The most serious competition originally came from one of the two separate proposals for the export terminals I just mentioned. The rate at which each was expected to progress depended, to a large degree, on their parent company's view of the global market. However, shortly after the last liberal government was defeated and the new minority government was sworn in, our primary competitor announced they would not be proceeding with their multi-billion dollar project due to significant changes in global market conditions. Although they attributed the decision to prolonged depressed prices and changes in the energy industry, it was widely speculated that the new government's stance on LNG development was a significant factor in their decision. Although the government dismissed the rumour and emphasized that the decision was based on global market pricing and nothing else, many in the industry found the denial hard to accept. However, the good news is that we now believe that we are the most likely project to succeed."

"And the major impediments to our successful completion?" asked the same director.

This time Damian quickly identified the voice as the former CEO of one of North America's largest oil drilling companies, who, as usual, brought a focused no-nonsense approach to any discussion.

"The two biggest local challenges for all parties remains satisfying the environmentalists and aboriginal bands. Of these two, it is management's view that environmental concerns are easier to address than the unknown nature of current, or future, possible aboriginal issues. Unfortunately, even satisfying the most straightforward environmental concerns continues to be made more challenging by the Canadian Environmental Assessment Agency's glacial decision-making process. Normally, this alone would have been enough disincentive to walk away from the project; however, we, and most of the other participants, are reluctant to abandon the projects having already devoted significant amounts of time and money. On the bright side, the current government under Dana Holmes, unlike their immediate predecessors, is once again bending over backwards to accommodate any major LNG export project."

"How will we get around the aboriginal issues? I assume they were a significant factor in the Prince Rupert project withdrawal?"

Damian immediately recognised the more senior of the two female board members who had spoken. "Correct, however, the Kitimat proposal, unlike those at Prince Rupert, requires shipping down a long, narrow channel. Although this poses greater environmental challenges, it comes with fewer aboriginal land issues and, most importantly, has the full support of the local population. We are confident this will keep any aboriginal issues to the absolute minimum. Additionally, Kitimat is the location of choice from an engineering and environmental perspective for the pipeline companies who will be bringing in the gas. This alone gives our project the greatest possibility of being the successful bid."

Without pausing, for further questions, Damian continued speaking. "Which brings us to the current issues before the board. One, a modification of our capital structure and financing arrangements to accommodate both the new government regulations and the bank, but which will reduce our parent company ownership in Woodstock LNG to below fifty percent; and two, accepting the financing proposal put forward by Monger Capital. If you could turn to the first of the two resolutions forwarded to you, I'll go over the details."

#

After almost an hour, the board was still engaged in a heated discussion regarding Monger Capital and how best to structure their proposed equity investment.

"Look," Damian said, barely concealed exasperation evident in his voice. "It's really quite straightforward. This is a big deal for the B.C. government, by way of jobs and economic stimulation, and for ECB for deal prestige. Last, but not least, it will be good for our Woodstock share price. Everyone wants this to succeed." Damian scowled. "Everyone that is except the environmentalists and the aboriginal bands—unless, of course, they get something major in return.

"So, let me summarize where we are now. Financing is 'on hold' by the bank and is contingent upon a satisfactory reduction in Woodstock LNG's debt when measured against the company's shareholder equity, otherwise known as our debt to equity ratio, and a ten percent local equity component to comply with the government's proposed requirement. Outside of these two items, the rest of their conditions are acceptable, as far as our finance department is concerned. We've no idea where this late provincial government condition came from, but suspect it's politically motivated. As a quid pro quo, we understand that they will find some way to trade-off this requirement with the onshore gas infrastructure groups by way of offering some yet unidentified tax relief. Although this reduced tax will improve the overall project returns, we are unlikely to see any of it trickle down and improve our shipping revenues.

"We were fortunate to have found Monger Capital, who have not only offered to inject the necessary ten percent local equity, which will satisfy the government requirement, but don't want any board representation. That's a big win for us. Their investment would of course also solve the bank's additional equity requirement, but does reduce Woodstock Marine's share ownership in Woodstock LNG to below the level for outright control."

"But we still don't know anything about who's behind them?" The upper-class British accented voice of the chairman of the audit committee echoed from the speakerphone. "Who are these people?" he added.

"Aside from being a Vancouver-based private investment fund, we don't know much about them," James Lee interjected.

Damian smirked, recognizing immediately what James was doing in trying to draw the conversation away from him. His executive team were well aware of his propensity to behave unpredictably when challenged.

"We know who runs the business locally, but any enquiries as to who their major investors or shareholders are simply runs into a dead end of holding companies," James continued.

"That said, it's not unusual for major investors to keep their names out of the limelight," Damian interrupted sharply, simultaneously taking back control of the conversation. "We only need to look at our own board, as far as that is concerned."

"I think he's looking at you, Gerry." The speakerphone filled with sudden laughter as the chair of the corporate governance committee took the opportunity to prick the conscience of one of the board's wealthiest directors.

"Perhaps we can—" James was mid-sentence when Damian again cut him off.

"We can continue to look," Damian said, "but in the end we need to get this deal done. This is too good an opportunity to miss. Without the Prince Rupert group, we are now definitely the front-runner, and what can really go wrong, irrespective of who their shareholders may be? I think unless anyone has a substantive argument, we should vote and move on."

There was a momentary silence before Damian spoke again. "Dan, can you read the resolutions and call for a vote."

#

Less than thirty minutes after the Woodstock LNG board meeting, Neil Mohle's telephone rang.

"Neil, good news," said Woodstock's VP Finance as Neil answered. "We're fine with the deal as structured by the bank."

"That's great. Who will be putting in the additional equity?"

"A Vancouver company, Monger Capital. That way we can cover off both the new government ten percent local equity component and meet ECB's debt to equity ratio requirement at the same time. We'll sign the term sheets and courier them over to you today."

"That is good news. Do you have any information you can send me on Monger? I'll need to tell the bank something about them before we paper the deal."

"Why is that?"

"FINTRAC requirements."

"Whose?"

"FINTRAC, the Financial Transactions and Reports Analysis Centre of Canada."

"Oh, them. Okay, what does the bank want to know?"

"Anything you've got to help establish Monger Capital's legitimacy. Ever since the introduction of mandatory reporting to FINTRAC, the bank has been hypersensitive about any possibility of 'funny money'. Much more so than in the past. However, if you people are satisfied with Monger, I'm sure they're above board; that alone should keep the bank happy. We may have some internal information that we can use as well. Just let me have whatever you've got so that we can cover all the bases."

"We don't have much, but I'll see what else Monger can give us and forward it to you when I get it. That said, if you turn up anything in your internal system that you can share with us on them as well, that would be great."

"Okay, I'll check. It'll be nice to get this wrapped up."

"Thanks, Neil. Chat soon. Bye."

CHAPTER 8

Kitty

Sitting quietly on the large deck of their coveted Yaletown condominium that evening, James Lee and his wife, Lian "Kitty" Lee shared their respective day's activities while sipping on two over-sized glasses of chilled Australian chardonnay. Despite Kitty's best efforts to appear attentive, she had little interest in the inner workings of the various Woodstock companies until James mentioned Damian's latest coup in pulling Monger Capital out of the bag when they needed it most. Suddenly fully attentive, but with no telltale outward change in her manner, Kitty's enquiries about Monger yielded little else from James, save that they were a private investment fund headed by a local businessman, John Ng—information she already knew and, as she did with anything remotely connected to her father, continued to keep strictly to herself.

CHAPTER 9

Vivian

Vivian Mohle gently massaged Kitty Lee's neck, Kitty's wet hair hanging down over her hands. It was still early by the salon's upscale clientele standards, and only one other of the eight crisp white stylist chairs was occupied, both women in muted conversation as short pieces of jet-black hair fell onto cloth draped shoulders. Within hours, the freshly painted salon, with its white walls and lavender highlights, would be filled with the chatter of animated wealthy women as they fussed over the latest hairstyles and colours, but for now, it was relatively quiet. Despite having requested an early booking, Kitty had been late for her appointment, and Vivian was already twenty-five minutes behind schedule.

At least Bobbie Ng hadn't arrived yet, Vivian thought. She'd be sitting on the edge of a chair, waiting, her foot tapping, furiously turning the pages of the most recent fashion magazine without reading, or perhaps without even seeing anything on the page. Seldom had Vivian seen a more agitated woman—always rushed, always nervous and bitchy; boy, was she bitchy. Pity her poor husband. Apparently, he was some sort of investment banking type. Maybe he was the problem. *Perhaps Neil knew him; I should ask.* The thought had barely crossed Vivian's mind when the light tinkle of a bell announced the opening of the salon door and Bo "Bobbie" Ng's arrival.

Dressed in a black and white patterned off-the-shoulder top, which accentuated her patently enhanced breasts, a flared black mini skirt and a pair of black stiletto-heeled platform shoes, she stood in the open doorway and scanned the salon like a hawk searching for prey. As her gaze swept past Vivian, she focused briefly on the stylist and client at the far end of the salon before sweeping back to Vivian's client, who, dressed in red sneakers, torn jeans and a white sweatshirt, she immediately dismissed as inconsequential. Finally, her stare moved back to Vivian.

"Good Morning, Ms. Ng," Vivian said. "Please have a seat. I'll be with you as soon as I can."

"It's time for my appointment," Bobbie announced. "Are you behind? I really do expect you to see me on time you know. It's why we make appointments."

As the only daughter of an affluent and powerful Chinese billionaire, women like Bobbie Ng were a dime a dozen to Kitty Lee. Under normal circumstances, she would have ignored the interruption and waited for Vivian to deal with it as she wished. Today, however, was different. She liked Vivian, and there was something very sensual about her neck massage, which had now stopped. Sensing Vivian wilting under the attack and unable to offer any defense without offending one or the other of her clients, Kitty interjected, in her flawless Canadian accent, "It's my fault, I'm afraid. I was late. I'm sorry. I think we're nearly finished, though."

"Yes," added Vivian, relief evident in her voice, "I'm almost done with Ms. Lee if you don't mind waiting a moment."

Surprised at Vivian's response and her apparent deference to the woman already in her chair, Bobbie looked at Kitty again. *Parents probably from mainland China,* she thought, *but brought up here.* No self-respecting Chinese person would have intervened with an apology. Not even someone from Hong Kong, like her. Secure in her assessment and assuming that in the unlikely event the woman spoke any Asian language at all it would be Mandarin, like most mainland Chinese, Bobbie switched to her native Cantonese to vent her anger. "Well, perhaps Ms.

Lee could try being on time for a change instead of inconveniencing her betters ... stupid bitch."

Fluent in both Mandarin and Cantonese, courtesy of the harsh demands of her father, Kitty may well have let the remark slide; however, the added "stupid bitch" uttered almost under Bobbie's breath caused her to snap.

Her response, delivered in accent-less Cantonese was swift and, gangland style, to the point. "It's Miss Hu to you, bitch. Now back off and leave us in peace, or Komodo will have you and your little Johnny's heads on a pole. He owns Monger Capital, you dumbass."

Having clawed her way to her current social status through peasant cunning and ultimately a suitable marriage, and with neither the education nor independent financial wherewithal for support, Bobbie was well aware of the fragility of her bravado. Accordingly, the effect of Kitty's direct verbal attack on Bobbie was profound. Her heavily made-up face, already pale, lost any semblance of colour, and her hand flew to her mouth as she staggered backward then turned and hurried from the salon without another word.

Stunned, Vivian watched the brief exchange. Other than the names, she didn't understand a word. Even if she had, the names meant nothing to her.

"What did you say?" Vivian asked. "And who are those people?"

"What people?"

"Those you mentioned."

"Me." Kitty Lee smiled. "It's my maiden name, but sort of secret. My father's quite a big deal in China, and I said he was a major shareholder in Monger Capital where that woman's husband works. I took a chance and guessed that she may have been married to John Ng, who I know runs Monger. She sounded abrasive enough."

"But what about the other names? I don't know what was said, but I heard several names."

"Oh, no one important. Just a scary character from mainland China. I pretended I knew him. It seemed to work, don't you think? I wonder why she left, though. I hope I haven't lost you a customer."

"Don't worry," said Vivian. "I'll call her later and book another appointment. I'm sure she'll get over whatever upset her soon enough. She probably just didn't have time to wait. Let's get you finished so you can get on with your day."

#

"You'll never guess what happened today."

"You have to give me more than that. Where? At work?"

"Yes," Vivian rotated her kitchen counter stool and stared at her husband over the rim of her wine glass, "at work."

"You got fired."

"Why would you say that? You know they like me there. They're my friends."

"I know. Just being a smartass I guess," Neil replied. "You got a new famous client."

"Better, but still wrong. It involves James Lee's wife."

"Really? I hope it's not bad news. You know I'm working on a deal with the Woodstock guys, right?"

"I know. That's why I'm telling you. It all ended well, so don't worry."

"Good, I'm having enough trouble with the deal without some personal stuff getting in the way. So, what happened?"

As Vivian recounted the day's events, she watched Neil continue the meal preparations. He enjoyed cooking and Italian was one of his favourites, but maybe that was because after eating spicy pasta and drinking red wine, they always seemed to end up in bed. Neil looked distracted as she spoke, but any possible disinterest abruptly disappeared when she asked if he knew Monger Capital.

"Who?" he asked, looking intently at her.

"Monger Capital," Vivian repeated. "Not really Monger Capital, but rather John Ng. Apparently, that's Bobbie Ng's husband, and he runs Monger. Do you know him?"

"No, they seem to keep a pretty low profile and haven't been in any deals I've put together in the past. I wouldn't mind finding out a bit more about them though. They're part of the Woodstock deal now, and I need some additional background on them. I'm going to check with the bank's security group to make sure that Monger's not on their radar for any reason at all. At least that way I can tell the credit department they're not on some internal 'bad guys' list."

"Why don't you ask James Lee?"

"Why would I do that? I already deal with Woodstock's finance department, and it's not really his area."

"Well he could ask his wife and then tell you."

"Huh? Why on earth would he ask his wife?" Neil suppressed a barely concealed laugh.

"Her father's a major shareholder," Vivian said.

"Really? In what company?"

"Monger Capital, dummy. Don't you listen to what I say?"

"Of course I do. How could you possibly know that?"

"She said so today after that strange exchange with Bobbie Ng. Kitty was speaking Cantonese, which I don't understand, but she said she told Bobbie that her father's a major shareholder in Monger Capital. I think his last name must be Hu. That's Kitty's maiden name anyway."

"What else did she say?" Neil asked.

"Nothing much, just some psychobabble about a criminal with a dragon name."

"A dragon?"

"Yes, you know, the famous one—the Komodo dragon. Kitty said she only made that up to scare Bobbie. I don't think it's got anything to do with Monger."

"Are you sure she said her father's a shareholder?"

"I don't know if what she said is for real, but why don't you just ask James. He must know."

"I might just do that. I guess I owe you one." Neil stared at Vivian as he spoke.

"Yes, you do," she replied, her face reddening slightly, "but I get to choose how you pay."

CHAPTER 10

Neil

Canada's banking system is widely considered as one of the safest banking systems in the world. Notwithstanding this, few people, bank staff included, were aware of the extent of their internal security expertise and contacts. Neil Mohle did not fall into this category. Both, through his longevity as a senior bank employee, and the international nature of many of his clients, he was not only aware of the banks security group's activities, but had, on occasion, requested and received their assistance in confirming the "good standing" of a potential client.

Thus, although not common bank practice, Neil's e-mail request on what the group may know about Monger Capital raised no specific concerns when it arrived in the inbox of Chris Broughton, manager of ECB's Toronto-based security department.

Blond-haired and ginger-bearded, at six feet two inches tall, his lanky frame would have looked more at home on a baseball pitcher's mound than it did draped inelegantly on the wheeled black-leather chair behind his desk. The whole image was exacerbated by the clutter of paper covering the desk's surface, the only apparent vacant space occupied by an oversized computer monitor and keyboard. Belying this image was Chris's extraordinary memory and attention to detail that made notes or orderly files superfluous.

Deciding the enquiry would likely be routine, he sent off a quick e-mail to one of ECB's correspondent banks in China, giving them Monger Capital's local details together with the list of their known shareholder companies that Neil had provided. His request was simple. Did the correspondent bank have any information they could share on either the company's shareholders or management, particularly the former? With China being twelve hours ahead of Toronto and allowing for some due diligence on their side, he anticipated an answer by his opening time the following day.

Chris then turned his attention to the publically available register of investment fund managers. Knowing any non-redeemable investment fund that has its head office in Canada is required to register as an investment fund manager, as are in certain circumstances international investment fund managers with head offices outside of Canada, he was confident that he would find Monger Capital's details there. He also recalled that buried deep within the definition of non-redeemable investment funds was the specific provision that they could not invest for the purpose of exercising, or seeking to exercise, control of an issuer or, with the intention of being actively involved, in its management.

As all indications from Neil were that Monger Capital would be a silent investor in Woodstock LNG, this provision strengthened his expectation that he would find Monger listed in the register—an expectation that ultimately proved to be incorrect. Surprised, Chris realized that despite Neil's belief regarding this particular transaction, by not having registered, Monger Capital was indirectly acknowledging that it primarily invested for the purpose of ultimately exercising control over the companies in which it invested, control which could be achieved in a number of ways, including by representation on the board of directors or a say in material corporate decisions. Although this, in and of itself, was not a cause for immediate concern, the absence of registration hindered Chris's search for readily available information on the company and its shareholders. He also knew that investors in funds of this nature usually expect a return of their initial investment, along with any profits, through either a public offering or a sale of the business.

Assuming these were all things both Neil and the company would already be familiar with, Chris turned his attention back to the various sources at his disposal to see if he could discover anything about Monger Capital's shareholders and management. It was only later that day, when the arrival of his take-out sushi order triggered his memory of the second part of Neil's enquiry.

"You won't believe this," Chris's colleague said, placing the package on his desk. "No spicy tuna rolls today. They made you a dragon roll for the same price as compensation."

"Shit," Chris replied.

"Hey, it's not a bad trade."

"No, sorry. Not the roll. Thanks for that; something I forgot."

"Okay, you're welcome."

With the sushi and his colleague quickly dismissed from his thoughts, Chris picked up his telephone and listened again to Neil Mohle's voicemail message that had arrived sometime after his initial e-mail enquiry.

> *Hi, Chris, as an aside, have you ever heard of an international criminal called Komodo? Maybe you could let me know when you reply to my earlier e-mail. Thanks, Neil*

Where had Neil come up with that? Assuming there was some relevance to the enquiry, although presumably unrelated to Monger Capital, and not wishing to concern his regular banking contacts with an enquiry into a possible criminal association, Chris decided to use his personal mobile and e-mailed a brief note to a hard-drinking former computer science classmate in London, who had links to several highly skilled hackers. Unlike China, London was only five hours ahead of Toronto. Unfortunately, Liam Riley had already been in his local pub for several hours and, given the extent of his subsequent hangover, did not check his e-mails at all until late afternoon the following day. By that time, ECB's correspondent bank in China had responded that they had no additional information on the shareholder companies in Monger Capital and knew nothing at all about John Ng. Chris forwarded this information, along with his own similar findings to Neil, who in turn advised his credit department. Satisfied that there was no reason to object to Monger's participation in the deal, by the time Liam finally opened his e-mail, ECB had already confirmed to Woodstock LNG that the signed transaction term sheets formed the agreed basis for the financing of four LNG vessels at a cost of one billion dollars. All that remained for funding to commence was completion of the final legal documentation.

When Liam's reply to his enquiry finally arrived, Chris had a hard time trying not to laugh. As usual, it was terse and to the point.

> *Komodo. Seriously bad Chinese underworld boss. No certainty on identity. Several possible suspects. Top of the list, but flying too far under the radar for anyone to be sure, is the highly secretive Chinese billionaire Quon Jin Hu. Sources alarmed at questions; will not provide any further information. Best advice. Stay the fuck away from this one, mate. Liam, out.*

As he re-read the message, real concern quickly replaced any humour Chris initially felt. What had Neil discovered? While the brevity of the message was typically Liam, the anxiety was not. If Neil's interest in this Komodo person was connected to the bank in any way, he'd better warn him. Hopefully, Neil was just curious. Many of the bank's Vancouver clients had Asian roots, perhaps one of them had mentioned Komodo? He would telephone Neil. No sense in creating a paper trail in the bank's e-mail system on this enquiry.

#

Neil sat staring at his office telephone, a very relieved Chris Broughton's voice still ringing in his ears. As far as Neil could tell, he'd skirted the issue quite successfully. Muttering excuses about how the Komodo enquiry had come from a name his wife picked up in her hairstyling salon. How he shouldn't have tagged it onto the end of his real enquiry about Monger Capital, but curiosity and opportunity had got the better of him—and he wouldn't do that again. Neil thanked Chris for the information and terminated the call. What he omitted, not without a little guilt, was Vivian's description of Bobbie Ng's reaction to Kitty Lee's outburst and the immediate and shocked connection he made on hearing Chris mention Quon Jin Hu's name.

According to Vivian, Hu was Kitty Lee's maiden name. Perhaps there were dozens of Hu's in China? Maybe the name was as common as Smith? Still, the coincidence bothered him. He'd check with Vivian tonight and, if necessary, follow up with James after that. If Quon Jin Hu was Kitty's father, he'd have no choice but to advise Damian of the rumour and, of course, the credit department of ECB. This development could potentially put the whole deal at risk and, with it, his sizeable annual bonus.

#

The discussion between James Lee and Neil Mohle took place by telephone early the following morning only minutes after Neil arrived at his office. After a handful of social pleasantries, Neil broached the question of Kitty's maiden name. Sounding surprised, but not alarmed, James confirmed that indeed, Hu was Kitty's maiden name.

"Not the same family as the billionaire," Neil asked casually.

"Would be nice," James replied. "What's this about?"

"Just doing some due diligence on Monger Capital and stumbled over a possible billionaire shareholder by the name of Quon Jin Hu. Thought I should check if he was any relation."

"How did you know Kitty's maiden name?" James asked. "It's hardly common knowledge, or were you checking on her as well?"

"Hell, no. My wife mentioned Kitty's last name was Hu, so I put two and two together, but it looks like I came up with five. Which is probably a good thing," Neil added.

"Why is that?"

"Well, just between us, it looks like Quon Jin Hu may not be as squeaky clean as he'd like folks to believe. I need to discuss this with the bank, but wanted to check whether you were related first. Depending on the bank's response to his possible involvement with Monger, we may have to revisit the deal. Worst-case scenario, the bank may withdraw. I should probably also talk to Damian and let him know where we stand."

"How can you guys withdraw?" James asked. "You've signed the term sheets."

"There's a material adverse change clause in them," Neil replied. "Always is. Your finance people will understand. If it transpires that a major shareholder in Monger isn't entirely above board, the bank could rely on the clause to withdraw from the deal."

"Let's not jump the gun," James replied. "Hopefully there's a simple explanation, or you're mistaken. I'll bring Damian up to speed while you talk to the bank, and we can regroup in the next day or two to see if we can clear this up. It's probably better for you if we do that anyway. Damian can be explosive, and you really don't want to have that discussion until absolutely necessary."

"Okay," Neil replied, relieved not to have to confront Damian with possible bad news. "I'll get back to you after I hear from the bank's credit guys."

It was several hours later before Neil realized that James had never really answered his question about his relationship with Quon Jin Hu.

#

James sat immobile behind his desk, staring at his closed office door. He'd managed to dodge answering Neil's question about Quon Jin Hu for now, but he knew that eventually the truth would be discovered. Neither he nor Kitty ever spoke in public about her father, Quon's extreme aversion to any form of publicity deeply ingrained in every member of the family. Hell, he had only met Quon after he had proposed to Kitty, and even then, he had to go to mainland China to ask for his approval. Moreover, while Quon had ultimately agreed to the marriage, that first meeting was strained and very formal. James always assumed the family obedience came out of respect for the man and his financial achievements, but perhaps he'd been mistaken and there was a darker reason. Thinking back, the household staff were almost subservient. Could it have been fear? He was so absorbed with making his own good impression at the time that he'd barely noticed anything else.

Checking his runaway thoughts, he decided he was being absurd. Most very wealthy and reclusive individuals probably faced the same rumours on a daily basis. He'd bought some time with his answer to Neil's question, but he'd better get on with clearing things up. Damian would go ballistic if the deal fell through, and who knew what sort of reaction he'd have if he ever discovered the identity of James's father-in-law. James needed to speak to Kitty about her father. There was no way he was going to call the man himself with questions that needed answering.

Leaving his office, James walked past his secretary without pausing, speaking as he went. "Jenny, I'm not feeling well, and I'm going home. I can be reached on my mobile if it's urgent, but I will probably try to get some sleep, so I may not answer immediately. Tell anyone who needs me that I'll call back as soon as I'm able."

CHAPTER 11

Kitty

Kitty Lee sat picking aimlessly at her evening dinner as her husband recounted all that had happened over the past few days, culminating in the call he'd received that morning from the ECB banker Neil Mohle about Quon Jin Hu. Had she not already been fully aware of her own part in this unfortunate disclosure of her father's identity, she may not have been able to follow James's somewhat disjointed account. Fortunately, given how matters had evolved, that was not the case. Pressing James on the need for absolute discretion until she had spoken to her father, she promised to get the information he needed without delay.

CHAPTER 12

Rachel

Despite the speed with which Rachel Burton received the requested security logs from the previous two months, the needle on her internal anxiety metre had already moved from medium to high. The excuse that she was confirming the time of certain visitor meetings seemed to have satisfied the head of security, who had quickly produced the requested reports. Declining his offer of assistance, she explained that it would be more efficient for her to do it alone, as only she knew which staff members had accompanied the various visitors. Although she had asked for several weeks of reports, there was really only one day, or rather only one early evening, that truly interested her: the evening Hayden had ignored her calling out to him as she watched him enter the restroom. Although she had waited in the corridor for a couple of minutes in the hope of speaking with him, he had not reappeared.

Taken in isolation, his behaviour was not particularly unusual; after all, he may simply not have heard her call. The problem was he'd been acting strangely around the premier ever since that day, and now Rachel was convinced he was hiding something. In her mind, she wasn't catering to her own infatuation with Hayden; she was doing her job and protecting the premier. If Hayden got hurt in the process, so be it. As far as Rachel was concerned, whoever the woman he was involved with was, she obviously couldn't be trusted.

Rachel's methodology was surprisingly simple. Starting with the day in question, she determined, from the security logs, which staff members were still in the cabinet wing of the building at the time, and then looked for any other similar occasions. Any days on which Hayden was away she automatically excluded. Within thirty minutes, she had two viable candidates. Outside of herself and the premier, only two women were in the office that same evening. They were also, on occasion, the only other persons in the building at the same time as Hayden. Both were members of the legislative assembly; however, one was not only unmarried, but also a member of the cabinet. The very attractive dark-haired French-Canadian was by far the most likely candidate.

Deciding it was time to start planting seeds, Rachel considered how best to proceed. Both women were currently on the LNG trip to Kitimat. She could call each with some excuse and see if she caught anyone unawares. Deciding that two calls for no particular reason might spark some discussion if they compared notes, Rachel decided to call Hayden. Maybe one of them was with him. She'd call Donna and pretend she couldn't find the premier, and then call Hayden. Barely able to conceal her excitement, she reached for the phone.

CHAPTER 13

Hayden

"Again, please."

"Again? You're insatiable this evening." Hayden smiled to take any sting from his words.

"It's the money. Huge globs of it make me horny."

"And what money is this?"

"A corporate donor. They made a major contribution to our party recently. Hugh Ruff provided a formal update to the cabinet this morning"

Hayden cupped her bare breast and gently chewed on the erect nipple protruding between his forefinger and thumb. "Why?" he murmured.

"Mmmm. They like our foreign investment program."

"The donor's from offshore?" Hayden asked, attempting to keep the surprise from his voice.

"No, a local investment fund, but I wouldn't be surprised if they have some foreign investors."

"Doesn't that concern you?"

"Yes, oh, do that again."

"You are concerned?"

"No, I'm not concerned, but, yes, I like what you doing. Can you please focus? The party has Hugh Ruff to look after the money issues.

It's not something I spend time worrying about. Having access to lots of it for our political purposes just turns me on."

Hayden focused. He would look into the money source later.

#

Hayden woke with a start. His left arm was numb. A head of dark, tousled hair rested on his shoulder while its associated warm body wrapped around him like a limpet to a rock. Reluctantly, he slid from the bed, trying not to disturb the still sleeping form. It was a big day in Kitimat, with the premier and several members of the cabinet in attendance, and he had several things to do before the day's events got underway. First and foremost, though, he needed to get back to his own room unnoticed. The still sleeping form barely moved as he extricated himself. He smiled. The sex had been good, almost too good, and they both needed the sleep.

"Remember, the better the accommodation, the better the sex," she had said when they discussed being away together.

Well, on this occasion, she was wrong. The accommodation was definitely average, but the sex had been great. Walking across the rough carpet in bare feet, he gathered up his clothes and slipped through the adjoining door into his own room. One thing he liked about small town hotels, almost every room had adjoining room doors and were easily available, without query, with some simple excuse.

As he showered then dressed, he ran through a mental checklist of things he needed to get done that day in between attending the several speeches and public appearances the premier would be making. He'd check in with her later to see what if anything she needed from him. The whole contingent was returning to Victoria together the following day, so, for today at least, everything would be focused on Kitimat and the one LNG deal planned for this area. Which reminded him, he still hadn't reached Woodstock LNG's banker. That was one call he'd make today as soon as he'd finished breakfast.

#

The ringing of Hayden's mobile phone interrupted the low morning conversation in the hotel dining area. Startled, he pushed his high-fat, low-carb breakfast to one side to answer.

"Jones."

"Gray."

"Very funny," Hayden replied, lowering his voice. "You scared the hell out of the locals. I think they have a no phones at breakfast policy."

"I'm sure they do, and it's a good thing too. You need to focus on all that fat you eat for breakfast. What do you call that diet you're on?"

"Banting... and you know it works. I'm twenty pounds lighter than I was three months ago."

"I know, and that's what pisses me off. No matter what I try, nothing works. Ugh, I hate you. Anyway, can you give Rachel Burton a call? She's trying to reach the premier and there's no answer. Is she at breakfast with you?"

"No, haven't seen her come down as yet. Some of the cabinet are here, though. I'm eating alone and trying to get some work done at the same time. Did Rachel say why she needs Dana? We've got a busy day ahead of us."

"No, she didn't say. She'll probably tell you, though; I think she's soft on you although I've no idea why."

"Why would you say that?"

"Woman's intuition. Don't say I didn't warn you. Well, must run. I have things to do. My boss is away, and the mice will play." With an audible click, Donna terminated the call, leaving Hayden speechless as usual.

Deciding that he had sufficiently disturbed most of the other diners, Hayden gathered up his laptop and mobile phone and headed for the exit. He was barely through the doors when his phone rang again.

"Jones." As Hayden answered, the elevator doors in the main lobby opened, disgorging several people, including the premier, who, without looking around, made directly for the dining room.

"Hello, Hayden. It's Rachel."

"Hi, Rachel. Donna said you wanted to speak to me."

"Actually I need to reach the premier, and she's not answering. Do you know where she is?"

"I just saw her heading in to breakfast. Do you want me to get her? I think they had a late night. Some cabinet discussion; I wasn't included. She'll probably answer now if you call her. Anything I can do to help?"

"No, that's okay. I'll try her again. You haven't seen Marie Bergeron have you? I have something for her as well."

"Yup. She's at breakfast with a couple of other members of the cabinet. I can let them know you're trying to reach them, which one do you want first?"

"The premier, please," Rachel blurted. "I've got the special donor list she wanted from Hugh Ruff. She asked me to call her with the names before her speech today."

Hayden was instantly alert. "I'd be happy to give her the names if you like," he offered. "How long's the list."

"Only three names, but it's supposed to be confidential. I'd better give it to her myself."

"Okay. No problem. I'll go back to the dining room and ask her to call you." Hayden disconnected the call. Rachel sounded agitated. He wondered who was on the list and what constituted a special donor. He wasn't a big believer in coincidences, but maybe the investment fund mentioned last night was on the list. He needed to find out more.

Returning to the dining room to deliver Rachel's message, Hayden tried desperately to remove any guilt from his face as he approached the table where the premier now sat with Marie Bergeron and two other cabinet ministers. While certainly adept at behaving like a chameleon and playing whatever role his job demanded, personal relationships were another matter altogether. Affairs only made things worse. Guilty feelings surfacing even in the most mundane circumstances, like now. Avoiding eye contact with anyone other than the premier, Hayden smiled broadly. "Morning all," he said.

Nodding in acknowledgement of the returned greetings, Hayden spoke again. "Excuse me, Premier. Rachel Burton is trying to reach you. She asked if you could give her a call. She has some information that you requested she get to you before your speech today."

There was a pause while Dana finished chewing. "Thanks, Jones. I'll call her a soon as I finish here."

"Great." Without another word, Hayden turned and walked quickly away. After months of seemingly fruitless investigation, he finally had a new trail to follow. Now all he needed was a reason to visit Hugh Ruff.

Choosing the stairs rather than the elevator for the short walk back to his second-floor hotel room, he arrived at his door only minutes after leaving the lower floor. Entering, he immediately checked the door to the adjoining room. Locked. No surprise there. Everything back to normal. She definitely controlled this arrangement. Not that he could blame her. She had more to lose than he did. For her, the political fallout would be disastrous. For him, maybe a serious reprimand. Any guilt he might have felt quickly faded with the recollection that she had started the whole affair. Sure, he had succumbed, but she was definitely the instigator.

With a couple of hours to kill before the first official meeting, and assuming he would not be needed before then, Hayden decided to try calling Neil Mohle. He wanted to get a fix on where things stood as far as the LNG project financing was concerned, and who knew what else he might discover at the same time. So far, the day had provided plenty of surprises.

CHAPTER 14

Quon

Thanks to the marvels of electronic communication, the fallout from Kitty Lee's outburst was almost immediate and, within an hour of Bobbie Ng leaving the Vancouver salon, Quon Jin Hu, closeted in his opulent office in mainland China, received the first of three critical messages. Not one to bother with telephones or computers unless absolutely essential, the messages were, as usual, communicated to him by his aging but astute and trustworthy personal assistant, Dong Lai.

The first, on this particular morning, came by text to Dong's mobile phone. It was short and to the point and, being first, made little sense at the time. It was sent by Jun "John" Ng, president of Monger Capital, a role that provided almost perfect cover for his primary employment as head of Quon's criminal activities in Canada. In it, Jun apologized most sincerely for any perceived slight to Mr. Hu's daughter by his wife Bo Ng. An incident had apparently taken place at Bo's regular hairstyling salon in Vancouver where, because of family illness, she was rushed and not her usual courteous self. While Jun was sure the person in question at the salon was unlikely to be Mr. Hu's daughter, he just wished to be certain that his wife had not inadvertently upset a member of Mr. Hu's family.

Despite its relative brevity, the text was a proactive attempt by the Vancouver crime boss to do two things. First, and most importantly, to determine whether Ms. Lee from the salon was in fact the daughter of Quon Jin Hu; and second, if she was, to minimize any damage to his reputation and standing with Quon from Bobbie's behaviour. Like the dragon that had prompted Quon's gangland nickname, if angered, his retribution would be swift and merciless. In order to best assess his position, Jun Ng sent the text. He had done nothing wrong, and in case it was necessary, he wanted to assure his employer of his continued silence regarding the location of any of Quon's family in Canada. He knew he needed to stay ahead of this incident. Thus, within minutes of receiving his wife's babbling phone message about the hairstylist altercation, he had drafted the text and, after reading it several times, sent it to Dong.

Unrelated to the salon incident, the second message, arriving by e-mail from the local head of Quon's personal investment company headquartered in the Bahamas, was sent directly to a seldom-used computer in the corner of his office. Retrieved by Dong shortly after arrival, the message was printed and delivered by hand to Quon. In it, his investment company management sought approval for the release of funds, beyond their current authority, for a significant investment through Monger Capital in a Canadian LNG venture. As chairman of the investment company, Quon needed to both sanction placing the matter before the full company board and set the timing for the meeting.

The third message, resulting from the same salon incident and affecting the same LNG venture, was left on Quon's home telephone voicemail several days later by his daughter Lian. Without doubt the favourite of his several children, he knew immediately when she identified herself as Lian that the news would not be good. Always Kitty when things were good, and Lian whenever they were not. Her message, like the others, was brief and to the point.

> *Father, it's Lian. We have an exposure issue in Vancouver.*
> *Please call me as soon as you are able.*

The Banker's Box

#

Quon's replies to each of these messages were, like their origination, provided in differing formats.

Jun Ng's enquiry resulted in two responses.

Dong Lai sent the first by text to Jun's mobile phone only minutes after he had discussed the enquiry with Quon, and it did not require any further discussion.

You must be mistaken. Mr. Hu has no daughter in Vancouver and does not wish to start a rumour of this nature. He suggests that as a suitable discipline for your wife for upsetting this unknown customer, you encourage her to find a new hairstylist.

Crime bosses rarely required being beaten over the head with a stick to get the message. Jun was getting off lightly. He would need to enforce the hairstylist ban, but that should be easy. More spending money or the threat of fewer recreational drugs would quickly keep Bobbie in line.

Quon's second response, resulting from this same enquiry, was made directly by him in a telephone call to his daughter. The call lasted for barely two minutes, during which time Kitty sat silently holding the phone, her head bowed. "Sorry, father, it will not happen again," was all she said as she replaced the receiver of the landline on the table alongside the large king-sized bed she shared with her husband, James.

"What was that about," James Lee asked his wife. "It's 3 a.m. What did your father want?"

"It's nothing," she replied. "Family squabbles. Go back to sleep. He can never remember the time zones. No emergency."

"Fuck," he said, "I'll never get back to sleep now."

"Okay," Kitty replied, purposely misinterpreting her husband's statement and sliding on top of him, her actions immediately terminating any further discussion of her father's call. That he had threatened to cut off James's head and return it to her in a box if she ever used his real identity again, she would keep to herself. As his favourite daughter, she knew he would never harm her directly, but those around her had no such sanctuary.

Dong Lai responded to the message received from the head of Quon's personal investment company using Quon's own office computer e-mail. In it, he noted that coincidentally the company directors were meeting at 7 p.m. that same evening, and if all necessary paperwork were received in time, they would deal with the necessary approvals. The recipient had no way of knowing that the board members of Quon's personal investment company were appointed in name only and would execute without question, either before or after an event, whatever authorities he required. Their acquiescence was assumed, almost as if their lives depended on it, which of course they did. As requested in Dong's reply, the necessary paperwork was subsequently provided well within the stated deadline.

Quon answered Kitty's voicemail three full days after his 3 a.m. call to her. Visibly shaken after listening to her message, he shuffled around his home with the cordless telephone in his hand, his entire short, squat frame radiating anger. After several minutes, he slumped heavily in an ornately carved hallway chair and sat unmoving until his face ultimately regained its normal colour. Neither his wife, nor any member of the household staff, ventured anywhere near him, and by the time he returned Kitty's call, his voice, while no longer reflecting his earlier anger, was filled with menace.

Unfortunately for Kitty, while Quon's initial anger from her message was once again under control, she was now obliged to explain to her father how the ECB banker, Neil Mohle, the husband of her hairstylist, Vivian, was probing a possible connection between Quon and Monger Capital. To make matters worse, the banker was also following a rumour that Quon was potentially the criminal boss Komodo. That this disclosure was clearly linked and followed so soon after Kitty's indiscretion at the hairstyling salon remained unsaid.

To say that Quon was livid would have qualified as the understatement of the year as once again Kitty sat silently throughout her father's tirade, any attempted protestations on her part immediately cut short by an abrupt command. Finally, after stressing to his daughter that no such family disclosure would ever be allowed to occur again, Quon's rage appeared spent and he lowered his voice until it was almost a whisper. "Here is what you will do," he said. "You will deny any connection between Komodo and our family. This to your husband or anyone that asks. You will also tell James that I need to speak to him about our family's investment in Monger Capital before he says anything to anyone about the information he has learned. Stress to him that he is part of this family now and he has a duty to protect our privacy.

"When that is done, you will arrange a meeting between this ECB banker and a very wealthy offshore investor. You will say that you do not yet have a name for this investor, but that he is a friend of one of your business associates who is visiting from Hong Kong and is looking to make a sizeable investment in Canada. He requires a banker, and you suggested Mohle because you knew his wife."

At this point, Kitty Lee could not keep quiet any longer. "Father, they will not be hurt will they? Please, Father. These are my friends."

"Perhaps you will keep that in mind the next time you feel the need to let your tongue run loose," Quon replied.

Despite the ambiguity of the reply, Kitty knew better than to ask twice.

"Now tell me," said Quon, "how strong is your marriage?"

"How strong?"

"Yes. Do you love him? Do you have problems?"

"No, no problems, and yes, I love him. Why do you want to know? What are you going to do?"

"Good. That makes it easier. I am only going to talk to him, but it is time for him to choose. I will ask him to tell you what I have said after we are done. Remember, though, you can only confirm what he tells you, for that is all he will know about our affairs. Only that and no more. If you have any questions, or if you are unsure, you will call me first before you say anything. This is not a mistake that you want to make twice. Do you understand?"

"Yes, Father."

There was a muted click as Quon disconnected the call without another word.

As she heard the sound, an enormous wave of relief swept over Kitty. She would make sure James understood the importance of listening to her father with care. She had known this day would come, but always assumed it would be much later in their married life, perhaps even only on the death of one of her parents. She had to make sure James did nothing rash, only that way could she keep him safe. Vivian and Neil remained a problem for which she had no immediate solution, but now was not the time to question her father. His tolerance would only stretch so far.

CHAPTER 15

James

A suitably forewarned James sat quietly in his living room, the telephone tucked between his ear and right shoulder as he listened to his father-in-law ramble on about how hard he had worked to become successful, how he had protected his family and how great wealth brought with it many challenging decisions and many detractors.

Kitty was at the gym, and between Quon's soft monotonous tone and his second glass of red wine after a long day at the office, James was almost dozing when Quon made the offer. As a result, all he managed to say was "what?" immediately followed by "I'm sorry. I didn't mean to be rude, but could you please repeat that? I'm not sure I heard you correctly."

Quon laughed; at least James assumed the short barking sound was meant to be a laugh. "Yes, you did," Quon replied. "I was saying that the time had come for you to take management of the trust fund that we have established for you and Kitty. Before we do this, I need to be sure that there is no conflict between your responsibilities to the company for which you work and our family. It is important to us that family comes first, and I need to know that you think the same way before we move ahead."

"I'm not sure I understand what you mean," James replied.

"Take for example, Monger Capital," Quon said. "It is true I have a significant investment in that company, and yet I would rather this not be made public. If people knew of my investment in Monger, they would make decisions based on my involvement rather than Monger's own performance. This is neither good for Monger nor for our family investments. To make matters worse, enemies, which I, like many others of great wealth, have gathered along the way, will try to use this information not only for their own advantage, but also against my family and me. Even to the extent, as you have now experienced, of trying to link me to this criminal Komodo."

"You mean there is no association?" James blurted out before he could stop himself.

"Of course not, but the rumours will persist and we must deny them at every turn, or else they will harm our family, you included, and that cannot be allowed to happen."

"I understand," said James, not really understanding, but at least managing to follow the logic of Quon's statements. "But how does one stop them?"

"I'm sure you'll think of something. Kitty assures me that you're very smart. You just have to decide whether you want to be simply very smart, or very smart and very rich. The answer seems quite easy to me. Now, I'm getting tired, so I'd like to go over the trust structure with you."

"Certainly," said James, still not quite sure what was going on, but with curiosity getting the better of him.

"Kitty will hold fifty-one percent of the shares, and you will hold forty-nine percent. I want you to have responsibility for the full day-to-day management, though, and to control any investments. You can employ whatever people you think are necessary to ensure you do this well."

"You want me to employ people? You mean people like investment brokers with whom we'd invest the money?"

"No, I mean direct staff to look after the daily affairs and report back to you, as required. They can engage as many investment brokers as you feel necessary."

"That seems to be an unnecessary expense and might detract from what we could earn," James replied. "Can you give me an idea of how much we're talking about?"

"One hundred million dollars."

"One hundred million?" Try as he might, James was unable to keep the shock from his voice. "Really? And what is it you want me to do?"

"Take care of Kitty, our family and the money, as your number one priority. Everything else comes second. Think you can do that?"

"That's it?"

"That's it."

"Then yes," said James, his head still spinning. "I'm sure I can. What does one say at a time like this? Thank you?" "Ha." Quon gave another cough like laugh. "Not necessary. You are really one of us now. Just take care of the family. No exceptions."

"I will," replied James.

"Good, now put your family hat on, and let's talk business. Our lawyers will contact you to set up the fund accounts in Vancouver. We will transfer the money to the accounts over the next few months, and I will contact a few select people that I know and trust and tell them in confidence of our family connection. New doors will open for you, and you will need to keep me informed of anything interesting that crosses your desk. Eventually, we will do some deals together, and you will become even wealthier. In the meantime, this is what I would like to do about this Monger Capital problem."

#

"One hundred million," James said quietly to himself as he hung up the phone. "One hundred bloody million." It was time to call Neil Mohle. He looked at the carefully crafted list of answers he planned to deliver. *Lies, all of them,* he thought, *except the one about there being no association between Quon Jin Hu and the criminal named Komodo.* At least that was true. He wasn't sure what he would have done if it had turned out that Quon and Komodo were the same person.

#

Neil Mohle picked up the telephone on its first ring. "This is Neil," he said.

"Neil, James Lee here. I've done some checking, and it looks like we can clear this Monger thing up quite quickly. How did you make out with your credit department?"

"Hi, James. Thought I'd wait to hear from you first. I decided there was no point in stirring matters up until I had all the information."

"Smart move," James replied. "I spoke to Kitty, and despite her family being pretty well-off, she's no relation to the billionaire Hu, I'm afraid. Would have been nice though; at least I got to dream for a while. I also checked with Monger Capital, and apparently, the billionaire is not connected with them at all. They were quite open about that. They didn't offer to tell me who their investors were, just confirmed Quon Jin Hu was not one of them."

"Believe it or not, that's good news as far as our deal's concerned. I was really worried about the possible Komodo connection," Neil replied.

"Yeah, I got that, so I thought I'd do you a favour and ask Kitty's dad if he'd heard any similar rumours in China. Although not in the same league as your Hu, he is pretty well connected in the business community."

"What did he say?"

"Laughed his head off. Apparently, it's quite a common rumour over there and completely false. Seems your guy is not only filthy rich, he's also very secretive and has as many people who like him as he does that don't. Kitty's dad said you can't amass a fortune in China without a great deal of political manoeuvring, and stepping on anyone who gets in the way."

"Not a lot different here," Neil answered. "Well, that's good enough for me. Onward and upward, let's get this deal done."

And get your bonus in the bank, thought James as he disconnected the call and slumped back with relief. The call had gone smoother than he anticipated. He had also delivered all the information Quon had asked, even the bit about Monger. Quon had assured him that he would speak with Monger, who would confirm the information James had given Neil if they were ever asked. Money was power, he had added, and James had little doubt that was true. He had done his job. The Hu family investment in Monger Capital would remain confidential, and he had put the ridiculous Komodo rumour to bed. Nothing further needed doing on that front. As agreed with his father-in-law, it was time to focus on Woodstock Marine. Just one more quick call to Quon to let him know how things had gone with the banker.

One hundred fucking million, he thought. He almost couldn't believe it.

#

Unlike James, who accepted his father-in-law's word without question, Quon Jin Hu left nothing to chance. Despite James's assurances, he needed certainty that his daughter's impulsive outburst would create no further damage than it had done already. Hearing from James that the banker had not shared the rumours with his internal credit department was good news and bought some badly needed time—time to take care of both Mohle and his wife before any further damage was done. All that was required now was for Kitty to confirm she had delivered the message about the offshore investor.

Not one to get his own hands dirty when arrangements of this nature needed to be put in place, Quon went in search of Dong. Where was that skinny old fool when he needed him?

CHAPTER 16

Drew

Rick "Vegas" Kolnick pushed his shoulder-length blond hair behind his left ear, his huge meaty hand, with its single red heart tattooed on the back of his ring finger, dwarfing the mobile phone cupped inside. "So tell me again, why we should do this for you?" he asked.

"Because we'll make it worth your while, and it's too close to home for us," John Ng replied.

"Upfront?"

"Upfront," John Ng confirmed.

"And how do we collect?"

"Same drop and timing as always."

"Money and information?"

"Both."

"Okay, send it over. We'll be in touch."

Disconnecting the call, Vegas tossed the phone onto the corner cushion of a nearby sofa and wandered into the kitchen to find the other members of the household and give them a "heads-up". They would discuss the details when the money and photographs arrived.

The Banker's Box

\#

To the casual observer, there was nothing remarkable about the exterior of the house on Airlie Road. Located in a respectable, predominantly blue-collar Vancouver Island neighbourhood, it looked similar to every other house in the street, right down to the dark red basketball hoop fastened above the double-garage doors. If it hadn't been for the three gleaming chrome-covered cruiser motorcycles securely locked inside and the carefully hidden cameras monitoring every inch of the property, the house could have passed for any other suburban residence. The presence of a large grey RAM truck and trailer parked in the driveway, its sides emblazoned with *Merlin's Mobile Motorcycle Repair*, completed the setting. Not that two of the three members of the household ever did any serious motorcycle repair work; it just supported their thin veneer of respectability. It also explained the occasional appearance of other motorcycles in the area, their real purpose masked by the strict enforcement of a "no gang colours" zone within a two-kilometre radius of the house.

Inside, Drew Jamieson, RCMP undercover agent and full-patch biker gang member, pulled on black Levi jeans over his boxer shorts and walked bare-chested and barefoot to the front door. As the most recent addition to "the Outpost", as the house was euphemistically called, Drew was responsible for the garbage and recycling routine, occurring on alternating weeks. The reason offered if any inquisitive neighbour asked why only Drew handled this chore was simply that the newest member of the shared household always got the crummy jobs. This, together with an accompanying laugh and smile, quickly put any further curiosity to rest. The fact that on certain days the garbage detail also carried with it the highest risk of exposure for their criminal activities remained unsaid.

Also unsaid was that each member of the household had their own specific responsibilities. Vegas, as the senior member of the Outpost, coordinated all of the gang's assigned activities and reported directly to the chapter president, his size and no-nonsense approach rendering his secondary role as discipline enforcer, a somewhat light duty. Next in line was "Scrubber" Barker, a qualified accountant, responsible for handling all financial transactions of the entire chapter through his office in the Outpost. He also directed the laundering of any illegal proceeds, a duty from which he derived his unusually appropriate nickname. Somewhat frail and frequently described during his youth as "that skinny runt", Scrubber was the antithesis of anyone's image of a biker. His particular skill set, however, kept him well protected from the usual macho bullying often directed at others of similar physical stature. Drew, son of a legitimate motorcycle dealer, coupled with his own almost legendary mechanical abilities, was the recipient of all the gang's most challenging motorcycle problems. It also afforded him the opportunity to move seamlessly, and relatively unnoticed, throughout the membership in search of information.

Accordingly, on this particular Tuesday morning, it was Drew that trudged to the curb with a bright blue recycling box filled with plastic milk jugs and a mixture of pop and beer cans. On top of the plastic containers rested the standard large yellow plastic bag filled with old newspapers and other paper products. With a brief wave to a similarly occupied neighbour directly across the road, Drew deposited the recycling on the curb and returned to the house.

Several hours later, with much banging, its yellow light flashing and its compacter motor straining, a recycling truck moved from house to house collecting the curbside piles. Orderliness was seemingly not high on their list of priorities as they flung boxes back onto the sidewalk with only the occasional box landing right side up. In Drew's case, in a move that would have taken a trained observer to notice, the blue recycling box, empty bar the yellow bag now stuffed inside, was casually but carefully flipped upright onto the grass at the edge of the property.

The truck had moved only a few houses down the road when Drew re-emerged from the house, coffee cup in hand, picked up the blue box, with its accompanying yellow bag in his free hand, and re-entered the house. Back in the kitchen, he placed his coffee cup on the counter, opened the bag and reached inside. There, neatly packaged were two thousand one hundred dollar bills along with two names, an address and a single photograph of Neil and Vivian Mohle. There was also a note with the anticipated location of an investor meeting, which, together with the date and time, would be confirmed within the next few days. Without any signature or name on the note, the sender's identity remained anonymous.

Two people, two hundred thousand dollars. Not a bad day's work if murder didn't bother your conscience. Drew wondered what the Mohles had done to upset the Chinese mob and how he could stop this before it was too late?

"Any coffee?"

Drew turned at the voice. "Yeah, Vegas. The package is here too. You should look."

Vegas reached across Drew for the package, the black club tattooed on the ring finger of his right hand clearly visible as it passed only inches in front of Drew's face.

#

Nolan Kulla, retired RCMP officer, recognized the distinctive throb of the Harley-Davidson exhausts long before he saw the motorcycles themselves. Without turning, he finished parking his metallic silver Yamaha V-Star diagonally at the side of the road in front of the oceanfront pub before looking to his left, just as they appeared at the crest of the road. Unhurriedly, he clipped his helmet to the side of the motorcycle and walked into the pub. He was a few minutes late and the "Shady" group, as they referred to themselves, were already all gathered at their usual spot, three tables pulled together to accommodate the almost dozen retired men engaged in animated banter. Sitting down at the last remaining space on the bench seats facing the ocean windows, he had barely settled when a passing server called out to him.

"Usual, Nolan?"

"Thanks," he answered and within moments was embroiled in yet another pseudo-serious disagreement on the merits, or otherwise, of the chosen topic of the day, a seemingly critical discussion interrupted only by the occasional brief pause to acknowledge the presence of any attractive passing female.

Meeting regularly every Thursday afternoon, the eclectic group, which arrived promptly at 4 p.m. and left like clockwork an hour later, provided the perfect backdrop for the occasional requirements of the retired RCMP officer and active field contact for Drew Jamieson.

Situated on the scenic beachfront road in Qualicum Beach, the pub was a frequent stop as motorcyclists and tourists alike travelled from one end of Vancouver Island to the other. Despite vehicle parking being readily available on the waterfront alongside the pub or in the parking lot directly across the road, most motorcycle riders parked diagonally on the shoulder of the road immediately outside the pub's front door. With the almost military precision of the arrival and departure of the Shady group, it was a relatively simple matter to coordinate face-to-face meetings. If personal contact proved difficult, a secondary message delivery protocol was automatically used.

So it was that afternoon, when Nolan Kulla left the pub that he found Drew Jamieson's motorcycle, along with two others, parked alongside his own. No opportunity had presented itself to make contact and Drew's helmet, routinely hanging by its chinstrap from his right mirror, dangled loosely from the left.

Nolan's pulse quickened as he started his motorcycle and headed down the road. A short distance away, he pulled into a vacant parking space facing the ocean and extracted a prepaid mobile phone from his saddlebag. Drew's helmet on the left meant there was message at the pre-arranged number. A number that, if anyone accidentally called, would identify the owner as Dolly's Massage Service, offering an outcall-only service. If by some reason Dolly's number was ever compromised, there was no location for anyone to check, and hopefully no one would ever be able to access the voicemails. Notwithstanding these precautions, all voicemails were wiped clean once heard. Everyone in this operation knew that Drew's well being hung by a very slender thread and that one mistake could have negative consequences on his longevity.

Dialing Dolly's number, Nolan retrieved the voicemail. The bikers had accepted a contract from an Asian gang. Payment had already been made; the location was likely somewhere downtown Vancouver, and they had a few days at most before the exact location was confirmed and the timing established. At that moment the hit would became active. The target was a Vancouver couple, Neil and Vivian Mohle. No reason was given. Urgent was the last word on the message.

Deleting the message, Nolan restarted his motorcycle and headed home. He needed to get to a secure line and pass this along.

#

Governed by the Witness Protection Program Act and administered by the RCMP, Canada's federal Witness Protection Program is a significant tool in the country's fight against terrorism and organized crime. Designed for the safety of those who assist the authorities, it provides everything from short-term protection to permanent relocation for victims, informants or witnesses. Known internally as protectees, participants in the program may be referred from any Canadian police service, a federal department involved in national security or defense, or even a foreign agency. Ultimately, almost all protectees are provided with a confidential new identity.

With these resources at their disposal, Nolan Kulla's call to his colleagues in the RCMP's Serious and Organized Crime Unit also set in motion an immediate request to the British Columbia Witness Protection Unit for assistance and the appointment of a dedicated coordinator to monitor this particular file. It also sparked a furious search for all possible information available on both Neil and Vivian Mohle. Given the nature and urgency of Drew Jamieson's message, there was little doubt the Mohles knew something or had done something that would hurt one of the local Asian gangs. Information that the RCMP would dearly like to have in their ongoing fight against organized crime.

To the chagrin of all concerned, while there was plenty of smoke around Neil Mohle's business and social activities, nothing was found to warrant the reported contract on his or his wife's lives. The most revealing aspect into Mohle's character was an apparent weakness for attending high-profile society functions often in the company of controversial Vancouver promoters. Outside of that, his financial affairs appeared to be in order, with only a house mortgage and the usual credit card debts. He was active in the business community, played tennis at a local club and was scheduled to testify as a witness at an upcoming commercial court case.

"It's early in the game, but there's a high degree of frustration to this investigation." RCMP Inspector Jack Bowie reported to his superiors. "We're trying to track down shadows at this stage. It's an unusual combination, a staid banker often hanging out with a bunch of flashy financial types. He seems to pull it off because of the business he generates for the bank, and there's no suggestion he ever acts improperly. Initial reports indicate that most of Mohle's friends are regular members of the community, and despite the seemingly loose business practices of some of his clients, none of them have known links to organized crime. According to all reports, he's as straight as an arrow. On top of this, there is almost no secondary information available on his wife. At this point, we think they might simply have found themselves in the wrong place at the wrong time.

"We've considered pulling them in and warning them, but without any knowledge of what they might be involved in, this could have serious consequences for our undercover biker gang operation that took years to develop. If the Mohles let anyone know we've contacted them, our agent will be compromised. Besides, what if we're wrong and they aren't as squeaky clean as they appear? What we need is someone the Mohles know and trust to get a message to them. If that's not possible, we can't make a move until we're absolutely sure of the timing and location of the hit."

CHAPTER 17

Kitty

Kicking off her running shoes, Kitty dropped her gym bag and light coat onto the entrance hall floor and walked into the living room. She felt great, and wearing only black tights, tennis socks and a sports bra, she knew she looked as good as she felt. James looked up as she entered, a guilty expression on his face.

"What wrong?" Kitty asked.

"Nothing. Just looking at some cars."

"Cars?"

James looked embarrassed. "Yeah, nothing important."

"Oh. Did you speak to my father?"

"I did."

"And? What did he say? Give me a break. I'm pooped. Don't make me keep asking questions."

"He wanted to chat about Monger Capital. Apparently, he does have an investment in them, but he wants to keep it quiet. He said he'd talk to Monger, but that he wanted me to deny any family involvement when I next spoke to the bank."

"Can you do that?"

"Already done."

"Really? You look smug; I assume that means it went well."

"I think so. I spoke to Neil Mohle, and he was happy to accept my assurance that you are not related to the billionaire named Quon Jin Hu. I also took the opportunity to mention that, in Chinese business circles, they were sure there was no truth to the rumour about Quon Jin Hu also being this criminal Komodo." James smiled. "Of course, at least on that point I knew I was on solid ground, after all I had asked Quon Jin Hu himself. Not something I could admit to Neil, though."

Kitty suddenly felt nauseous. How could James ask her father if he was a criminal? What kind of question was that? "Did you really ask my father that?" she said. "What did he say?"

"As I told Neil, he laughed his head off. Apparently, it's quite a common rumour over there and obviously completely false. Seems because your dad's filthy rich and very secretive, he has as many enemies as friends. He said you couldn't amass a fortune in China without a great deal of political manoeuvring, which is bound to create animosity in some quarters. He figures it's these people who make up the rumours about him."

Relief flooded through Kitty. "And Vivian's husband was happy?" she asked.

"Very. I'm sure he's more worried about getting his big fat bonus from this deal than some far-fetched rumour."

"So your deal is good."

"Seems to be. On another note, your father had some interesting information for us."

Kitty's heart skipped a beat. Walking over to the kitchen island counter, she kept her back to James as she reached into the fridge below the counter top and removed a small bottle of sparkling water. "About what?" she asked.

"He's handing over a trust fund to us, and he wants me to manage it."

Kitty smiled. "No wonder you were looking at cars. What kind was it?"

"An Audi R8," James replied sheepishly.

Kitty laughed. "Welcome to the big leagues," she said. "I thought he'd do that someday. How much is the trust fund? Enough for the Audi?"

"One hundred million."

Kitty almost choked mid swallow. One hundred million! She knew her father too well. He wouldn't part with that much money without something serious in return. She'd need to play along for now to keep James from suspecting anything, but she knew it was only a matter of time before he was asked to do something in return. There would be a price to pay for all that money; of that, she was certain.

#

Kitty lay staring up at the ceiling, sweaty and spent. Alongside her, James, one arm loosely draped over her stomach, breathed heavily, his face buried in the pillow. Her father's news and James's resultant euphoria at their newfound wealth had, as she expected it would, culminated in a frenzied bout of lovemaking, immediately after which James had collapsed into deep untroubled sleep while she lay awake, stewing.

As instructed by her father, she had spoken with Vivian Mohle about a meeting between her husband and a wealthy offshore investor. Vivian, in turn, had promised to speak to Neil and get back to Kitty with some possible meeting times. She'd have to follow up in the morning and get the details back to her father before he became impatient and had that dreadful man Dong call her; he gave her the creeps.

CHAPTER 18

James

James awoke with a start, morning sun streaming in the bedroom window. Next to him, Kitty lay sleeping, flat on her stomach with only her feet covered by the duvet. The sight of her naked body immediately stirred in him all the desires of the previous evening. Deciding not to press his luck, he rolled out of bed and headed to the kitchen to brew some much needed morning coffee. He had a lot to do today, not least of which was to set in motion Quon's somewhat strange request regarding Woodstock Marine.

#

"Morning, Damian." James walked into Damian's office as he spoke.

Behind his large, but relatively uncluttered desk, Damian looked up from his laptop at James. "Morning. You seem cheerful. Something on your mind?"

"A couple of things, actually. Do you have a few minutes?"

"Sure, sit down. What's up?"

Despite the lightness of the exchange, James well knew how quickly Damian could change. He hated setbacks and coming to him with an unresolved problem was a sure way for the conversation to go downhill in a hurry. The old mantra "don't bring me problems; bring me solutions" really applied when it came to keeping Damian on an even keel.

"Well, the first one's kind of strange, but it's all resolved now and I just thought I'd let you know in case it ever comes up again. Earlier this week, I received a call from Neil Mohle from ECB, who wanted to meet with you about Monger. He's been doing some digging and came up with the idea that a possible Monger shareholder may have criminal ties."

"Shit, is this true?"

"Fortunately not, which is why I waited until we knew where we were before we bothered you with this stuff. Turns out the rumour is false on two counts. The person in question is neither a shareholder nor a criminal. It's also a good thing he called me first and didn't go straight to our finance department, who would probably have immediately called Monger to check. According to the grapevine, they are a touchy bunch and would be pretty pissed off if stuff like that were being bandied about. I suggest that if the topic ever comes up with the bankers again, just tell them you know about it and kill the discussion right there. We'd be in trouble if Monger starts looking at ways to drop out of our deal simply because we, or the bank, upset them. Our profitability on this deal is skinny enough already."

"Good call. What else?"

"I've been thinking about the Woodstock LNG vessels themselves. Right now, we've priced the whole deal based on the option pricing we obtained to build the ships at an as yet unspecified future date. We also can't give the shipyards a firm commitment to build until we know we've secured the long-term shipping contract for the gas, which won't be until the government awards the LNG terminal contract. Unlike years ago when we used to get these options at almost no cost, the shipyards now load the option pricing in order to protect themselves in case we don't exercise the options and let them expire. Essentially, they're covering their potential loss of other business by holding building slots open for us. To increase our profitability on this deal, I wondered how you felt about going firm on the contracts now, assuming we can get a reduced price, and we take the risk of the LNG deal in Kitimat not going forward."

"What do we do with the ships if our consortium isn't awarded the terminal contract?"

"We trade them on the spot market. The LNG market is picking up all the time, and if we don't have a long-term contract, we can either trade them ourselves or possibly even sell them off to some investment fund. Better yet, maybe Monger would agree to buy them at some predetermined price if the Kitimat contract falls through. They could structure some kind of deal around the ships and then flip the whole deal to their investor group. I know it's risky, but it's probably worth looking at and would restore some of the profitability we've lost by the enforced restructuring of this deal to meet the bank and government demands. At worst, maybe you could get the finance guys to re-run the models based on whatever pricing break the shipyards would give us if we commit to build immediately and then take a look at the incremental risk."

"Perhaps that's not as crazy as it first sounds," Damian said. "Let me think on it. Anything else?"

"No, that's it, thanks." James turned and walked slowly from Damian's office. He had done as Quon asked and delivered both messages. Only time would tell how things panned out. If Damian behaved as expected, he'd probably reject the spot market idea for now and then, after he'd made a few modifications, re-present it as his own. While this behaviour usually irked James, in this case, he certainly didn't mind. Although Quon had asked how James thought Damian would respond to the ideas, he hadn't elaborated why he had wanted the suggestions made. With nothing to lose and a sizeable trust fund to gain, James was more than willing to plant Quon's requested seeds.

CHAPTER 19

Kitty

When Kitty woke, James was long gone. Sleepily she picked up her mobile from the bedside table, the small flashing red light alerting her to a waiting text.

Morning, Hon. Early start. Gone to office. Call you later. James xox

Relieved to be alone, Kitty wondered what she should do next. Her own work could wait; there was nothing important happening. On the floor, Lulu, her tiny Shih Tzu, still slept, curled up in Kitty's discarded pajama bottoms. Deciding to take care of Lulu first, Kitty pulled on sweatpants and a top, woke the sleeping dog and headed out of the condominium for a quick walk. She needed to finalize the arrangements with Vivian; that was her first priority. Although still worried about what would happen at the meeting, she was even more terrified of upsetting her father again by not doing what he had asked.

#

What at first appeared to be a simple meeting request eventually proved quite difficult to accomplish. Between Neil Mohle's apparently busy evening schedule and her father's insistence of specific meeting parameters, Kitty and Vivian went back and forth over the course of several days before they were able to finalize the arrangements. In the end, their perseverance prevailed and the meeting was set. Dinner at the finest waterfront restaurant in Coal Harbour, where Neil had been a regular customer for years, at 8:30 p.m. on August 10th, to discuss a possible business deal with an as yet unnamed businessman who had ten million dollars to invest.

CHAPTER 20

Hayden

"I honestly never thought we'd end up like this," Hayden said.

"It was bound to, sooner or later," she replied. "We've been skirting on the edges for ages, and it all sort of came together in Kitimat—excuse the pun."

He leaned on his elbow and stroked her bare stomach. "Do you think we'll change?"

"Probably."

"Really? Is that good or bad?"

"I don't know, but I think sleeping with someone always changes things. You can get pretty intense without messing up a relationship, but that last step always makes things different."

"So what do we do?" Hayden asked.

"Nothing. Why don't we just see where it goes and how we feel. Are you okay with that?"

"Is there a choice?"

"Not really unless you want to end it now. I'm not in a position to let this become public."

"Then I'll take whatever I can get." Hayden smiled and simultaneously reached for her breast.

"Hmm... wait. I have a question. Didn't you say Woodstock's banker for the LNG deal was named Neil Mohle and that you knew him?"

"What? Where did that come from? I'm trying to deal with the task at hand," he gently squeezed her breast, "and you want to talk work."

"Answer and you may get lucky."

"Yes, I did. I didn't register having met him before until I called about the deal while we were all in Kitimat. I was trying to get a fix on how the Woodstock LNG financing was progressing, and we were dancing around how much he could tell me. Neil reminded me at the time that I should be familiar with the bank's confidentiality rules because I was working at its Toronto head office when he and I attended the same in-house credit course. I remembered him then; he's quite different from your usual banker. It was immediately after that call that I mentioned it to you, but no one else. Is there a problem?"

"No, no problem. He and his wife's names are in a note I received attached to an upcoming cabinet briefing memo. All it says is that the solicitor general will be providing further information tomorrow. There's no other detail, and as usual, the material is highly confidential. Unless you're also sleeping with the solicitor general, there's only one place you could have heard this, so you'd better not tell anyone."

"No chance of that, a sentiment which I'm sure he shares, but maybe can we focus on this other pressing issue for now," he said, sliding against her.

CHAPTER 21

Rachel

Rachel surveyed the room; everything seemed to be in order for the cabinet meeting. She was looking directly at the open door when Marie Bergeron walked in, a thin brown briefcase hanging from a long leather strap draped casually over one shoulder and a white take-out coffee cup in her hand.

"Hello, Rachel."

"Hi, Marie."

"Everything ready?"

"Yes. I think so. Apparently, there may be someone else dialling in to the meeting, but I haven't been given the name. I've left a note for the premier to call me if you need any help linking them in."

"Okay. I know I'm early, but I wanted to beat the traffic. If you're finished, I'll just sit here and go over the material before we start."

"I'm done," said Rachel. "Let me know if you need anything. I'll be at my desk until the meeting is over."

Gosh, she looks good, Rachel thought as she left the room, her mind immediately jumping to her last call with Hayden Jones. She was so sure he'd be with Marie when she called, and yet she'd found him apparently alone and Marie at breakfast with other members of the cabinet. Her pent-up anxiety had evaporated immediately. Perhaps she'd been mistaken; maybe they weren't having an affair after all. The unexpected outcome caught her off guard, and in her desperate attempt to think of some appropriate reason for calling, she had stupidly blurted out the first thing that came to mind—the confidential special donor list. Hopefully, Hayden would let it go and not ask any more about it. At least, she'd resisted the impulse to give him the names.

Back at her desk, Rachel's hand hovered over the shredder as she took one last look at the list included in the pile of documents the premier had left on her desk to be shredded. She was familiar with the first two names, both well-known international corporations with ties to local industries. The third name was new, Monger Capital—she hadn't seen that one before. It also had that funny Ng notation in brackets behind the name that she'd seen on the premier's scribbled note a few days earlier. Maybe it was a name? She should have realized that before. Perhaps it was the same donor?

Rachel knew that under Canada's Elections Act, corporations and foreign entities were strictly prohibited from donating to a federal political party. She also knew that unlike the federal regulations, and until very recently, the British Columbia Elections Act had no such prohibition or limit. B.C. was, at the time, reported to be one of the few democratic jurisdictions in the world that actually welcomed such political donations. Over time, the subject had become a major issue for all political parties, with polls indicating that the majority of British Columbians would prefer a total ban on foreign and corporate donations.

Against this backdrop, the previous provincial government had amended the legislation imposing similar prohibitions on provincial party election financing, as had their federal counterparts. As a stopgap measure, transition rules were also established to govern political contributions received before the amending legislation received Royal Assent. Specifically, political donations received during the transitional period from an organization who would no longer be eligible once the new legislation was in place could not be used towards election expenses or specified communications. By default, therefore, and fortuitously leaving an enormous hole in the legislation to accommodate the generosity of past corporate and foreign donors, the money could be used for all other political purposes. Irrespective of the actual legislation, the sensitivity of the voting public on this topic remained another matter altogether, and it was for this reason that the premier had Hugh Ruff maintaining two lists of donors for funds received prior to the legislation coming into force. No great effort was expended on keeping local corporate donations under wraps. The law allowed for their specific usage, and Dana's government would comply appropriately. In the meantime, they provided a significant, albeit somewhat compromised, portion of the war chest for ultimately fighting and winning elections.

The special donor list was different. This comprised the names of those donors who were known or suspected of being funded by foreign individuals or corporations. This was much harder, even impossible at times, to justify to the electorate and, as such, was kept as confidential as possible. No voter would ever accept that the donations were made without some expectation of favouritism, and probably at the expense of somebody local. There was, of course, also the risk that the original source of such foreign funding, legal or otherwise, was unknown. Slipping the list into the shredder, Rachel listened to the comforting grind as the paper was reduced to unrecognizable strips.

CHAPTER 22

Dana

Dana Holmes looked around the room at her cabinet members. Carefully picked, they were loyal to a fault. This was the one place where she could be entirely candid without fear of leaks. This was her team, and even if she had to say it herself, they were damned good.

Also in attendance on this particular morning, despite not being a member of the cabinet, was Hugh Ruff, strategist and chief fundraiser for the party. A job made significantly more difficult by the recent changes to the provincial Elections Act. Changes that in their current form would really only benefit the smallest and traditionally least effective party—a typical case of catering to the lowest common denominator in order to stay in power.

Because of the clear voter sentiment on the political donations issue and the constant sniping of the opposition parties, Dana and her cabinet received regular monthly briefings from Hugh Ruff on anyone on the special donor list. Unfortunately, on this particular morning, the solicitor general had asked to move his agenda item forward and, due to the sensitivity of the matter, that Hugh be excused from the meeting. With only one name on the list for discussion on this occasion, Dana saw no reason not to acquiesce to the request, suggesting that Hugh save any update until the following month's meeting.

After a brief pause while Hugh gathered his papers and left the room, Dana spoke. "Okay, let's get started. I believe the solicitor general has the floor. Go ahead, Charles. What's happening that is so urgent?"

Charles Crofut leaned back in his chair, ran his fingers through his grey hair and looked slowly around the room. "Despite my many years practising law, this is new ground for me," he said, "and likely also for everyone else at the table. While I'm not sure there is anything we can actually do about the matter that isn't already being done, we need to be aware of the circumstances and prepare ourselves for any possible repercussions if it takes place."

"Very mysterious, Charles. Now you really have our attention," Marie Bergeron interrupted.

Charles frowned. "Sadly, that's probably true. I thought Canada was above things like this. We're supposed to be a civilized society."

"Come on, Charles. Spit it out."

Charles looked directly at the MLA from Vancouver's Kitsilano neighbourhood who had spoken. "It's in your back yard, I'm afraid. Apparently, there is a contract in place on two members of your constituency."

"What?!" Dana's face paled. "Do you mean what I think you do by 'a contract'?"

"Yes, I do. The contract killing of two of our citizens. The RCMP are all over it, but were concerned enough to advise me of the possibility. I, in turn, thought you should all be aware of what is going on. You will naturally need to keep this strictly confidential. People's lives are at stake."

"Do you know their names?" Dana asked.

"Again, on a strictly confidential basis, it's a husband and wife from the Kitsilano area: Neil and Vivian Mohle."

"Why don't we just tell them?"

"Do they have criminal connections?"

"Who wants them killed?"

Dana, seated opposite Charles, watched his head turn quickly from side to side like a tennis match spectator as the cabinet members seated around the long conference room table rattled off questions. Before he could respond, she held up her hand, palm outward. "Hold on, let's do this slowly and allow Charles to brief us as he thinks best. There may be information that the police don't want to share at this time, and I'm sure you have dozens of questions; I know I do."

"Here's what I know," Charles said. "The Mohles are an apparently normal couple with no known criminal ties. Despite apparently dressing somewhat stylishly, he's an otherwise regular banker, and she's a hairstylist, but quite a bit younger than he is. Both work in Vancouver. The best guess at this point is that they have somehow stumbled into something, which, if exposed, would cause serious harm to some criminal network."

"Do we know which criminal group is involved?" Dana asked.

"Two, it seems. An Asian gang set up the contract, but farmed out its execution, my apologies for the term, to a biker group. I've not been told which biker group or why. Perhaps this is normal gang modus operandi; it's certainly well outside my experience."

"What connection do the Mohles have with any Asian gang?" Dana asked.

"Apart from Ms. Mohle being of Chinese descent, none that we know."

"So why don't we just tell them and put them in protective custody for a time?"

"A couple of reasons. Firstly, we don't know what they know and, as such, don't know how long we would need to keep them in protective custody before any danger had passed, if ever. Secondly, the RCMP have an undercover agent embedded deep within the motorcycle gang. The agent has been undercover for several years and, along with putting his life at risk on a daily basis, is one of very few people who are aware of the contract. Apparently, the timing has not yet been established. Contacting the Mohles now will immediately put the agent at serious risk of discovery, particularly if there is something about the Mohles that the police don't know. The risk of a leak also increases exponentially after they have been contacted; no one is currently in a position to gauge whom they may tell. The RCMP even had serious reservations about my informing you of this matter. A leak at this time could be disastrous for all concerned. Bottom line, we are currently between a rock and a very hard place."

"So what are you asking the cabinet to do?" Marie Bergeron asked.

"Nothing for the time being, but we ought to be thinking about what we might say if this gets away from us. We can't have gangs murdering our local population without expecting a great deal of voter anger at our inability to safely protect them."

"What are the police doing in the interim?" Dana asked.

"Trying to establish when this might take place, what the reason is and, if possible, how to get the Mohles into some form of protection without jeopardizing the agent's life. I believe they are currently looking for some contact that both they and the Mohles would trust to deliver the message. All of this is predicated on the Mohles having become inadvertently involved and having no direct criminal connections themselves. If it turns out they do, I'm sure the matter will be handled differently."

Realizing the topic was one that allowed for endless speculation, Dana stepped in and redirected the group's attention to the remaining outstanding matters on their agenda. Charles Crofut was tasked with providing the cabinet with regular updates on the Mohle affair, which would henceforth be added to the agenda under the heading "Burrows". No one was ever going to accuse her of not maintaining her sense of humour in the face of adversity.

CHAPTER 23

Hayden

As any billionaire will tell you, financial success, whether achieved through legitimate or dishonest activities, requires not only hard work and meticulous attention to detail, but also a reasonable slice of luck. As such, Quon Jin Hu was confident that, with even a modicum of luck, his careful plans to mitigate his daughters error would prevent the further exposure of his involvement in Monger Capital and, in turn, Monger's ultimate source of financing. In this instance, however, Lady Luck had other ideas.

Unbeknownst to Quon, just ahead of the change in provincial legislation, and in order to facilitate the company's legal investment opportunities, John Ng had donated a sizeable amount to the provincial government directly from Monger Capital. Because of the possibility of offshore funding, that investment then appeared on Hugh Ruff's special donor list.

The matter may well have ended there, but for two other seemingly unrelated events. Hayden Jones became privy to the confidential list through the offhand comments of the premier's assistant while simultaneously learning of a sizeable political donation made by an unknown investment company.

Once again, with just a little luck, Monger may have slipped under the radar. Hayden had not yet learned the company name, and with the passage of time, the provincial government's somewhat cursory examination may have been satisfied and Monger Capital's name removed from the list.

Perhaps it was not surprising then that luck, having already chosen her side, dealt Quon one further fateful blow. The planned contract killing of the Mohles was discovered and placed on the provincial cabinet agenda by the solicitor general. This event in-turn resulted in the ejection of Hugh Ruff from the meeting, an action that bruised his already fragile ego and rendered him, albeit briefly, off guard.

#

Hayden watched Hugh emerge from the cabinet room and walk hurriedly towards him down the long corridor. Hugh's shoulders were slumped, and he looked decidedly unhappy.

"Morning, Hugh. You look like someone turfed you out of the meeting. Cheer up, bud. It can't be that bad."

"Says who?" Hugh replied. "It's always the same with these bloody cabinet meetings. Anytime anything supposedly important turns up, it's flagged as confidential and I have to leave. Unless we receive a significant investment, I only attend one of these damned meetings a month and my material hardly takes any time at all. You'd think they could stick to the schedule. It's not as though the special donor list is irrelevant. One wrong donor and we'd all be buried in shit."

Hayden could hardly believe his luck. Not only had Hugh provided the opening he needed, in his anger, he had overlooked the fact that Hayden may not be aware of the list or its contents despite his frequent access to the premier. Trusting his instincts and despite the risk of exposure, Hayden tried to sound knowledgeable using the threads of information he had already discovered. "I guess you had planned to brief them further on the new investment fund that came on board."

"Yeah, and it's about as clear as mud. This Monger Capital bunch are a closed shop, as far as their ultimate ownership are concerned. They're probably fine, but the cabinet needs to know where we stand."

Suddenly, as if realizing he had spoken out of turn, Hugh's anger seemed to dissipate and his voice dropped to a conspiratorial whisper. "Probably said too much," he muttered. "Keep it to yourself, will you. Can't have the premier thinking I'm not onside."

Before Hayden could respond, Hugh patted him on the arm as he brushed past him and continued his hurried walk down the corridor.

Finally, a name. While he'd give anything to see the whole list, Hayden recognized this was the first real opportunity he'd uncovered. Rachel had mentioned there were three on the list. Why were they different? All three could be entirely legitimate, but at least now he had one name he could report. There were others at CSIS headquarters who could investigate the company while he continued to ferret out information right here. Furthermore, one important question remained: whatever the reason for the list, if there was something unusual about the companies, were Hugh Ruff, the premier and the cabinet just sloppy or were they somehow complicit?

CHAPTER 24

Kitty

Kitty shivered as she replaced the telephone. Dong Lai did that to her. She rubbed the goose bumps that covered both her arms. She really didn't like that man. Although she had called her father on his office line, it was Dong who answered and Dong who then asked for the details of the meeting arrangements. Kitty hadn't argued; she wanted to get off the phone as quickly as possible.

Scooping up Lulu, she tucked the little dog under her arm and headed out to the coffee shop. Perhaps a latté would make her feel better. She needed time to think. Beyond the meeting, she didn't know what her father had planned, but the fact that Dong was involved filled her with dread. Maybe if he hadn't stressed that neither she nor James was to attend the dinner, she'd have felt better. Dong's only response when she'd asked why was that Quon had instructed him to pass on the message. As he fawningly answered whenever pressed, he was only doing his job.

One good thing had come out of this whole mess, though. Outside of any knowledge of her father's illicit activities, James was now truly one of the family, and he was like a kid with a new toy as the trust fund arrangements started falling into place. No longer did she have to listen to him whine about Damian and the Woodstock group. With his ego now bolstered by their recent and unexpected good fortune, he brushed off the usual office politics with ease. Like it or not, James had a newfound confidence and a seemingly insatiable sexual appetite to boot.

CHAPTER 25

James

"What did you think about Damian's board presentation, James? Can you believe they agreed?" Dan Fortin asked.

"I only read your minutes. Although Damian usually invites me to sit in on these meetings, I wasn't asked to attend this one. Based on the minutes, I'm okay with it, with the exception of the bit about giving John Ng a seat on the Woodstock Marine Board of Directors. That's our parent company. Why do you think Damian offered that up?"

"Beats me unless that's what he ultimately had to trade to get Monger Capital's agreement to take the ships if the gas deal falls through. If it all works out, though, he's going to look like a hero. Outright ordering of the ships now rather than pricing the deal off the options certainly improves the profitability, and one board seat out of nine only gives them a seat at the table. It doesn't affect control. Ultimately it shouldn't make much difference."

James nodded. As expected, Damian had initially rejected the spot market idea and then, after making a few minor modifications, represented it to the board as his own. The board seat was an unexpected twist, though. James wondered if somehow Quon had been behind that too.

CHAPTER 26

Dana

With the cabinet meeting over, Dana returned to her office, dropping a small pile of papers onto Rachel's desk as she passed. "Can you shred these for me, please? I don't want to leave them in the general bin. There are a few sensitive items in there."

Instinctively, Rachel looked down at the papers before replying. Stapled to the front page was a note with the name Neil Mohle highlighted in yellow. "Oh," Rachel said.

"Something wrong?" Dana asked.

"No, Premier, sorry. I didn't mean to read the material. The name just jumped out at me. I worked with a Neil Mohle when I was at ECB."

"You did? Somehow I'd forgotten you worked at ECB before joining us. How well did you know him?" Despite the casualness of the enquiry, Dana listened very carefully to the reply.

"Pretty well inside the office. Enough to share a few personal details from time to time. I never saw him socially outside the bank, nor did I ever meet his wife. He was a bit different from the rest of the staff."

Dana laughed. "I keep hearing that comment. It's enough to make me want to meet the man." Realizing that she had said as much as she should on the topic, Dana picked up the paper with the Mohles' names and fed it directly into Rachel's shredder before continuing to her own office and closing the door behind her. The shredder had destroyed any comments she may have scribbled on the note; only the formal minutes of the meeting would remain.

Flopping down awkwardly into the ergonomically designed chair behind her table-like desk, Dana kicked off her shoes. It had been that kind of day. It was moments like these that made her realize how empty her life had become. Everything revolved around the job. Without that, who was she really? The closest thing to normality were her occasional trysts, and even those were born of need and familiarity. At some point, they too would need to end. Exposure to any sexual indiscretion was a political liability she could not afford.

Wiggling her toes, Dana slid down her chair and stretched out her legs while pressing her stockinged feet against the top edge at the back of her desk, her mind turning to her conversation with Rachel. How coincidental that Rachel knew Neil Mohle from ECB. Perhaps she knew Jones from there too? If so, why hadn't she mentioned it? Charles Crofut said the RCMP needed someone both they and the Mohles could trust to deliver a message, why not one of his former colleagues from ECB? Dana reached for the telephone and looked at the list of speed dial numbers fastened alongside. Charles Crofut was number eight. Dana pressed eight and listened to the distant ring.

CHAPTER 27

Neil

There was something strange about the meeting request. Always on the lookout for new business, Neil usually jumped at any opportunity to meet a potential new client. In fact, if his memory served him correctly that was precisely what he had done when first asked to meet this colleague of the Lee's. It was only after that initial confirmation that an inordinate amount of time had seemed to be spent narrowing down the perfect location and a precise time for dinner. Several times he had offered to make the arrangements himself by speaking directly to the other party, but on each occasion, he'd been rebuffed with one excuse or another. Perhaps that was it; even now, he still didn't know the name of the person they were to meet. If James and Kitty had not also been attending, he probably would've cancelled before now.

Despite his misgivings, the matter had eventually been settled. The dinner would take place at his favourite restaurant in Coal Harbour, and he would finally meet this unnamed businessman. Even though the Lee's had made the arrangements, he couldn't resist calling the restaurant and asking the maître d' for their best window table, the one overlooking the harbour and the North Shore mountains. As a regular and valued customer, he was promised that it would be available.

Still, he couldn't shake the feeling that this investor sounded too good to be true. The idea that a legitimate businessman had ten million dollars that he didn't know what to do with struck him as pretty weird. And why offer to send a limousine over to pick them up? This was Neil's home turf. Sending a limo was overkill. Still, having decided that declining would have looked petty, unless some reasonable excuse presented itself, he was pretty well stuck with the arrangement for now.

CHAPTER 28

Drew

Stretched out full length on the floor of the garage, Drew peered at the awkwardly located oil tank sight glass of the Harley-Davidson motorcycle. Like many others without a centre stand, the Harley's sight glass location at the bottom of the engine required either a mirror on a telescoping rod or someone sitting astride the motorcycle to keep it level while another checked the oil. In this instance, Vegas had the former task while Drew checked the level.

Because of the arrangement, Vegas's attempts to extract his suddenly ringing mobile phone from the back pocket of his tight jeans rocked the motorcycle from side to side.

"Hey, Vegas, keep it steady, will you?"

"Yeah, sorry." As he finished his brief apology, Vegas flipped open his old-style mobile and answered the call. "Vegas."

As Vegas sat silently listening, Drew finished checking the oil, then stood waiting. A moment later, Vegas disconnected the call. "We've got the location and the date," he said.

"When's that?" Drew asked.

"August 10th evening at Coal Harbour, a waterfront restaurant."

"Who called?"

Vegas stared intently at Drew in response. "Why?" he asked.

"That's less than a week," Drew replied, attempting to draw attention away from his earlier question. "Can you get set up in time? Who will you use?" As he finished speaking, Drew reached down and fiddled with the motorcycle fuel tap. His attempt to find out more about the contract had been worth a try, but Vegas had been instantly alert.

"It'll be close," Vegas replied. "I'll talk to the twins. If it doesn't look right to them, they can pick their own time and people. The Chinese won't be happy, but I'm not risking our guys for their shit. If we can't get away clean, then no deal until we're ready. You finished?"

"Yeah, thanks. Oil's fine; fuel's on. You're good to go."

Moments later, Drew watched as Vegas roared out of the driveway, his long blond hair flowing out behind his black beanie helmet. That had been close. Vegas protected his contacts almost as well as he protected the club.

Drew was still watching when he heard Scrubber's voice behind him. "Where's he off to in such a hurry?"

"Target timing is set. He needs to get organized. It's only . . ."

"Don't tell me," Scrubber interjected. "I don't want to know. The less I know about these things, the better I sleep."

"Works for me. My bike's not running quite right. I'm going to take it for a hard ride and see if that will clean it out. You need anything?"

"Which way are you going?"

Drew looked at his watch: 3 p.m. "Don't really mind. Probably up the highway to Qualicum and back. The limit's one twenty on that stretch, so it's good for the bike. Shouldn't be more than a couple of hours."

"No, I'm good. See you later."

#

As Drew exited the long lane entering the highway to Qualicum Beach, he gently twisted the throttle and the deep roar of the Harley-Davidson exhaust echoed off the nearby cliffs as the motorcycle responded flawlessly. *Good thing Scrubber can't hear this,* Drew thought and smiled as he accelerated away.

#

Drew walked into the brown wooden oceanfront pub in Qualicum Beach shortly before four o'clock and looked slowly around. Brown tables with their red Formica-topped surfaces were dotted throughout the partitioned room. Darkened pub to one side and waist-high windows running the full length of the room and facing the ocean on the other. At each end, a TV featured the day's highlighted sports event, rendered almost irrelevant alongside the expansive and spectacular ocean view. Back dropped by distant mountains and interrupted only by a single low-lying island somewhere in-between, the ocean stretched as far as the eye could see. At one of the tables, on a black leather-topped bench seat facing the ocean and sandwiched between two semi-bald grey-haired older men, sat Nolan Kulla.

"Fuck," Drew muttered to himself. There was no time for the usual message protocol, and as it was Thursday, he had taken a chance on being able to deliver the information in person and while alone. Sitting down at a nearby table, he ordered a drink and, in a voice loud enough to be heard several tables away, asked the server directions to the washroom. His drink ordered, he stood and, leaving his gloves and keys on the table, walked across the room to the small washroom at the back.

As he hoped, minutes later, Nolan Kulla squeezed inside.

"Sorry, kind of cramped in here," Nolan said, as he manoeuvred alongside Drew, who was standing facing the urinal.

"No problem," Drew replied, by which time Nolan had confirmed that the single stall in the small washroom was empty.

"You have more details?" Nolan asked.

"Coal Harbour, waterfront restaurant, dinner, on evening of August 10th. That's the first contact. Outcome will depend on what opportunities present themselves. The Evans twins have been given the job."

"Those crazy bastards," Nolan replied. "That's scary. The only thing they've got going for them is when they're all cleaned up, they look like every other executive in town." Then, realizing the impact of what he had just said, he muttered, "Oh, shit."

Zipping up his pants, Drew stood washing his hands as he spoke. "Unless something changes, don't expect more from me. Tell HQ they need to get these two out of town in a hurry. Give me a minute before you leave." With that, he walked from the washroom and returned to his table where a single bottle of Corona, a slice of green lime jammed in its neck, waited alongside his black leather gloves and keys.

Several minutes later, Drew watched as Nolan returned to his group and, after a brief apology and excuse for his early departure, left some money on the table to pay for his drink and walked out of the pub.

His task complete, Drew sat quietly staring out to sea while he finished his drink before leaving. His message delivered, he'd enjoy the ride back and, if asked, could honestly report that his bike was running beautifully, whatever was wrong with it before presumably cured by the extended high-speed run along the highway.

#

By the time Drew reached the Outpost, his message too had reached its destination. Wasting no time after leaving the pub, Nolan had returned home where he immediately phoned in his report from the secure landline in his comfortable office located above the double garage and well out of earshot of the main house. That done and satisfied that there was nothing further he could do about the matter, he joined his wife in the living room downstairs. One more cold beer before dinner would round out yet another perfect day of an otherwise uneventful retirement.

CHAPTER 29

Jack

Within minutes of receipt of Nolan's message, the RCMP group responsible for the Mohle case had assembled in Inspector Jack Bowie's office to review their options, which, after several minutes of circular conversation, appeared to be severely limited.

"So, in summary," Inspector Bowie said, "without any crime having been committed and to protect our undercover source, at this stage its either offering witness protection now or conducting ongoing surveillance with the intent of preventing the crime as and when it happens. Anyone have any further thoughts on these two options?"

"Surveillance takes a lot of manpower and has a significant risk of failure to prevent the actual event. While we have the first contact information, we still don't know exactly when and where the actual hit is expected to take place."

Jack looked at the young RCMP corporal standing near the door of his office who had spoken. "True," he replied. "With that in mind, we had better assume it will take place at the very first meeting. We have that location, we know the Evans twins are involved in some way with the arrangements, and we know the Mohles are meeting for evening dinner."

"Why not offer them witness protection just before the dinner?" Sergeant Kate Harrington asked. A member of the RCMP Serious

Crime Unit and in this instance the assigned Witness Protection Program coordinator for the Mohles' case, she was both prepared and anxious to get them into the program and out of harm's way. "If we could meet them somewhere before they go out, at least the offer would be on the table. We have no idea what these thugs may have planned for during or after the dinner. The dinner arrangements are the only certainty we have at this time. Anything we decide to do will have to take place before that time."

"A meeting immediately before dinner may not be a bad idea," Jack replied. "According to the solicitor general, there are two current members of the premier's staff who previously worked at the same bank as Neil Mohle. We could conceivably use them to deliver the offer."

"Why both? Why not just one?"

"It lends more credibility," Jack answered. "One person could look like a set-up of some sort. It's much harder to fake something with two apparently unrelated parties delivering the same message. It doesn't leave us much time, though."

"That's okay," Sergeant Harrington said. "We can stash them out of the way while we sort out the longer term details. Who are the two? And what do we know about them?"

"One is an executive assistant to the premier; the other has some sort of special advisor role. According to the solicitor general, the executive assistant's background is straightforward, but apparently, the premier became quite evasive when he pressed her for more detail on the advisor. Let's get their names into the system and see what comes up. Assuming it's all good, we can set things in motion to get the Mohles off the street and into your program."

#

Several hours later, Inspector Jack Bowie looked up from the document he was reading at the sharp knock on his open office door. "Come in, Kate. What's on your mind?"

"You're not going to believe this, Inspector, but we ran the names and guess what? The premier's advisor is from CSIS. We've no idea what he's doing here, but it's right under our noses, and as far as we can tell, nobody in our network knows why. I'm not suggesting we get into an argument with CSIS, but shouldn't they keep us informed? What are we supposed to do now?"

"Could we still use him without letting on that we know where he's from?"

"We could try, but I'm not sure that would work. We'd probably be better off telling him we know where's he's from and make sure that whatever he's up to, our paths don't cross. We wouldn't want to expose him no matter how upset we are that we're out of the loop, as far as his activities are concerned. If it's ok with you, I'd rather approach him directly than through some indirect back channel. We really don't have time to let this get bogged down in a territorial argument."

"What are the chances we're both on the same path?"

"That seems unlikely. Mob violence is not normally on the CSIS radar, but I'll sound him out and report back. Putting my initial irritation aside, his being involved may even work to our advantage. He'd understand our issues and should know how to present the facts to the Mohles."

CHAPTER 30

Hayden

Hayden's pace slowed as he joined the steady stream of people filling the sidewalk along Victoria's inner harbour. Situated across from the legislature buildings, the harbour's marina provided a magnificent and tranquil backdrop as Victoria's citizens, from either the nearby residential areas or downtown transit stops, headed to their offices.

Despite anything Murphy's Law might say to the contrary, Hayden had a feeling that the day would be perfect. He felt energized after his morning run. There was nothing on the premier's calendar that required his immediate attention, and his report to CSIS had been received with interest. So much so, that some back-room technical wizard was already hard at work digging into Monger Capital's shareholder details. A quick shower at his downtown apartment, then a coffee and a smoked salmon bagel on the way to his office in the legislature building and he'd be good to go. Absent any interruptions, he planned to spend the majority of the day looking through the various LNG deals under consideration by the government and investigating their funding sources. No point in only focusing on the Woodstock deal and letting the others languish. Smiling to himself as he headed for his apartment, Hayden wondered who the original Murphy was and how the saying "whatever can go wrong, will go wrong" arose before becoming Murphy's Law, or Sod's Law as the Brits would say. For that matter, who was Sod and how had he come up with the same law as Murphy? Loving trivia, Hayden decided he would look it up as soon as he reached the office.

#

As Hayden walked through the large entrance doors of the grey stone legislature building, Rachel Burton rushed up to him.

"Where have you been?" she asked. "The premier's been looking for you for almost thirty minutes. There's an RCMP officer here who wants to meet with you and me. She wouldn't say what it's about, and she wouldn't meet with me until she had spoken to you. Do you know what's going on?"

"No idea," Hayden replied. "What does the premier want?"

"I don't know. She just told me to find you before you spoke to the RCMP."

"Okay, I'll just drop my bagel and coffee in my office and head straight there."

"I'll do it for you. The premier's already upset because you weren't here when she needed you."

Hayden looked miserable as he handed the requested items to Rachel and headed directly to the premier's office. A hot coffee and bagel at the end of his run was his reward for completing his morning exercise routine. Somehow a cold version after his meeting didn't have the same appeal. Reaching the premier's office, he knocked on the doorframe and walked through the open door without waiting to be invited. "I hear you are looking for me," he said.

"Yes," Dana replied. "Close the door, will you. I need a quick word before you meet with the RCMP."

Hayden turned and closed the door before returning to stand behind the chairs in front of the Dana's desk. "Any idea what they want?"

"Yes. They need someone who knows Neil Mohle to give him a message. I told Charles Crofut that both you and Rachel had worked with Mohle at ECB. Charles gave your names to the RCMP, and Sergeant Harrington turned up this morning asking to speak with you and Rachel. She wants to speak to you first, though, although she wouldn't say why."

"You didn't tell them . . . ?"

Before Hayden could finish his sentence, Dana interrupted. "No. I didn't tell them anything about you, other than you had mentioned working with Neil Mohle at ECB. I also told them that neither you nor Rachel are privy to the information Charles gave to the cabinet."

"Well, at least that part's true. What's this all about?"

"I gave her my word that I'd let her fill you in. She's in the conference room and probably tired of waiting around. Why don't you go there now and find out for yourself."

#

Hayden looked through the glass wall of the conference room before entering. Inside, Sergeant Kate Harrington, petite with blonde hair pulled tightly back in a short ponytail, the complete antithesis of anyone's image of a rugged RCMP officer, stood looking down as her thumbs moved rapidly over the keys of her mobile phone. She stopped typing and looked up as Hayden entered.

"Hi. I'm Hayden Jones. Sorry to have kept you waiting, but I wasn't expecting you and had a late start. I understand from the premier that you wanted to speak to me about getting a message to Neil Mohle."

Kate stood and held out her hand. "Sergeant Kate Harrington, RCMP," she said. "What else did the premier tell you?"

"That's about it, except you also planned to speak with Rachel Burton although I don't know why it would take two of us to deliver a message, or for that matter why you couldn't do it yourselves. Oh, yes, and one more thing, she said you needed to speak to me before you spoke to Rachel. Quite frankly, it all doesn't make much sense."

Hayden watched closely as Kate placed her mobile phone on the table, then paused for several moments before speaking.

"Look," she said, "we are faced with a situation where we need to get a message to Neil Mohle within the next few days, and we need to have it delivered by someone he trusts. Without the luxury of time, we have fortuitously stumbled over the fact that both you and the premier's assistant have worked with him in the past."

"So why both of us? Surely one would suffice."

"I'll get to that, but bear with me for a moment. Having discovered the two of you, we needed to make sure that there was nothing about you that could jeopardize our plans."

"You mean you dug into our backgrounds."

"Yes. As I said, we don't have the luxury of time. Both Neil Mohle and his wife's lives are at stake."

"And what did you find? I assume if you telling me this, you were satisfied with the results of your investigation."

"Well, almost. Rachel Burton is an open book; you, however, appear to work for CSIS."

Hayden sat back in his chair, trying hard not to let the surprise show on his face. "Why would you think that?" he asked.

Kate leaned forward. "It seems that you've worked with us in the past. Look, we don't want to know what you're doing, nor do we want our investigation to conflict with yours. The only reason I'm telling you that we know of your CSIS link is to prevent any problems."

"Who else have you told?" Hayden asked.

"No one," Kate replied.

"What about the premier?"

"No one," Kate repeated. "We need to get the Mohles into witness protection, and as long as this doesn't interfere with your own investigation, we would like you and Rachel to make the offer. Apart from that, any information we have about you will stay buried."

"Okay, why don't you tell me about the Mohles and we can take it from there. On the surface, I don't see how the delivery of a message could negatively affect my own activities, but I'd like to defer committing until I have the whole story. Should we get Rachel and you can brief us both at the same time?"

"Actually, given your background, I'm willing to tell you everything we know. Once we have your agreement to help, we plan to give Rachel an abridged version. Her role is more one of adding credibility and providing some additional cover. She really doesn't need to know all the details."

"Fine. Why don't you start?"

As Hayden listened to the details of the RCMP information, he was struck by the parallels to his own money laundering investigation. Although there was no evidence of a direct link, the Mohle contract had apparently been instigated by a Chinese criminal group and yet, because of some "association" with the intended victims, had been passed on to a biker gang for its execution. As far as the RCMP were aware, Neil Mohle had no Chinese mob association, and further, they had not been able to ascertain why a contract had been issued on the Mohles' lives. Hayden knew that it was unusual for Chinese criminals to go after family members of their primary target unless somehow the family members themselves had information that could hurt the gang. This probably meant that both Neil and Vivian Mohle shared knowledge that was prejudicial to this particular organization.

His own investigation into illegal Chinese money flows had led him to Monger Capital and a transaction where Neil Mohle was the banker. Perhaps the two were linked? While the RCMP had uncovered his CSIS connection, they were unaware of the nature of his current investigation and he planned to keep it that way. He would agree to deliver their message to the Mohles, but he wouldn't lose sight of his own objective, nor would he reveal any details of his own activities.

#

Rachel burst into Hayden's office. "Can you believe what's happening?" she asked rhetorically. "Sergeant Harrington said you have already agreed to deliver the message to the Mohles, but that they would like me to go along to complete our cover as two couples merely out socializing. Apparently, you are going to present the Mohles with an offer of protection by the RCMP. I thought this kind of thing only happened in movies. What would they have done if we hadn't both been working here?"

"I guess they'd have found another way to get the message to the Mohles. Kind of scary, though. It seems their lives are in danger."

"I never thought of it that way," Rachel replied. "It felt exciting for a moment."

"Didn't mean to rain on your parade, but I was just sitting here wondering what will happen to them if they don't accept the offer."

"Do you know what they are involved in?"

"No, the RCMP didn't say. It seems the less we know, the better. Just deliver the message and then forget about it, they said."

"How on earth can we forget about it? I understand what they mean, though, but it's hard not to be curious. How will you set up the meeting? Sergeant Harrington didn't give me any details; she just asked me to follow your lead. Apparently you'll stay in touch with her as to how things work out."

"Yeah. I'm supposed to call Neil Mohle today and press for a meeting on the evening of August 10th. I'm going to use the need for a quick discussion on the Woodstock LNG project as the reason. It seems the Mohles have a business dinner that same evening, so it will probably end up being drinks before dinner. Don't ask me where the RCMP got the information. I didn't ask."

"That's only a few days away. What shall I wear?"

Hayden laughed, and then turned serious. "Actually, that's probably not as frivolous a question as it sounds. If we assume the Mohles do have a dinner later that evening, they will probably be dressed in business attire for the occasion. Why don't we do the same to make sure we blend in and then treat ourselves to dinner in downtown Vancouver afterwards. Maybe we can even get the RCMP to pay although that's probably highly unlikely. Unless your other half would be upset," he added quickly.

"No other half to worry about, and dinner would be great," Rachel replied. "No sense in wasting an evening in Vancouver. Do you plan on us catching the last ferry back to Victoria? If so, we'd better watch the time. I'm not sure when it stops running."

"We might as well stay over. There's no certainty how things will develop and how much time we may need. Would you mind checking with the premier and then, assuming it's okay, booking us accommodation at a hotel downtown? I'm sure she'll agree to the government picking up the tab. I think we should try to keep this under the radar as much as we can. The premier is already in the loop, and that way it will look like regular government business. In the meantime, I'll try to get hold of Neil Mohle and make the meeting arrangements. I'll get Donna to let you know as soon as I've heard."

"Okay. I can do that." Rachel turned away, speaking over her shoulder as she left the office. "By the way, I didn't see Donna when I came in earlier. That's why I walked straight in."

Alone in his office once again, Hayden stared blankly at his desk blotter. No matter which way he examined things, he couldn't believe this was all mere coincidence and that the threat on Neil Mohle's life wasn't somehow tied to the recent financing arrangements for the Woodstock LNG project. Monger Capital had Chinese connections; they were on Hugh Ruff's special donor list, and suddenly, according to the RCMP, there was a threat on Neil Mohle and his wife's lives from a Chinese gang. In his experience, these were all indications of the Mohles, unwittingly or not, being either in possession of highly damaging information or complicit in whatever was taking place. For Hayden, the RCMP request for help could not have come at a better time. His own investigation was moving slowly, and assisting the RCMP without revealing his real objective provided the perfect opportunity to gather additional information for his own purposes.

"I see you and Rachel finally have a thing going."

"What?" Hayden looked up to see Donna Gray standing in the doorway.

"Didn't I just see her sneaking out of your office on my way back from getting coffee?" Donna held up her Starbucks coffee cup in evidence of her statement.

"I don't think she was sneaking out, and no, we don't have a thing going. We're going over to Vancouver together, and I've asked her to make the hotel arrangements for staying overnight." Hayden grinned as Donna faked an exaggerated surprised expression. "Have a seat, and I'll fill you in. I have to try and schedule a meeting with Neil Mohle, and once that's done, I'd like you to coordinate the schedule with Rachel."

Donna flopped down into one of the chairs in front of Hayden's desk, almost spilling her coffee out of the small hole in its white covering lid. "Staying overnight, how interesting," she said. "Okay, boss, fire away. I'm all ears."

#

"Hayden." Donna's voice came from directly behind Hayden.

He spun his chair around and placed the file he had been reading on the desk.

"I think you're all set with Neil Mohle," Donna continued. "The strategy of arranging the meeting through his assistant worked. Apparently, he had all sorts of questions, which she of course couldn't answer and could only relay our basic request. It would probably have not been quite as easy if you had made the call yourself."

"Thanks. It was good suggestion of yours. How did you present it?"

"I'm still not certain his wife will be there, but I said that you had some questions for the bank on the Woodstock deal and would be in Vancouver on August 10th. You were busy all day, but as you had discovered that one of your female colleagues had worked with Neil at ECB . . . floated the idea of a dinner with him and his wife. I said that the questions were neither onerous nor lengthy, so it would probably be a mostly social evening. Oh, and I also said you would pay." Donna smiled as she waited for Hayden's response.

"Cheeky, but probably smart," Hayden said. "What happened then?"

"As you expected she got back to me saying dinner wouldn't work and tried suggesting other dates, all of which I rejected due to your busy schedule. After a bit of fussing, I offered drinks before dinner as an alternative adding that both you and your colleague would be there and hoped his wife could join."

"And he agreed."

"Yes. You're set for six. His dinner's around eight-thirty at the waterfront restaurant in Coal Harbour, so I've arranged for you to meet in the lounge of the hotel next door. I talked to Rachel, and she's booked the same place for your overnight accommodation."

"That's perfect, and you think his wife is coming?"

"I believe so. His assistant confirmed they were both going to the dinner and that she had extended the invite to both of them. It was the best I could do without getting too obvious."

"That's great, Donna, thanks."

"You're welcome. I'll pass this along to Rachel and keep my fingers crossed that they don't try to change anything. There's not much time anyway, so hopefully it will hold up."

As Donna left his office, Hayden tilted back in his large black leather chair and stared vacantly out of the window, past the manicured green lawns and busy road, at the boats in Victoria's inner harbour. Always something of a control freak and despite his ready acquiescence to the RCMP's request and his earlier enthusiasm, he wasn't entirely comfortable with the way things were unfolding. Historically slow and painstakingly detailed, his investigations usually involved lengthy reports, checked and crosschecked until no uncertainty existed. Ultimately, these reports would be followed by a broad series of arrests carried out by others while he stayed far out of sight, buried deep within several layers of bureaucracy to preserve his ongoing value as an undercover investigator. This was turning into something very different.

Two impulsive decisions, and as far as he could tell, unless he very carefully extricated himself, he would quickly become well and truly tangled in the same web he was investigating. If the Mohles were involved with Monger Capital and if Monger was linked offshore money laundering, presenting the RCMP offer would potentially place him in a very visible position.

Then there was the affair. What was he thinking? No, that wasn't correct; he wasn't thinking... not with his head at least. It was a mistake on so many levels. They worked together, she was in a political position where even a hint of scandal could ruin her career and last, but by no means least, she might potentially be involved, directly or inadvertently, in the matter he was investigating. He also knew that in the longer term, the relationship wasn't going anywhere. The only real love in her life was her career, and she pursued it with a single-minded focus. He was a periodic and seemingly welcome distraction, whose own obvious attraction to her had existed ever since they first met. Maybe he just had a thing for older women, not that she was that much older. Proximity and opportunity had done the rest. Given how things were now unfolding, he knew he had to end it before it became public, which by then would be far too late.

Turning back to face his desk, Hayden pulled a yellow legal pad from his drawer, picked up a pen and started writing. It was time to focus. He'd made his decision. He would extract himself as gently as possible from the affair and press forward on the Monger Capital connection. One meeting with Neil Mohle was all he would do for the RCMP; after that, they were on their own. While the risk of exposure remained, his cover as an ex-employee of ECB would stand the test of any scrutiny, however thorough, and the potential rewards for his own investigation were substantial. He started listing names, drawing boxes around them and then linking the lines.

CHAPTER 31

Damian

It wasn't often that Damian was reflective, but things were going well. *Almost too well*, he thought, then, catching himself, he decided that they were no better than he deserved. Despite the stock market's belief that Woodstock's corporate direction stemmed from the board, Damian was satisfied that it was primarily through his efforts that the company had achieved its global presence. Sure, the board had offered guidance, but they were generally risk averse, and if he hadn't pushed, they'd probably still be seen as a large but conservative company. Being "a safe pair of hands" didn't suit him. He wanted recognition as an innovator and leader despite the potential reputational risks involved. Damian had heard the derogatory whispers calling him arrogant and a bit of a gunslinger, but those came right alongside others that he preferred, like self-assured and charming. Irrespective of what others may think, he knew it was a blend that served him well in negotiations where he was never happier than when his opponent was off-balance.

Although having never served in the military, Damian viewed business like warfare and his language was littered with words like retaliation and skirmishes, all forming part of the larger battle the company was waging. Conflict suited him. Not everyone can smile while making a threat; it takes a particular personality, and then almost before the threat was out of his mouth, the charm was back on. When once told that the resultant effect was disturbing, as he appeared either too charming or somewhat irrational, he argued that there are theatrics in all negotiations and he saw no reason to change.

This latest deal with Monger Capital was a prime example, he thought. The board was still going on about how little they knew about Monger Capital rather than the fact that the deal with Monger had enabled them to close the bank financing and meet the government's local equity requirement. If he'd listened to the board, those two items would still be unresolved. Then the appointment of John Ng to the Woodstock Marine board—what a battle that had been. Once again, they seemed to overlook the benefit to the company and instead focused on some unknown and likely irrelevant risk. Damian smiled to himself; at least they'd acknowledged his creative idea to fix the vessel costs now and improve Woodstock LNG's deal profitability, with an assured take-out purchase of the vessels by Monger if their consortium wasn't awarded the Kitimat LNG contract. What they didn't like was Monger Capital's resultant requirement for a seat on the parent company board, a seat that would be filled by John Ng. It had only been his repetitive reminder that it was only one seat of nine and couldn't really influence the direction of the company that had finally swayed the vote. In the end, John Ng's appointment was approved, with only two votes against.

That the original idea to fix the vessel costs now had stemmed from James Lee remained unsaid. Unless sharing credit was unavoidable, Damian saw no reason why he should not take it all. In private, he may acknowledge some input from James, but in public, and certainly as more time elapsed, the idea would be solely his.

CHAPTER 32

Neil

Dressed in a maroon velour tracksuit over his white shirt and shorts, Neil walked through the house in his socks, a tall glass of red wine in his right hand. Vivian had not arrived home yet, and he probably still had time for a quick shower before preparing dinner. He had left the office early for his weekly tennis game but, unlike most weeks, had declined the post-game socializing to get home early. He needed to speak to Vivian. There was something odd going on, and he wanted her opinion on whether he was being paranoid or not.

Leaving his half-empty wine glass on the kitchen counter, he walked to the bathroom, stripped off his clothes and stepped into the shower. With no one else in the house, he didn't bother to close the bathroom door, and his discarded clothes were easily visible to anyone approaching the bathroom down the short corridor.

Arriving home only minutes later, Vivian looked at the wine glass, heard the shower, saw the pile of clothes and walked directly into the open bathroom. "You're home early," she said.

"Jeez, you scared the hell out of me," Neil replied over the sound of the water. "I'm almost done, but I haven't started dinner. Give me a moment, and I'll join you in the kitchen. My wine's there already."

"Perhaps I'll join you in the shower instead. It's been a long day."

There was a brief silence before Neil spoke. "I'll get out," he said. "I've got something on my mind that I need to discuss."

"Sure." Vivian's expression soured as she left without saying another word.

Joining Vivian in the kitchen a short time later, Neil found her furiously chopping red peppers to add to an already overflowing salad bowl on the counter. He eased behind her and placed his arms around her waist. "Hey," he said. "I didn't mean to upset you; I'm just worried about this meeting." He squeezed his arms tighter. "I'll pour you some wine, and then you can help me decipher what's going on, then dinner, then . . ." Neil stopped talking and stepped away.

Vivian looked at him, squinted her eyes and faked a frown. "Okay. I'll give you one chance to make up for rebuffing me. What's worrying you?"

#

"And that's it?" Vivian said as she sat curled into the corner of the sofa, her salad bowl balanced on one knee, her wine glass on the coffee table in front of her.

Neil looked at her from the opposite corner of the sofa where he sat. "Yup. That's it."

"Okay, let me see if I've got this right. I get a call from Kitty Lee suggesting a business dinner between you and one of her wealthy colleagues. Outside of Kitty fussing about arranging the perfect meeting place and time, which, by the way, turns out to be your favourite restaurant, your biggest worry is that you don't know the client's name and that Kitty insisted I also be at the dinner. Do you really think that's enough reason to be paranoid about the meeting?"

"What about the limo?"

"What about it?"

"Don't you think it's strange that someone wants to send a limo to pick us up for dinner when we already live here?"

"Not at all. Maybe they want us to be able to relax have a few drinks. Without the limousine, we'd need to have someone else drive or take a cab. Then again, maybe they just want to impress you with their generosity. After all, you're meeting them as a favour to Kitty Lee."

"I don't know. It still feels like overkill to me. Honestly, if Kitty and James weren't joining us, I'd probably cancel."

"Oh God, I almost forgot." Vivian lifted her hand and covered her mouth with her fingers.

"Forgot what?"

"Kitty called me earlier today. They've run into some sort of problem and may not be able to make the dinner. She hasn't cancelled completely, but said that at this point, it looks unlikely they will be able to join. She'll said she'll call me if things change."

"You're kidding, right?"

"No I'm not."

"That does it. I'm not going."

"Don't be silly. I promised her you would meet with this person. If we don't go, it's going to make me look bad and I may lose a client."

"Okay, but no limo. We'll get ourselves to the restaurant. You'll have to phone and tell her, as we don't have any contact details for this mystery man. Maybe she can give you those or at least some information so that we'll know who he is when we get there. This may end up better anyway because we also have an invite for drinks before the dinner with two of my former colleagues from ECB, who now work for the government. They called my office and my assistant set it up at the hotel next to the restaurant so we can go straight from there to dinner. Apparently, they were insistent and had originally suggested dinner, but I was already booked. Seems the tenth was the only night they could make it, so we settled for drinks instead. They have something to discuss regarding the Woodstock LNG deal. Whatever you do, don't mention anything about it to Kitty when you call her. She's sure to tell James, and then he'll have all sorts of questions for me. Just tell her we have an earlier arrangement and will make our own way to dinner."

"Why didn't you tell me this before?"

"I was about to when you suddenly remembered that the Lee's had cancelled and we got side-tracked. Besides, that doesn't really matter now; it's providing us with the perfect excuse to decline the limo."

"And make you feel better about the whole arrangement."

"Yeah. It still doesn't feel quite right, though. Don't ask me why, just some gut instinct. I'll probably feel better when I know who this contact of Kitty's is that we're meeting, and after we've had drinks with Hayden and whomever he's bringing. My assistant didn't know who the other person was besides being a woman. I think you'll like them, at least him anyway. He's one of those sophisticated and good-looking 'suits' you sometimes comment on."

"Like you."

"No, not like me . . . you know what I mean."

"I know; no one's quite like you." Vivian grinned at Neil and held out her hand. "Come on, I've been distracted thinking about this ever since I saw your clothes on the bathroom floor."

CHAPTER 33

Kitty

"Aargh." Kitty Lee threw her mobile into the soft pillows of a large living room chair. "What's the matter with these people?" she asked.

There was no one else in the condominium, and both her exclamation and question went unanswered. Her conversation with Vivian Mohle had been brief and, in most cases, would have been nothing more than a minor blip in any social arrangement. Unfortunately, this was not a normal social arrangement, and once again, she would have to deal with that dreadful man Dong and explain about the limo. Moreover, as if that had not been bad enough, she had almost peed in her pants when Vivian asked for the name and contact details of the man she and Neil were to meet. Caught unawares and not having a ready answer, she had mumbled something about not worrying and that she would send them the contact details. What was she supposed to say now? She had no idea what her father had planned, and with the Mohles originally being picked up by limo, having a name or contact details for the investor had not been an issue. With the arbitrary change Vivian had just made to the arrangements, everything was different. She'd have to call Dong and take it from there. She wondered what the time was in China, then, deciding she didn't really care, searched through the cushions, picked up the phone and called her father's office.

With a fifteen-hour time difference, Dong Lai's day had just started when Kitty called, and as she expected, it was his voice that she heard answering her father's phone. Without any pause or social greeting, Kitty launched into a babbled explanation of the change in arrangements and her frustrations of trying to deal with Dong's requested meeting set-up. That her own indiscretion had resulted in the necessity for these arrangements never for a moment entered her head. She had apologized for those, her father had remonstrated with her, and as far as she was concerned, there the matter ended. This meeting was just a major inconvenience in her otherwise pampered life.

After listening without interruption, Dong promised to get back to Kitty with the requested information or an alternative arrangement before the following morning, Vancouver time.

"No," Kitty said. "No more alternative arrangements. Just get me the contact details so I can pass them along. I've had enough of this mystery. If you've got a problem, speak to my father." Without allowing Dong any time to respond, Kitty terminated the call, her shaking fingers barely finding the appropriate button.

#

Unbeknownst to Kitty, her call set in motion a domino-like series of events. Dong knew there was nothing in Kitty's message that required further input or direction from Quon Jin Hu. Despite his trusted position in the family, he knew he trod a fine line when dealing with Quon's favourite child. The arrangements would need to remain in place and an alternative method of isolating the Mohles would need to be established. Sighing, Dong picked up the phone and called John Ng.

#

"Do you have to answer that thing at dinner?" Bobbie Ng asked as the quite buzz of a vibrating mobile phone broke the silent tension at their upscale downtown club table.

"Depends who it is," replied John Ng, glancing down at the mobile phone he held in his lap and out of sight of the other diners. "Yes," he said, rising from his chair at the same time. "Be right back."

Walking quickly from the club dining room, the phone held at his side, John pressed the connect button, lifted the phone to his ear and spoke. "Hold on, Dong. Be right with you." Continuing at a fast walk, John exited the club before once again lifting the phone to his ear and speaking, only this time in fluent Mandarin.

#

Not long after John Ng finished speaking to Dong Lai, Vegas Kolnick's phone, lying unattended on his bed, rang several times before falling silent, the ringing replaced by a small periodically flashing red light. Returning to the room some fifteen minutes later, Vegas noticed the light, picked up the phone, listened to the waiting message, cursed and then called the twins. The subsequent discussion was brief and to the point. Their original plan to pick up the Mohles by limousine would no longer work. The initial contact would have to be at the restaurant, and he needed to pass along a name.

#

Lounging in the living room of the shared North Vancouver house inherited from their parents, identical twins Garrett and Griffin Evans listened to Vegas Kolnick's voice echoing eerily from the tiny speaker of the mobile phone balanced on the top of an empty beer glass. Six-feet three-inches tall, with matching blond haircuts, the twins had not an ounce of fat on either of their rangy bodies. It was almost impossible to identify one from the other when they were together or alone, a feature they often used to their advantage. Chameleon-like in their behaviour, they had an uncanny ability to blend into almost any setting, as long as they were alone. Together, the double effect was so startling that no one could ever forget seeing them. They also shared another trait—explosive tempers and a mean streak a mile wide.

"Fuck, this was going to be so easy in the limo," Garrett said.

"It's okay," Griffin interjected holding up his hand to stop his brother speaking. "Vegas, do you still have that thirty-three-foot Grady White?"

"Yeah, it's at the marina in West Vancouver. I never moved it over to the island."

"We're going to need it moored as close to the restaurant in the harbour as you can get it on Wednesday night. We're also going to need someone to run the thing and make sure the cabin is unlocked. We won't have time to mess about getting it ready ourselves once we arrive. We just need to have a shitload of power in case we have to make a run for it. I've got an idea about how we can pull this off, but I need to speak to Garrett before we settle things."

"That's fine. I'll take the ferry to Horseshoe Bay that afternoon and run the boat myself, but I still need a name."

"How about Twiss?" Garrett interjected. Like that Oliver character who wanted more food. "It's a restaurant so more food . . . get it?"

"That was Twist, you idiot," Griffin said, "not Twiss."

"Well, I like Twiss," Garrett replied, his voice rising. "Twist sounds funny."

"Okay," Vegas interrupted before things got out of hand, "Twiss it is. Do we need two names?"

"No, just one. Only one of us will be at the meeting."

#

Kitty was asleep when Dong Lai called back with the contact information that Mr. Twiss, a tall blond-haired gentleman, would meet the Mohles at the waterfront restaurant in Coal Harbour on Wednesday at 8:30 p.m. As a result, it wasn't until later the following morning that Kitty retrieved her voicemail and then called Vivian to pass on the information. Vivian, in turn, although busy with her second customer of the morning, sent a quick text to Neil with the details.

CHAPTER 34

Neil

Stepping out of his car in the parking lot of his brother's Vancouver business office, Neil Mohle looked down at Vivian's text message mere seconds after it arrived on the screen of his phone. While still uncomfortable with how things had evolved, he was now somewhat appeased by having a name and a general description of their dinner contact for Wednesday evening. Pocketing the phone, he entered the small quayside office building sandwiched between a looming historic sugar refinery and the ocean.

"Hi, Neil."

"Hi, Boet."

Neil watched his brother's face transform with a huge smile. He'd called him "Boet", the Afrikaans word for brother, as far back as he could remember. Philip's success hadn't changed that. Despite establishing a global logistics, freight forwarding and storage service business to the point where his company was now regarded as the market leader in this niche industry, Philip Mohle was still "Boet" to his older brother. Renowned for their high quality packing and safety standards, as well as total discretion, the company handled fine art and high technology products for the who's who of these industries.

"I'm glad you called. What brings you down here today?" Philip asked. Tall, dark-haired with a neatly trimmed goatee and glasses, he was the complete antithesis of his brother.

"Well, you're not in town that often, and I needed a break. I thought perhaps I could scrounge a cup of coffee, and you could show me what you're moving around that brings you back to Canada. I don't see enough of you since you moved your headquarters to London."

Philip laughed. "Got to go where the business is, Neil. We're moving a damned expensive item, that's what. Come upstairs and grab a coffee, and then I'll show you the crate. Cost an arm and a leg just to build the thing, and this time it has to go by ship, so it had to be almost indestructible. I tried everything I could think of to meet the requirements to go by air, but no luck."

"What on earth can't go by air?"

"Can't really tell you that, but you can make a few guesses after you see the container."

As Neil followed his brother up the stairs to the mezzanine of the steel-framed building, he looked down at the large pristine space below where several workers in spotless white overalls moved in and out of a very large pale-blue shipping container, its outside covered in distinctive yellow and black "sensitive electronic devices" warnings symbols. "Is that the container you were talking about?" Neil asked, pointing down.

"Yes. Do you think anyone would miss the warnings and storage instructions? Don't worry, there's nothing inside; the goods are here, but haven't been loaded yet."

"Glad to hear it."

#

A short time later, Philip Mohle and his brother stood looking into the pristine interior of the large container. "Impressive isn't it," Philip said, running is hand along the smooth insulated panels lining the container. "We're installing the air conditioning this morning."

"You could live in this thing," Neil replied. "All you need is plumbing, and you'd be good to go. Isn't it overkill for whatever it is you're shipping?"

"Not at all. It's going to be at sea for almost sixty days, and the cost of this container and the shipping is negligible compared to the cost of the contents."

"What kind of vessel is being used?"

"It's a regular container ship, but the container will get priority placement and will certainly be handled with care. The stickers will make sure of that. Look, Neil, I hate to rush you and I'm glad you dropped in, but I'm pretty stretched today. Any chance of dinner tomorrow? I leave for London on the weekend, and it would be nice to catch up before I go."

"I can't do tomorrow. We already have a dinner, but I could do Thursday. Is that any good?"

"That's fine. It's probably better anyway, because I understand, tomorrow is one of the fireworks displays for Vancouver's Symphony of Fire, and apparently, the evening traffic will be horrendous. We wanted to bring some equipment through downtown Vancouver, and they suggested we choose another day."

"Okay, Thursday it is. I'll call you with the place and time later."

"Actually, can you rather send me a text? I'll check that whatever I'm doing. I don't answer my phone or check my voicemail as regularly as I should."

"Fine. Text it is then. You carry on with whatever you have to do. I'll find my own way back."

Neil shook hands with his brother, reached up to pat his shoulder and handed him his empty coffee cup. "See you on Thursday," he said as he left.

CHAPTER 35

Hayden

"Nice car," said Rachel as she slid into the plush leather interior of the silver Mercedes early on the morning of August 10th. "I love that new car smell."

"One of my few indulgences," Hayden replied. "This and travel."

"Travel?"

"Archeological sites, islands, historical buildings, art galleries, as long as there's an objective, I love travelling. I'm not very big on crowded tourist venues or trying to cover as many cities in a week as I can. How about you?"

"I'd go anywhere. I haven't done much aside from the major European cities and the States; it's always hard to find enough time and money."

Both lapsed into silence as Hayden navigated his way out of the downtown core and onto the highway to the Vancouver Island ferry dock at Swartz Bay. Finally, the traffic thinned. "How well do you know Neil Mohle?" Hayden asked.

"Well enough to swap stories periodically. Except for bank functions, I never saw him socially or met his wife. Do you know him well?"

"Hardly at all. He even had to remind me when I last spoke to him that we'd attended a bank course together. According to the RCMP, I'm being used because we've had some recent contact over this LNG deal and it provides a useful cover story. Remind me again what they told you about what's happening."

"Not much at all. They swore me to secrecy, said the Mohles were in serious trouble and that you would be delivering an offer of protection to them from the RCMP. I was along because he knew me and, if needed, to be able to confirm that the offer was legitimate. Other than that, I was to follow your lead. They seemed to have quite a bit of faith in your ability to pull this off. Have you been involved with them before?"

"No," Hayden lied as he pulled up at the BC Ferry ticket booth. "I'm as green at this as you are. Let's hope we don't mess it up."

#

Spectacular as always, the scenic ferry trip was soon underway. Preferring to avoid the crowds, Hayden and Rachel opted to pay the additional all-inclusive entry fee to use the facilities of the onboard Seawest Lounge.

"This is nice," Rachel said. "I haven't used this before. I normally join the breakfast line and then end up eating too much. Coffee and pastries is plenty, and it's much quieter in here."

"I like it," Hayden replied. "I usually work on board, and I find it's similar to a business class lounge at the airport. Without the booze, of course." As he finished speaking, he lifted his small laptop from his briefcase, opened the cover and turned it on. "Don't mean to be rude," he said, "but I need to check a couple of e-mails while there is still an internet connection. Can you give me a few minutes?"

"No problem," Rachel replied, standing up at the same time. "I didn't bring any work with me, so I'll go and find a few magazines and bury myself in them until you're done."

Hayden watched Rachel walk away to the magazine racks, his laptop and pressing e-mails momentarily forgotten, then looked down and quickly started typing. He'd sent off a report to CSIS headquarters the previous evening, along with a request for any information they may have uncovered regarding Monger Capital. If they'd found anything new, he'd like to have that information before his meeting with Neil Mohle.

#

When Rachel returned to her seat, Hayden's laptop was once again safely stored in his briefcase and his attention was focused on the nearby coastline as the large car-carrying ferry transited Active Pass, a narrow and treacherous passage between Mayne and Galliano islands, on its way to its final destination at the Tsawwassen Ferry Terminal on the Lower Mainland.

"All done?" she asked.

"Yes, thanks. Find anything interesting?"

"Not really, mostly gossip. You know, who's having an affair with whom."

"Anyone you know?" Hayden asked, smiling.

"No, although you did get an honourable mention."

"Me? Nice try, but you have to be famous."

"So, you are having an affair, but you're just not famous enough to be in the magazines?" Rachel replied, looking directly at him.

"That's not what I said," Hayden answered, looking slightly embarrassed before bursting out laughing at Rachel's serious expression. "How about you?"

"Am I having an affair?"

"No, are you involved with anyone, and if so, what do they think about your running off to Vancouver for dinner with a colleague? Despite our working together on two separate occasions, I know very little about you. Maybe you could tell me something about yourself."

"No one important enough to worry about," Rachel replied. "What would you like to know? Remember, though, fair's fair; anything you ask I get to ask as well. It will be a while before we dock, so there's plenty of time for sharing."

Unsure of what he had got himself into, Hayden nodded. What could Rachel possibly ask that he couldn't answer? What was more, he had noticed that the more time he spent with her, the more he enjoyed it.

#

Having pre-booked their ferry tickets, Hayden's vehicle was one of the first loaded, as well as one of the first to exit from the upper car deck, down the ramp and onto the long highway leading to Vancouver.

"That trip seemed to go far too quickly. It was nice to get to know something about you," Hayden said. "Strange that we never connected before when we worked at ECB."

"I think you were too busy climbing the corporate ladder," Rachel replied. "I noticed you, though."

Hayden turned to look at Rachel, who immediately averted her head and stared fixedly out the side window. Not sure how, or if, he should respond, he chose to say nothing. Then, after a short pause, he spoke and changed the subject. "We'll probably be checked into the hotel by lunch time. I was going to skip lunch and go for a run around the Stanley Park seawall. I've still got some work to do and planned to work in my room when I got back. Are you okay to meet at around five forty-five in the lobby? That way we can go to the lounge together to meet the Mohles. It's probably best that we arrive at the same time."

"That's fine," Rachel replied. "The premier said I should take some time off and go shopping for clothes." She gestured at her casual skinny jeans, short, fawn suede boots and white blouse. "I don't know if she thinks it might be fun or was suggesting that I dress badly. Either way, I plan to take her up on her suggestion. I'll see you at five forty-five."

The slightly awkward moment having passed, the trip continued in comfortable silence broken only by the occasional observation of some pertinent landmark or the heavy downtown traffic until they arrived at the hotel. After leaving the car with the valet parking attendant and completing their requested early check-in, they headed to their respective rooms, once again agreeing to meet later as previously arranged.

CHAPTER 36

Rachel

Alone in her room, Rachel sat on the end of the bed looking at her reflection in the full-length mirror. Why hadn't she made more of an effort? What happened to her promise to herself to have a makeover, something to make Hayden sit up and take notice? She'd enjoyed spending time alone with him and even managed to keep her infatuation in check. Well, almost in check anyway. Only two glitches as far as she could recall. Once pressing him about having an affair, and then foolishly admitting that she had noticed him at ECB. Fortunately, both remarks appeared to pass uneventfully. He'd even laughed at the notion of his having an affair. Maybe she'd been wrong about that. Well, tonight would be the big test. She wasn't going to let this opportunity pass. Once they had delivered the police message to the Mohles, it was dinner alone and she planned to do everything in her power to make herself irresistible. Smiling, she flopped back onto the king-sized bed and started pulling off her boots. "Makeover here I come," she said aloud.

CHAPTER 37

Dana

Dana noticed how quiet it was in the office with Rachel gone. Not that her assistant was noisy, but the usual sounds of another person working in reasonably close proximity were somehow comforting. Like any work environment, the top job was, by definition, a lonely one. Despite regular cabinet meetings and many specialist advisors, the final decisions were hers. And if that isolation wasn't enough, Jones had come along with a CSIS request for him to remain completely anonymous. Just another political appointee whose need she couldn't quite explain.

Dana sighed and leaned back into her tall-backed chair, its design decidedly at odds with the light-brown antique table that served as her desk. Despite her best efforts, Hugh's warning continued to hover in the forefront of her mind. At first, she had assumed he was merely venting his displeasure at being asked to leave the last cabinet meeting without delivering his usual update. However, of late, she was more and more convinced that perhaps he was right. If Hugh couldn't get sufficiently comfortable with whoever was behind Monger Capital to take them off the special donor list, maybe she should take notice. If Monger was heavily funded by offshore money, this was a political issue she didn't need. She had barely finished the thought when her telephone rang. She picked up the receiver and answered, "Dana Holmes."

"Dana? It's Hugh. I didn't expect you to answer your own phone."

"Hi, Hugh. I was just thinking about you. Rachel's away on business with Jones."

"Oh, no wonder I can't find him. I wanted to get him to ask the LNG bankers about Monger Capital. I'm sure they could give us the information we need to clear them from the list." No sooner had Hugh completed his sentence than Dana's stomach twisted into a knot.

"I have to talk to him later," she said, "so why don't I ask him to give you a call? I've been thinking about your concerns and agree that we'd better go carefully with this Monger group until you are comfortable that they're not funded by some major offshore bunch that could cause us trouble with our supporters."

"Thanks, I'd appreciate that. I'll leave it with you and get out of your hair."

"Thanks, Hugh. Bye."

Dana disconnected the call, the knot in her stomach now replaced by an awful empty sick feeling. Hugh didn't know about Jones being undercover and investigating economic espionage, whatever that was supposed to mean. Maybe his investigation included offshore political donations? The CSIS request was so unusual that she'd never even thought to ask. What if asking him to look into Monger uncovered something sinister? While she had no reason to suspect anything was amiss, bringing him into the loop was far too close for comfort, as far as she was concerned. If Monger was not all that it appeared to be on the surface, how would Hayden handle it? And would he assume she was involved?

"Jones, Jones, Jones," Dana said aloud. Then, resting her chin in her hands, she stared unseeing at the far wall of her office. Hayden had been attracted to her ever since she'd first tutored one of his university classes. Five years his senior and despite his flirtatious advances, she'd enjoyed the experience, his obvious intelligence making up for his sometimes awkward approaches. Despite a few years of close proximity, nothing had ever developed and each had gone their separate ways. Now, unexpectedly and significantly more mature in his late thirties, here he was back in her life and this time she had been the pursuer. Not that it had taken much pursuing. One over-indulged office function and her less than sober and very direct actions had set the stage for everything that had happened since.

No matter how she felt about him, however, things were getting out of her control, a state she couldn't allow. Her career came first, it was time to end the affair, however painful or difficult it might be for them both. Her mind made up, Dana reached for the telephone and punched in Hayden's number.

#

As she listened to the distant ringing, Dana tried to recall her one conversation with Hayden about the special donor list. Distracted at the time and confident in his discretion, she hadn't paid too much attention. *What did I say? And was it anything he could use?* She should never have let this happen.

"Jones," the abrupt greeting followed by very heavy breathing.

Despite the seriousness of her call, Dana smiled. "What on earth are you doing, Jones? or shouldn't I ask?"

"I'm out for a run around the Stanley Park seawall. I only stopped to answer the phone."

"Why don't you call me back when you're done?"

"We can talk now if you like; I'm about finished. I've just arrived back at the Rowing Club, which is roughly where I started. I can talk while I cool down and walk back to the hotel. What's up?"

"You know I like you, Jones, but . . ."

"If this is one of 'those' conversations, we can probably skip having it," Hayden interrupted. "Your work is important, and I always suspected I was on borrowed time. Unless you really need to, can we rather not say anything we may later regret? If you do want to discuss it, that's fine, but I really don't expect you to have to give me an explanation. If it's strictly business from here on in, I understand."

Dana sighed deeply before replying. Hayden seemed almost to have read her mind. "Thanks, Jones. You're a good friend," she said. There was a pause before both gave a brief relieved laugh.

"Wasn't that how this whole thing started?" Hayden asked gently.

"It believe it was," Dana replied. "Good luck with the project and enjoy your dinner. Thanks for understanding. I'll see you when you get back." She had barely disconnected the call before remembering that she was supposed to ask Hayden to call Hugh Ruff.

Dana leaned her head back and stretched with relief. Hayden's easy acceptance and understanding was welcome. She hated messy endings. Their next few meetings might be somewhat tentative, but she expected things would quickly settle as they both got back into a regular routine. With a bit of luck, there was also the chance that his investigation would end sometime in the not too distant future, and the old "out of sight, out of mind" adage would take over. For now though, she would turn her attention to working with Hugh on clearing up this Monger business and ensuring they were as clean as possible.

CHAPTER 38

Neil

The Wednesday evening was warm and not a breath of air flowed through the open windows of the house as Neil Mohle prepared himself to meet the mysterious Mr. Twiss. A man who needed his help to invest ten million dollars. Standing partially dressed in his walk-in closet, Neil placed a large gold ring on his right hand and a gold band on his left little finger, followed by a smooth circular gold, black-faced watch on his left wrist, and a gold bracelet on the right. Finally, he draped a gold chain with a diamond pendant around his neck. Satisfied with the resultant image, he removed a freshly laundered and lightly starched white shirt from its wooden hanger and slipped his arms into the waiting sleeves.

His tennis game had run late, and he would have to hurry if he was going to be on time for his meeting with Hayden Jones. If Vivian didn't arrive within the next few minutes, she was going to have to join them at the hotel.

His dressing completed, Neil ran through a mental checklist as he walked through the house. All windows and doors closed and locked, their calico cat *Anitya* sitting peacefully in a small patch of sunlight and the car in the garage. Vivian should be home momentarily; she was rarely later than six o'clock. He couldn't wait much longer; maybe she was walking home from her evening bus journey. He would check.

Shortly thereafter, he hurried out of the front door, which he closed but left unlocked.

Removing his mobile phone from his pocket as he strode the short distance to the intersection of their street and the main bus route, Neil scrolled through his contacts. He needed a cab and quickly. The traffic would be awful at this time of night. Besides if he was going to drink, he wasn't going to drive.

After being told that the next available taxi would take twenty minutes to arrive, Neil looked at his watch and then at the large downtown bus heading directly along the road towards him. Punctuality overriding his aversion to both public transit and his concern at leaving the house unlocked, he sprinted to the nearby bus stop and held out his arm. Vivian would soon be home, and no one would break into the house in that brief time; Kitsilano wasn't that sort of neighbourhood. Last, but certainly not least, a bus, with its preferred lane access, would get him downtown before 6:30 p.m., just in time for his meeting. After boarding the bus, he had barely paid his fare and sat down on one of the few remaining hard dark-blue seats when he felt the vibration of his mobile. Pulling it from his shirt pocket, he looked at the text on the screen.

Still stuck at work. I'll come directly to the hotel. Running about half-hour late. Vox

Irritated that the house would now remain unlocked until they returned after dinner, but still satisfied that no break-in would occur, Neil edged away from the sweaty fellow passenger next to him and focused on staying in his seat as the bus jerked its way through the busy traffic. *At least I'm still fit and healthy,* he thought. Several of his fellow passengers looked decidedly old and tired. The difference in his and Vivian's ages popped into his mind, upsetting him more than he expected. Not that she had said anything—any anxiety was of his own making.

#

Neil felt a surge of relief as he stepped off the bus at its first stop in the Coal Harbour area of Vancouver. He really hated public transport, little germ-laden cabins moving people from one point to another. He brushed imaginary lint off his clothing and looked directly across the road at the hotel. It was 6:25 p.m.; he'd be right on time. Smiling for the first time that evening, he headed toward the traffic lights and the crosswalk.

At exactly 6:30 p.m., Neil walked through the entrance of the hotel lounge and scanned the room. Had Hayden Jones been alone, Neil may have missed him on his first pass. Not that Hayden had changed that much in the intervening years, merely matured. He looked fit and healthy. It was the woman with him that caused Neil stop and look twice at the couple seated in front of the oceanside windows. *Drop-dead gorgeous; her slinky blue dress and shining red hair would have made a priest look twice,* Neil thought. She was supposed to be a former colleague. Neil didn't recognize her at all. He was still standing silently gawking when Hayden looked across the room and waved.

As Neil reached the table, both Hayden and the woman stood. "Neil, good to see you. I'm sure you remember Rachel Burton from ECB."

"I remember Rachel Burton," Neil replied, "but I don't think we've met." He held out his hand to Rachel, a broad smile now plastered on his face.

"I see you haven't changed," Rachel answered, returning his smile.

"Well, you sure have," Neil said. "I don't think I'd have recognized you at all. Sorry, that was supposed to be a compliment. I'm starting to get tongue-tied, and I'm sure I'm going to say the wrong thing, so perhaps I'll just shut up at this point."

Both Hayden and Rachel laughed aloud as the trio sat down. "Is your wife not joining us?" Hayden asked.

"She is, but she's running a bit late," Neil replied. "She should be here in a half-hour or so, if that's alright. Maybe we can get the business end out of the way before Vivian arrives?"

"Why don't we order our drinks first, and catch up a bit before we do that," said Hayden.

#

When Vivian arrived at the hotel, the trio was on their second round of drinks. This, coupled with the sharing of their individual experiences with some of the ECB's more well-known characters, had quickly broken down any initial awkwardness, and the conversation flowed freely. So much so, that the suggested business discussion had still not been broached. Neil, sitting with his back to the entrance, had almost forgotten he wasn't with his current ECB banker colleagues until he felt a squeeze on his shoulder and heard Vivian's voice.

"Hi, Neil. Sorry I'm late."

Neil looked over his shoulder at Vivian, immediately recognizing the real reason she was late; she'd been shopping. Her red dress, with its thin black piping, was new, and he had to admit it was set-off perfectly by her dark eyes, black hair and black leather choker necklace, from which hung a gold star-shaped pendant with a black stone in its centre. A gold wedding band with three large diamonds in a row, almost-black nail polish and dark red lipstick completed the picture. She looked ravishing, and he was delighted. Any remarks he may have had about their unlocked house, or her lateness, dying unspoken in his head.

"Hi, hon," he said, standing. "Let me introduce you to two of my former colleagues." Neil turned back to find both Hayden and Rachel standing, and after a quick introductions, the group resettled themselves around the table. After Vivian ordered a drink from a nearby attentive waiter, Neil spoke again. "Well, I guess even though I thought we could cover off the LNG deal questions before Vivian arrived, we'd better do it now, Hayden. This is fun and probably more enjoyable than our dinner date will be, but we have to be at the restaurant by 8:30 p.m., so we'd best get started." As he finished speaking, Neil looked from Hayden to Rachel, whose face paled as he watched. "Are you okay?" Neil asked.

The Banker's Box

"Fine," Rachel answered, but before she could offer any further explanation, she was interrupted by Hayden.

"Look, Neil, any LNG questions can wait. I'm afraid we used that as a bit of an excuse to ensure we were able to speak to both of you this evening before your dinner."

"Both of us? What's Vivian got to do with any LNG deal?"

"Actually we don't know if this has anything to do with the LNG deal, but it definitely concerns both of you, and we have been asked to deliver a message to you from the RCMP."

"The RCMP. What kind of a message is that? And why ask you two to deliver it?"

Hayden paused, and Neil waited anxiously while the waiter appeared to move in slow motion as he delivered Vivian's glass of white wine and then checked whether they required anything else. As he finally walked away, Hayden continued, "I'll tell you everything we know, which isn't much. Anything after that, I'm afraid you'll need to get from the RCMP."

"You're joking, right? This is some kind of ECB stunt. Some kind of peculiar work anniversary humour. Like a singing telegram or something."

"No, I'm quite serious," Hayden replied. "Apparently, your lives are in danger. Rachel can vouch for that. It's why they asked both of us to deliver the message. They thought as former colleagues, we might have some credibility with you."

"Our lives are in danger?" Neil repeated, the skepticism he felt clearly evident in his voice.

"Why don't you let me start at the beginning, and I'll tell you everything I know," Hayden replied. "We can try and answer any questions once I'm done. It won't take long, and apparently, time is critical. Perhaps there is something you can add that will allow this to make more sense."

"Okay," Neil replied, turning to look at Vivian, disbelief written all over her face. "Go ahead."

#

As Hayden spoke, both he and Rachel leaned forward. Neil looked from one face to the other. He couldn't believe what he was hearing. Vivian sat quietly alongside him, still apparently in shock, while Rachel periodically looked as surprised as he was as Hayden filled in the details of the RCMP witness protection offer. It was obvious Hayden knew more than she did about this whole affair. One thing was certain, as the story unfolded, they weren't joking.

To Neil's surprise, Vivian, who had not said a word since Hayden started speaking, asked the first question as he finished. Despite her shock, she had obviously been listening carefully. "What I don't understand is why a biker gang would be trying to harm us," she said. "I don't know any bikers, and as far as Neil's concerned, I've never heard him speak about having biker clients. I thought you said you suspected this had something to do with the LNG deal Neil's been working on. What do bikers have to do with LNG?"

"Vivian's right. As far as I know, I don't have any clients who are part of a biker group. I realize that sometimes these things are well camouflaged to look legitimate, but I've known the majority of my clients for years," said Neil.

"How about someone recent or a new deal that's not yet complete… like the LNG deal in Kitimat and the whole group behind the bid?" Hayden suggested.

"I've known the Woodstock guys for years," Neil replied. "And why would they want to harm us? We've just finished papering the deal." As he finished speaking, Neil suddenly recalled Woodstock's new arrangement with Monger Capital and Chris Broughton's comments about Komodo. Could the association be true? And even if it was, what did that have to do with a biker gang? He wasn't going to raise this now. That was a conversation he and Vivian would have in private. Maybe one of his promoter clients had got into trouble? He knew they sometimes flew pretty close to the wire, but he was never directly involved; he was just their banker. Neil looked at his watch; it was already a little after eight o'clock. "Look," he said, "I realize you mean well, but this is just a bit too much to take in right now. We need time to discuss it. You're asking us to give up everything we have because of a threat we know nothing about. How sure are the RCMP about this? Without being stupid about it, I've no interest in rearranging our lives just because someone thinks there may be some danger. Is there anything else you haven't told us?

Before Hayden could answer, Vivian's mobile phone rang.

"Sorry," she said, looking at the screen but not recognizing the number. "I should take this." Standing up, she pushed back her chair and walked quickly away, the phone pressed hard against her ear.

Neil looked at Vivian as she walked away. "Her parents sometimes call from China, and it's usually at an inopportune time," he said, a wry smile appearing briefly on his face.

"There may be a Chinese connection to this," Hayden said, seizing the opportunity in Vivian's absence.

"Chinese?" Neil repeated.

"Yes. According to the police, a Chinese group placed the contract. Can you think of anyone that may want to harm you or Vivian?"

"We've quite a few friends from a variety of Asian countries, and I have several Chinese clients, but none that I can think of that would want to harm us."

"We don't have much time," Hayden replied. "The RCMP want to get you into protective custody before your dinner appointment. Seems they're nervous about the people you plan to meet. They have the restaurant staked out, and another group here in the hotel. They're waiting for you in Room 207."

"We can't just leave," Neil protested. "The house isn't even locked, and the cat's inside. This is crazy."

"Why don't you at least talk to the police?" Rachel interjected, looking at Hayden for support. "I'm sure they must have ways of dealing with things like this."

"I agree," Hayden said. "We'll go with you and leave once you get to the room. There's still a bit of time before your dinner appointment, and Vivian's on her way back now."

Neil turned and looked over his shoulder. Vivian was walking back, her face ashen and her arm, with the phone still in her hand, hanging limply at her side.

"Everything okay?" Neil asked as she arrived.

"Kitty called," she whispered. Then in a normal voice, "Can I speak to you for a minute . . . outside?" Without waiting for a reply, Vivian turned and once again walked toward the lounge entrance.

"Sorry," Neil said, rising from his seat. "We'll be right back."

CHAPTER 39

Kitty

Kitty walked slowly away from one of the increasingly rare public payphones attached to the grey concrete wall of the downtown Vancouver high-rise building, her shaking hand still wrapped tightly around the few extra quarters she had brought. She couldn't remember having defied her father before, but these were her friends and they hadn't done anything wrong. Not that this was an open defiance. As far as Kitty was concerned, she was just interfering in his plans. Seemingly, just in time too. Who were the people Vivian was meeting for drinks? She hadn't offered much, only that they were old colleagues of Neil's. Kitty wondered if that were true? Her father had tentacles everywhere.

In the end, after a brief greeting, her message to Vivian had been simple and one she would deny having ever made. "Run. Don't trust Neil's colleagues and don't go to dinner. Better yet, don't trust anyone. Your lives may depend on it." Without further explanation and before Vivian could ask any questions, she had ended the call and walked away. One way or another, she knew she would never see the Mohles again.

CHAPTER 40

Hayden

Puzzled but not concerned by Neil and Vivian's sudden departure, Hayden looked over at Rachel, who sat quietly sipping on her drink. "What do you think?" he asked.

"I think they believed us, and I don't think they were hiding anything although Vivian wasn't around when you mentioned the Chinese connection."

"Yeah, I wasn't sure when I should bring that up. In the end, it seemed opportune while she was away just to see how Neil responded. I thought she might have Asian connections he doesn't like or trust."

"I was also surprised how much you knew. The RCMP obviously told you more than they told me." Hayden didn't respond, and after a moment's silence, Rachel continued, "I'm still not sure that it wouldn't have been better to have the police deliver the message, or at least come along to the meeting with us."

"They really aren't sure whether Neil and Vivian may be involved in something illegal and didn't want them rattled by a police presence. They're working on the assumption that if the Mohles have nothing to hide, they'll still have ample opportunity to organize things after we make contact. My instructions were to get them to Room 207, and then for you and me to leave and forget this ever happened."

"That sounds good to me," Rachel replied. "I wonder what's wrong, though? Vivian looked absolutely stunned when she returned from her call."

"I don't know, and it's almost 8:30 p.m. Either we can give them another few minutes and then I'll go and look, or better yet, perhaps you'd like to visit the restroom? Maybe if you walk past them, it will prompt them to return."

"Why don't I do that," Rachel answered. "I'm not good at waiting." As she finished speaking, she immediately stood up and walked toward the lounge entrance.

Hayden watched Rachel leave, surprised at how much he was enjoying her company. He wondered where the starchy Rachel that he knew had gone, or if she really ever existed. Whatever the reason for the change, he was certainly enjoying this new version, as were several other occupants of the lounge, judging by the number of heads that turned to follow her path through the room.

Rachel had barely passed through the lounge doors into the hotel lobby when she returned, hurrying back to the table where Hayden sat waiting. "They've gone," she said.

"What do you mean 'gone'?" Hayden replied.

"Gone. The lobby is empty."

"You've got to be kidding me."

"Look for yourself."

Hayden hurried to the lobby and looked around. Rachel was right. The Mohles were nowhere in sight. "You check the ladies' restroom," he said. "I'll check the men's and meet you back at our table."

Minutes later, they were back at their drinks table without either Neil or Vivian Mohle.

"I don't believe this," Hayden said. "I know we had nothing resolved, but I thought we were reasonably on track. It has to be something to do with that call Vivian took. Did you hear who she said called?"

"No. She whispered something to Neil about who called and then asked to speak to him outside. I couldn't hear the first bit."

"Shit. Sorry about the language, but this is not good news."

"Perhaps they went straight to dinner. I know that would be rude, but it was almost 8:30 p.m. Maybe Neil sent you a text?"

Hayden looked at his phone. Nothing. "We need to get in touch with Sergeant Harrington," he said. "The RCMP better take over. I've got her mobile number here."

#

Immediately after receiving Hayden's call, Sergeant Kate Harrington had mobilized her group. Undercover police scoured the hotel and surrounding grounds, taxi drivers were questioned and the police team in the restaurant were put on alert. No sign of either Neil or Vivian was found; the Mohles had simply vanished.

#

It was nine o'clock before Kate Harrington finally reappeared in the lounge where Hayden and Rachel continued to wait. "Looks like you're free to go," she said.

"Find anything?" Hayden asked.

Kate shook her head. "Strangest thing," she replied. "Makes me wonder how innocent they are, though. Our people will stay in the restaurant for a while. We have two members of the biker club under surveillance in the restaurant just in case the Mohles do show later. We don't know the extent of their involvement in the contract, and even though we assume they are up to no good, there's nothing we can do at this stage; no crime has been committed. There was only one of them at first, but his brother just joined him; they're twins, so easy to spot. Well, thanks, you two. I'd better get back to work. This is where the fertilizer really hits the fan. Everybody's an expert on what we should have done once something goes wrong."

"Sorry how things turned out," Hayden said. "For a while, I thought it was going to work. That call Vivian received definitely threw a wrench into things."

"Not your fault. Enjoy your meal. We'll take it from here."

As Kate left, Hayden turned to Rachel and looked down at her high-heeled shoes. "Can you walk in those? I wouldn't mind a stroll along the waterfront before we go and eat. I need to settle down. My head's still buzzing."

Rachel looked at him then reached down and pulled off her shoes. "The weather's gorgeous, so barefoot okay?" she asked taking his arm.

"I'm game if you are."

Hayden grinned. More and more he liked this new Rachel Burton.

CHAPTER 41

Vegas

Lounging in the cockpit of his Grady-White 330 Express, a faded-blue baseball cap pulled low over his eyes, Vegas Kolnick sipped on a cold can of beer and watched the restaurant entrance. From his posture, he looked no different from any other boat owner relaxing at the end of a long day on the water. No outward evidence indicated the rising tension he felt as the evening progressed, and the texts from the twins started to arrive.

#

Vegas had arrived at the marina around five o'clock that afternoon. *There was a benefit to having bought the boat from a dealer located right here in the Coal Harbour Marina,* he thought. *How else could you find moorage at such short notice?* Anxious to please potential repeat customers for their very expensive products, dealers had reserved spaces to provide moorage, for a few hours at least, without much haggling. As things transpired, he had managed to position the boat within fifty metres, and in direct line of sight, of the restaurant entrance. Once moored, Vegas sent a brief text to the twins confirming his location. As far as he was concerned, the rest was up to them and the boat's two powerful 350 horsepower outboard engines. He had no clear idea of what the twins planned, but he had done his part. All he could do now was wait. He would use the time to get a few things done around the boat. By his estimate, as long as he was ready to leave any time after eight o'clock, that should be fine.

#

The first text arrived from the twins at 8:35 p.m.

> *No sign of the people meeting Mr. Twiss. I'm at another table supposedly waiting for my brother to join me. Their table is still empty.*

With nothing to add, Vegas didn't bother to reply. The second text arrived fifteen minutes later.

> *I'm starting to look stupid sitting here alone. Where the fuck are they? Mr. Twiss*

Realizing that whichever twin was in the restaurant was starting to lose control, Vegas answered. *Probably just delayed. Sit tight.*

No reply was forthcoming until the third text, which arrived at exactly nine o'clock.

> *We are both here now. Going to eat. If those fuckers don't show, we'll see you at ten. Looks like their table is being given to someone else. We'll text again if they turn up. This is not good, and we're not happy.*

Vegas's reply was short and to the point.

> *Okay. You'd better hope I've forgotten that last comment by the time you arrive. Don't ever threaten me again, you assholes. Vegas*

Vegas silently shook his head. Despite his irritation with the twins, they were right. This wasn't good. He needed to contact John Ng and find out what had gone wrong. He was looking for the number in his contacts when a woman's laugh echoed across the water. Straining to see the couple approaching along the walkway from the hotel on the opposite side of the restaurant, Vegas watched as they walked past the restaurant entrance before crossing the grass verge and heading towards the street. He couldn't be sure from this distance and with only the streetlamps for illumination, but it appeared that the woman was barefoot and carrying her shoes in her hand.

#

Before the Evans twins left the restaurant, Vegas had already spoken to John Ng and decided to spend the night onboard. He would leave at first light rather than cross back to West Vancouver in the dark. Deciding to avoid having the two irritated and, by now, possibly drunk brothers on the boat, Vegas stepped onto the dock and walked casually toward them.

Reaching the intersection of the dock and the foreshore path at almost the same moment as the twins, Vegas found it impossible not to smile. Identically dressed in black suits, white shirts and black ties, the two looked like large versions of the Blues Brothers, all they needed were hats and sunglasses. The twins, for their part, seemed to have mellowed after their dinner and presumably sufficient booze to blunt their former irritation.

"What now?" Griffin asked, pointing at the boat. "Want to go on board?"

"No. Let's talk here," Vegas replied. "I'm still trying to find out what happened. How did you two get here?"

"Car," Garrett answered. "It's parked a few streets away. We still get paid, right?"

"Yes. You'll be paid, but for now the job's not finished. Go home. I'll be in touch."

"As long as we get paid," Garrett repeated.

"And don't forget you owe us for dinner," Griffin added, at which point both brothers burst out laughing as they turned and walked back toward the restaurant.

Vegas watched them walk away before turning and heading in the other direction. The weather was perfect, and he needed to stretch his legs before turning in. There was nothing more he could do until he heard more from John Ng.

#

The two undercover RCMP officers, assigned as backup in case the Mohles turned up late for their dinner invitation, had immediately recognized the Evans twins on their arrival in the restaurant. Later, with no sign of the Mohles or their expected guest and after learning of the Mohles disappearance from the hotel, the officers had switched their attention to the two bikers. Continuing their discreet surveillance throughout the twins' dinner, they had finally left the restaurant shortly before 10 p.m. and directly on the heels of the two men.

Standing concealed in the restaurant entrance, they watched as the twins walked along the waterfront before stopping and speaking with one of the boaters leaving the marina. From their gestures, it looked as though they were commenting on his boat. After a brief conversation and some laughter, the twins returned along the waterfront before heading up to the street, presumably, to where they had parked. The boater, meanwhile, strolled along the waterfront in the opposite direction in no apparent hurry.

Suspicious at first, but influenced by the nonchalance of the group, the officers decided that the meeting was coincidental and that there was no point in wasting any time following the owner of the boat. Requesting their vehicle from the valet parking attendant, they continued their surveillance of the twins.

CHAPTER 42

Rachel

Alone in her hotel room, Rachel once again flopped backwards onto her bed as she had done earlier that day. What an evening it had been, her whole body was tingling. Excitement didn't begin to describe the feeling. Wriggling off the bed, her tight blue dress now rumpled and pulled up almost to her hips, she looked down at her feet; the soles were filthy. She looked like a tramp, but the evening had been a blast and she wasn't done yet.

Hayden had been more disappointed than she expected over the Neil Mohle business, and it had taken as much charm as she could muster to shake him out of his initial lethargy. After all, she pointed out, it wasn't as if this was his job; they were doing the RCMP a favour. Even though the police seemed to have placed a lot of faith in his abilities to convince the Mohles, it still wasn't his responsibility. As for herself, her role was minor, but she had tried her best, and if Neil and his wife decided to take off for some reason, neither she nor Hayden were to blame. In fact, if she had to bet on it, she was sure they had run off because of the telephone call. She had no idea what it was about, but Vivian had looked shocked, and immediately after that, they were gone.

Dinner had proved the final catharsis. The food was great; they had drunk a little too much and the conversation flowed freely. She had learned a lot about Hayden, and him about her. That said, she still couldn't quite make sense of his career choices. With his qualifications and obvious intelligence, she would have thought he would be in some senior legal position by now, not that his job in the premier's office wasn't important. He just seemed capable of so much more.

And then, there was still the affair; that really bothered her and she had struggled to keep her jealous streak under control. At some point in the evening, they had, as most couples of a similar age, asked the inevitable relationship questions. While she had confessed to having no current romantic attachment, he had provided a somewhat embarrassed and circuitous answer. She interpreted this as his having been in some form of relationship that had ended very recently. Whatever the truth, the explanations, temporarily at least, cleared the air of any lingering doubts on both their parts, and the rest of the evening passed in relaxed flirtatious banter. Between the wine and her recent makeover, she was fully expecting a late night knock on her hotel room door.

Stripping down to bright red underwear, which she had carefully matched to the colour of her toenail polish, Rachel headed for the bathroom. She wasn't ending up in bed with filthy feet from her barefoot walk and a quick shower wouldn't hurt. If she hurried, there should still be time.

CHAPTER 43

Hayden

Sitting on the end of the king-size hotel bed, Hayden stared at his ghostly reflection in the dark TV screen facing him. He looked strained and worried. Usually careful and controlled, this unsettled feeling was new territory for him; everything it seemed was a little out of balance. For the first time in his career, he had allowed outside events to override the focus of his own investigation. Talk about a mess. A recently ended affair with the premier of the province, who, to make matters worse, may or may not be directly involved in accepting offshore financing through Monger Capital. An aborted effort to assist the RCMP in offering witness protection to a banker who may or may not be involved with the same company. A strong suspicion that the company in question might in fact be a Chinese money-laundering conduit in his own investigation. Now Rachel, where had that come from? Something about her was very different from the person he thought he knew from work. Bright, bubbly and fun. He couldn't remember ever feeling quite like this about somebody, and there was no mistaking the invitation in both her words and actions as they had left for their separate rooms.

Hayden continued to stare blankly at his reflection. Every fibre in his body told him to get up and go to Rachel's room while every brain cell fought the urge. He sat unmoving for several more minutes, then sighed and hung his head. He knew what he had to do as far as his work was concerned, and the realization that he really liked this woman and didn't want to ruin things did the rest. Maybe this was would prove to be a missed opportunity he would always regret, but for tonight at least, he would try to do the right thing. Getting up from the bed, he headed to the bathroom. Shower, then bed; tomorrow he would develop his plan.

CHAPTER 44

Neil

Neil and Vivian Mohle sat huddled together in the dark corner of the building entrance, thankful for the warm August weather. Several hundred metres away, the looming shape of the historic old sugar refinery hummed and throbbed with mechanical noises as if alive. It was eerie on the waterfront at this time of night, and because sound would travel far across the water, neither spoke. Philip should be here shortly, and they could go inside. Any discussion on what to do next could wait until then.

Their flight from the hotel had been instinctive, and neither had spoken much during the journey. Kitty Lee's call to Vivian provided the trigger; fear had done the rest. Vivian's whispered message as they walked from the hotel lounge played repeatedly in Neil's head.

"Kitty called from a payphone. She sounded frightened, but wanted to warn us. I told her we were meeting with some of your old colleagues that you hadn't seen in ages, and all she said was we should run. Not to trust anyone, including your colleagues, and not to go to dinner; our lives may depend on it. Then she hung up."

The message had terrified Vivian, and Neil had fed off her fear. Although Kitty's warning collaborated Hayden and Rachel's message about their lives being in danger, why would the police use them to deliver the offer of witness protection? Their rationale had sounded plausible until Kitty's message, now he wasn't so sure. And what about Kitty's earlier use of the name of some criminal called Komodo to scare that woman in the hair salon. What if there really was a connection between him and Kitty? According to Chris Broughton's sources, this Komodo person was very bad news. Even if the offer of witness protection was real, could it keep them safe from some international criminal? Spending the rest of their days living under a false identity with their lives in some bureaucrat's hands gave him no comfort at all. His overriding instinct was to run, get somewhere safe and worry about the repercussions later.

Even before they reached the hotel lobby, Neil had already made up his mind. No sooner were they out of sight of the group in the lounge than he grabbed Vivian's hand and hurried to the exit at the rear of the hotel and out into the nearby parking lot. Weaving through the parked cars, they made their way to the walkway leading to Stanley Park. Even before anyone missed them, they had flagged down a passing cab and headed back in the opposite direction toward Vancouver's busy cruise ship terminal.

Blending easily with the multitude of passengers milling around Canada Place, Neil called and left a brief message for his brother, Philip, to meet them at his office as soon as he was able, not say anything to anyone about their whereabouts and wait for them if they were not there. That done, they had taken another cab to the east end of Gastown before commencing the long walk along Powell Street, past dozens of Vancouver's homeless people until they almost reached the far end of the old sugar refinery building. There they had slipped through a convenient and well-used hole in the railroad property's wire fence.

"How did you know this would be here?" Vivian asked as they clambered through, crossed over the railroad tracks and walked down Rogers Street to Philip's dockside office building.

"In this part of town, there's always a hole in the fence," Neil replied, without any attempt at humour.

As anticipated, they had arrived at Philip's office building before him and now sat huddled in the corner of the recessed entrance, waiting.

CHAPTER 45

Philip et al

Philip Mohle was exhausted as he watched the dockside crane lift the large pale-blue container onto the waiting flatbed truck. They had less than three hours to get it delivered to the Deltaport container terminal at Roberts Bank. There, somewhere along its eleven-hundred-metre contiguous berth, one of the port's high-speed, super post-Panamax cranes would load the container onto an enormous transpacific container vessel, the MV *Ubekamanzi*. Travelling down the west coast of the United States, the vessel would pass through the Panama Canal arriving at Freeport in the Bahamas sixteen days later where the container, along with several others, would be discharged for transfer to another vessel and arrive at its destination—Cape Town, South Africa—after sixty-six days at sea.

Calling on engineering skills he thought he'd long since forgotten, Philip had worked alone and through the night to get the container ready. He'd also been on the phone, waking people from their sleep and requesting favours he'd someday have to repay to amend the container's original delivery schedule at short notice. Fortunately, two things had worked to his advantage. The container's air conditioning and ventilation system had already been installed, and the expected contents for shipment had been delivered to his office several days earlier. Ultimately, he had everything he needed to meet the new shipping deadlines, everything that was except for the agreement of his brother and his wife, who, anxious and exhausted, had curled up together on the one small red-leather sofa in his office and fallen asleep.

"Okay, you're good to go," Philip said to the driver. "I'll see you at Deltaport. You're cleared to go straight alongside. It'll be the last container loaded at the stern." As he finished speaking and the truck pulled away, Philip looked at his watch: exactly 6:30 a.m. He'd done well. Just time enough to lock the office building and head for the dock. At this time of the morning, both he and the truck would get there before the terminal gates opened at eight o'clock.

#

"So, without putting too fine a point on it," said Inspector Jack Bowie, "it appears we've fucked up. That about sum it up, Kate?"

"Yes, sir," replied Sergeant Kate Harrington, deciding that any attempt at an excuse would likely fail miserably. "We thought we had every eventuality covered for their protection, both at the hotel and the restaurant, but we did not anticipate they would take off of their own accord."

"Do you think they have something to hide? Or do they know something we don't and are running scared?"

"Hard to know although I would have thought if they were scared, they would have taken our offer."

"I assume there's no way of knowing if they're still okay?"

"Not really, but given that they didn't appear at the restaurant and the Evans twins left alone, it's probably a reasonable assumption that they're safe. For the moment at least."

"Alright then, let's put a watch on their home and work locations and also monitor any missing person reports. Coordinate this with any municipal police forces as well. If anyone reports them missing, we want to know immediately, and when you find them, bring them in, whether they like it or not. No more dancing around. We need to get to the bottom of this before I find the solicitor general waiting on my doorstep."

#

Kitty Lee, still suffering the mixed guilt and anxiety resulting from her recent call to Vivian Mohle, decided she would stay in bed for the day. Pushing away James's warm body, with its now seemingly ever-present erection, she feigned a stomach ailment and curled into a fetal position. Pulling the duvet cover up to her chin, she lay unmoving, staring sightlessly out of the bedroom window.

James, on the other hand, despite having his early morning advances rebuffed, couldn't wait to get to work. His newfound wealth, or "fuck-you" money as it was more colloquially known, even made working for Damian enjoyable. He had quickly discovered that there was little that could match the secret enjoyment of knowing that you could walk away from your job at any time without regret.

#

Damian Slater was late as he drove slowly down the ramp to his reserved parking space below the Burrard Street office tower. Although he didn't notice, his was the only reserved executive space still unoccupied, not that he would have cared. As far as he was concerned, being last to the office was one of the privileges of rank. Besides, he was preoccupied. Today was the first full board meeting that John Ng would attend, and he planned to make sure that it went as smoothly as possible. It was clear the directors already regarded Ng as one of "Damian's men", so direct attacks would be unlikely, but he still intended to shut down any snide remarks should any director attempt to continue their expressed opposition made before Ng's appointment.

Carefully opening the door of the sleek black Mercedes S-Class sedan to avoid scraping it on the rough surface of the concrete wall alongside, Damian locked the car before making the short walk to the parking area elevator. Exiting the elevator in the building lobby, he joined the noisy babble of dozens of people moving in and out of the adjacent bank of elevators to the offices on the floors above.

#

Rachel awoke with a start; she was naked and lying on top of the bedcovers. Momentarily nonplussed, she looked at the hotel room door, which still appeared unlocked. Confused as to whether she had merely fallen into a deep sleep or passed out, she struggled to remember what had happened the previous evening. She recalled finishing her shower and then, after unlocking the deadbolt on the door in anticipation of Hayden's probable appearance, she had laid down on the bed exhausted from the day's events. With the bedcover carefully but loosely twisted around her body to add some modesty to her staged scene, she had rested her head on the pillow... and that was the last she could remember. She didn't know whether to be relieved that no one had entered her unlocked room or disappointed that Hayden had not accepted her less than subtle invitation. Rolling onto her stomach, she looked at the clock. She had missed breakfast and barely had time to meet in the lobby as arranged. She had better hurry, or they'd miss the ferry.

#

Hayden watched from the deep wing-backed chair in the lobby as Rachel hurried to the checkout counter, pulling her carry-on case behind. She looked flustered, and he wondered why. There was still plenty of time, and meeting at 9:30 a.m. had been her suggestion. He looked down at his newspaper, but his mind was elsewhere.

What was it she had said the previous evening? *"I know you said you have a few calls to make, so I'll see you in the lobby at 9:30 a.m. tomorrow, unless of course I see you before. I'll leave my door unlocked for a while in case it's not too late and you feel like a nightcap."* That was it.

He smiled. Somewhat inebriated after a glass of wine or two too many, her less than subtle invitation had been obvious. After saying goodnight at the elevator, he had fought the urge; it was only after he had showered and was about to get into bed that the questions began. What if she was waiting and he didn't arrive? He really wanted to do the right thing, but hadn't felt this nervous about a possible relationship in years. Maybe he should telephone, but perhaps she would already be asleep? With her room on the same floor and only a short distance down the hall, he decided to dress and then quietly try her door. He would leave whatever happened after that to fate.

"Oh, there you are. Have you been waiting long?"

Hayden looked up at Rachel standing in front of him. "No, not long at all. I checked out a few minutes ago and then sat down here. Sorry, that sounds a bit vague; my mind was elsewhere. Did you sleep well?"

"I think so," Rachel replied warily. "I remember putting my head on the pillow and that was it. Next thing I knew it was morning, and I had missed breakfast. I either slept like the dead or passed out."

Not ready to explain his own actions the previous evening, Hayden quickly changed the topic. "Never mind, we can have breakfast on the ferry. I wonder what's happened to the Mohles?"

"I don't suppose the RCMP will give us any more information now that they don't need our help," Rachel replied.

"Shouldn't think so," Hayden said as he stood up. "Well, we'd best get going. Why don't you meet me at the front of the hotel? I'll get the car delivered from the valet parking."

CHAPTER 46

Dana

Dana Holmes hung up the telephone. She felt better after speaking with Hugh Ruff. His assurance that nothing bad had surfaced about Monger Capital, and that he was doing his utmost to confirm their ultimate ownership, lifted her spirits. With the Monger question in Hugh's capable hands and her affair with Jones out of the way, she could once again focus on her job. There was a lot she wanted to achieve while in still office, and while the affair had proved to be as enjoyable as she had anticipated, it was definitely a distraction. A distraction that, in her position, she could ill afford. Strange as it may seem, and while she would certainly miss the intimacy, with it out of the way, she felt recharged. Her life was once again her own.

Getting up from her chair, Dana walked out of her office and placed a list of files on Rachel's desk. She looked at her watch. The midday ferry should be arriving shortly and with it, Rachel and Jones. There were things she needed Rachel to do, and she hoped they would be on time.

CHAPTER 47

Andre

Andre Malherbe, master mariner and captain of the Panamax container ship MV *Ubekamanzi*, was decidedly unhappy as he stood on the bridge and looked down at the waiting gap in the neat rows of containers below. He hated disruptions to the orderly loading of his ship, and the company message received late the previous night, requesting a loading delay for the last minute arrival of a single container destined for trans-shipment in the Bahamas to Cape Town, South Africa, had soured his mood. To make matters worse, its contents required specific placement above deck so that its internal battery-operated air purification system could be accessed during the voyage if necessary. That no one on board had any familiarity with the system did not seem to concern anyone at headquarters, as they assured him that suitable shore-side assistance would be available if required.

Several hours after the company's request, he received two private calls. The first, a frantic message from his mother literally begging him to help her younger sibling, Neil Mohle, who apparently was in fear for his life. The second, which did nothing to alleviate his anxiety after the first, from her youngest brother, Philip, with a convoluted plan to help Neil that if it failed, would not only end Andre's sea-going career, but probably also land him in jail. The only comfort he received from either call was that both his mother and Philip assured him that Neil had done nothing wrong or illegal.

Turning away from the bridge windows, Andre addressed his chief officer and fellow South African, Kobus Koch. "Kobus, we need that bloody container on board as soon as it arrives at the dock. We can still get away on schedule if all goes well. Oh, and make sure the lashings don't obscure the container's air system. It's supposedly clearly marked on the outside. It needs to face the walkway in case we need access during the voyage."

"Will do, Skipper."

"Okay and one other thing while I remember: I have some corporate stuff to go over while we travel down to Freeport. There are a number of large plans, and I don't want to have to pack up each time I take a break. I thought I'd use the spare cabin alongside mine, but I don't want anyone going in there, so advise the crew, will you. I'll let you know when I'm done."

"Fine, I'll have them post a sign on the door. Anything exciting you can share?"

"No, it's confidential at this stage, but nothing to worry about. It doesn't affect us directly. Just corporate shit, but they want a seagoing opinion. Covering their butts, most likely."

Both men stood silently for a moment before Andre spoke again. "Another thing: can you get two of those emergency ration pails delivered to my cabin? I want to take a careful look at the contents. I've got some ideas about better provisioning for the life rafts, but need to know a bit more about the food packaging."

"Are you sure you want two? I think the contents are all the same. Each pail holds about thirty day's food supply, with about eighteen hundred calories a day."

"Okay, one then; unless the contents are different, then two."

"Will do."

"Fine, I'll leave you to finish the loading. I'm going below." Andre turned and walked from the bridge. He'd taken the first step. Once the container was loaded, there'd be no turning back.

#

"Stay in the truck," Philip Mohle said to the driver. "I'll just check the ventilation and then you can move down to the loading dock. Five minutes max."

Climbing up the back of the truck and out of sight of the driver, Philip tapped lightly on the container's ventilation grill. Moments later, a small carefully-concealed door swung open revealing the strained faces of his brother and Vivian. "Are you ok?" Philip asked.

"Yes, it's cramped in this space, but when we open the inside panel and can move around the whole container among the equipment, its fine."

"I need to pee," Vivian interjected.

"Can you wait?" Philip asked.

"No. Why can't I climb down and go behind those containers?" she said, looking past Philip at the seemingly endless rows of containers stacked nearby.

"Too risky."

The words were barely out of his mouth when Vivian now dressed in dark sweatpants and top, courtesy of one of Philip's former roommates, stepped through the door and climbed down the back of the truck. "I'll only be a minute," she said, running over to the stacked containers and disappearing into the shadows.

"Fuck, Neil. We don't have time. She's putting the whole thing at risk," Philip complained.

"Give her a minute, Boet. It's pretty scary for us too."

"Okay. Two minutes, then you have to close the door, and we get this thing loaded. Have you got your phone, just in case?" Philip asked.

"Vivian has it in her pocket. We got rid of hers earlier and didn't plan to use mine unless absolutely necessary. We didn't want to be traced. Are you sure Andre's okay with this?"

"I'm not sure okay is the right word, but he's agreed to help. That's probably as good as it gets right now." Philip fidgeted nervously. "Close the door, Neil. I'm going to look for Vivian. She needs to hurry. If we're not back in a couple of minutes, they'll need to load, and I'll find another way of getting her out of here."

Philip pushed the small door closed and listened for his brother to turn the latch. Climbing off the back of the truck, he looked around; there was no sign of Vivian. Hurrying over to the stacked containers, he peered into the shadows. Nothing. Where the hell was she? He walked back to the truck and signalled to the driver to start his engine. "Take her over and load her up," he yelled over the roar of the diesel motor. With his brother taken care of, he'd continue his search; Vivian couldn't have gone far.

#

Despite over four-hundred monitored video cameras strategically placed around Vancouver's port facilities and the addition of high-tech security gates in most areas, a basic port pass issued to employees allows wide access to the tens of thousands of containers stacked in supposedly secure locations. Without security checks for these employees, it is difficult to determine how many port pass holders have criminal links. Certain dockworkers also possess a higher-security Transportation Security Clearance pass issued by Transport Canada that allows them inside restricted zones on the waterfront. While these workers are screened for criminal records and links to organized crime before the TSC passes are issued, the restricted zones are small compared to the highly-populated rows of containers able to be accessed with only a general pass.

Several gangs are known to use shipping containers to smuggle cocaine, heroin or precursor chemicals used to make ecstasy and crystal meth. While the number of incidents is thought to be low relative to other trafficking routes, the quantities, when discovered, are typically very large. The operations are also clearly linked to known or suspected gang members working in key positions among dockworkers, equipment operators, truckers and supervisors, providing them with the ideal means of transporting the drugs internationally. Often being among the first to board arriving ships, they are perfectly positioned to unload the goods, place them in storage and prepare the necessary documents for transportation to their final destination. Any co-workers not involved in the illegal operations are readily intimidated into a forced code of silence with threats of violence.

Accordingly, on this particular morning, Willy Sands, who had spent the late hours of the previous night drinking and commiserating with the Evans twins about their failed rendezvous, had just finished transferring the last of a cocaine shipment from an open container into the trunk of his bright red Chev Camaro ZL1 when Vivian Mohle appeared around the corner of the stack. Seeing an Asian woman in a sweat suit in the dockyard at this time of the morning, Willy immediately thought "hooker" and responded instinctively. Small, but powerfully built, like most dockworkers, his fist connected with the side of her head before she had a chance to utter a single word, and she fell limply to the ground. Scooping her up, Willy bundled her into the trunk of the car and a short time later drove slowly and unchallenged through the port gates and onto the highway heading to Vancouver. He didn't know what she might have seen, but he'd drop her off somewhere and then complete his delivery. Where was the only question. It needed to be quiet. She couldn't be allowed to see either him or the car again. Realizing he was out of his depth, he called the only people he knew who would help.

"Griffin, Willy here. I've got a bit of a problem and could use some help."

"Do you have any idea of the fucking time?"

"Yeah, sorry. I was taking care of business, and this Asian chick walked right into the situation."

"So why call me?"

"Well, I knocked her cold, and now she's in my trunk, but I can't risk her identifying me or the car. It's full of product."

"So what do you want me to do?"

"I thought maybe you could rough her up and then let her go somewhere. She's cute too, so maybe you'd even enjoy it. Whatever you boys want to do is okay with me. I just need her out of the car. I'll also owe you one." Willy laughed. "Maybe you could even substitute her for the one you lost last night."

"Fuck you, that's not funny. Bring her to the house. Pull into the garage, and we'll bag her and then you can leave. She'll never see you or the car, but you'll owe us big time."

#

Standing quietly on the quayside, Philip watched as the giant container ship left the dock. Outwardly calm, internally he was frantic. His sister-in-law had vanished and his brother, securely locked inside a container without any means of communication had been loaded aboard the MV *Ubekamanzi*, which was now underway to the Bahamas under the captaincy of his nephew, Andre Malherbe.

Extremely reluctant to be involved, Andre had been adamant that, after their initial conversation, no further communication take place between them until the container was offloaded in Freeport. If things went awry, Andre wanted as much latitude as he could get to protect his own position. No traceable communication with each other was the first rule and one that Philip could not break. If Philip couldn't locate Vivian, neither his brother nor Andre would know until the ship was in the Bahamas.

After a lengthy and fruitless last search of the terminal, Philip returned to his car; he had a plane to catch and documents to collect. His brother's escape was underway, and he needed to follow the agreed protocol. Timing was critical. He could only hope that Vivian hadn't changed her mind and was going to try her own escape. That could potentially screw everything up. She'd hated being confined to the container, and it had taken all of Neil's persuasive skill to get her initial agreement. Philip had no idea of what he would do when he found her. All he knew was that the plan couldn't wait. If he were going to keep his brother safe, he'd have to carry on as agreed. If Vivian couldn't be found so be it, there was only so much he could do.

CHAPTER 48

Garrett and Griffin

When Willy Sands arrived at the Evans twins North Vancouver house, both men were already waiting in the garage. As the car approached, they opened the automatic door and closed it immediately after Willy had entered. Tapping on the driver's window, Griffin said, "Don't turn off the engine, and when I bang on the back, pop the trunk."

Willy did as instructed and moments later watched in his side mirror as a limp female body was dropped unceremoniously into a large dark blue hockey equipment bag, which was then zipped closed.

"Okay, you're out of here," Garrett said as the garage door opened again.

"Was she still unconscious?" Willy asked through the car's now open window as he backed out.

"Nope . . . just thumped her again while she was trying to orient herself. She's out now, and we'll be on our way before she wakes up."

"What are you going to do?"

"Do you really want to know? Or do you want to get going?" Griffin asked.

"I'm on my way. Thanks. I owe you one."

"We know. We'll call you sometime."

Willy finished backing out of the drive and once again went on his way.

As the garage door closed, Griffin said, "Let's look at her again. We need to make sure she can breathe, and we should tape her up. Can't have her kicking and screaming while we move her."

Unzipping the bag, the twins looked down at the still body of Vivian Mohle, two darkening bruises marking her otherwise unblemished face. There was a stunned silence before Griffin spoke. "It's the woman."

"Are you sure?" Garrett asked.

"Absolutely. I'll tape her up. You go get the picture."

"What are we going to do if it is her? And what the fuck was she doing in Willy's drug drop?"

"Who knows, but we need to get her on Vegas's boat and then find out where her husband's hiding. Go get the picture. We'd better get moving."

#

A little before 10 a.m. that morning, Neil Mohle's assistant recognized his mobile number on her telephone display before she answered. Surprised that he was not yet in the office, on answering, she found it even more unusual to hear a woman's voice until Vivian identified herself. Her message was brief. Neil was going to be away for a few days and he would call later to explain. At the time, Neil's assistant was juggling another call and did not ask any questions. Half an hour later, deciding she needed more information to reschedule his various activities, she first called Neil's mobile and then his home number, only to receive automatic voice messages on both phones. Assuming that unless she heard from him before the weekend, he would return on the following Monday, she made no further effort to contact him and rearranged his few scheduled appointments accordingly.

Shortly after the call to Neil's office, the manager at Vivian's hair salon also received a call made from Neil's mobile. With a garbled reference to a family emergency that she was unexpectedly required to attend, Vivian said that she was unable to come to work until the following Tuesday. Her request that someone reschedule or take over any outstanding appointments was received with frosty acceptance. Both women knew that the days before weekends were always busy and that Vivian's clients would, at best, be unhappy with whatever alternative arrangements were made to have someone else see them.

#

Anchored a hundred metres off the rocky and heavily-treed North Shore, in one of the many small deserted inlets scattered along the coastline, Garrett looked at Vivian Mohle, her legs and hands still taped together as she sat on the passenger side of Vegas's spotless Grady White powerboat. "There, that wasn't so bad now was it?" he said, finally letting go of Vivian's left nipple, which he'd squeezed firmly throughout both calls, with a final sharp twist.

Vivian yelped with pain, then stared defiantly at him, not answering.

"Cat got your tongue?"

"No. Why are you doing this? Why did I have to make those calls? And what do you want?" Vivian looked from one man to the other and then back again. They looked identical; it was weird, really weird.

"We need to find your husband?" Griffin said.

"Why? What has he done?"

"That doesn't concern you. What were you doing at the docks? Was he there? Will he be looking for you?"

"I told you I don't know where he is. We'd gone to the docks for him to check on some shipment, and all I did was go behind a container for a pee when some man attacked me. Was it one of you?"

Vivian's head rocked back with the force of the flat-handed blow to the side of her head. Tears welled up in her eyes as she struggled not to cry.

"Don't bullshit me, lady. Where's your husband? Those two calls you made will buy us plenty of time to find him before anyone starts looking for either of you." As Griffin finished speaking, he tossed Neil's mobile over the side of the boat. "And if you're not careful, those are the last calls you'll ever make," he said ominously.

"Why don't we chuck her overboard as well?" Garrett said. "If she knows nothing, she's no use to us anyway. That way we can at least claim half the money. We also promised Vegas to get his boat back to him before lunch."

"We've still got a couple of hours, and I'm sure this little lady has plenty more to tell us before we've finished with her. Right, honey?" Griffin leered at Vivian and, grabbing her sweatshirt, pulled her roughly behind him and into the cabin below deck. "Now," he said. "No one can see or hear us here. Let's try again, shall we?"

#

Even an experienced pathologist might have had difficulty determining which of the three earlier blows to the side of Vivian's head had caused her carotid artery to rupture, the resultant symptoms often delayed by hours or even days after the initial blow. In Vivian's case, the first indication of a problem came as she tumbled into the cabin behind Griffin.

"I can't see," she cried, the terror in her voice causing Griffin to pause.

"Don't fuck with me, lady," he snarled, any threat in the words erased by the puzzled expression on his face as he watched Vivian flounder helplessly on the bunk where he had thrown her.

"I'm not. I can't see. I can't see," Vivian screamed before falling on her side, her whole body jerking spasmodically. Then, just as suddenly, the movements stopped and she lay still, her mouth open in a suddenly muted cry.

#

Vivian's naked and mutilated body, wrapped in thirty feet of anchor chain, slid off the swim grid with a loud scraping sound before sinking quickly below the surface to the ocean floor. Any trace of her passage quickly erased by the wash of the powerful engines as the boat surged forward heading out of the inlet and back to its berth at the West Vancouver marina.

The dark blue cotton equipment bag containing Vivian's clothes and weighted down by the boat's anchor was discarded in a similar fashion to her body several hundred metres further along the route.

Vivian's head, hands and feet, now concealed in a heavy plastic fertilizer bag, were stored in a convenient fish locker as the twins first cleaned their tools and then washed down the boat, returning it to its former spotless state.

As if connected by a single brain, Griffin and Garret went about the tasks with silent efficiency, neither uttering a single word during the voyage back. The job was only half done, and they had reputations to uphold.

CHAPTER 49

Hayden

As he walked away from Rachel to pick up the car, Hayden realized his hands were trembling. Something about her had gotten under his skin, and he felt like a nervous teenager on a first date. Even more strange was the fact that although he had worked with Rachel previously, he had never seen her in this light. He knew it wasn't a rebound reaction from the end of his affair with Dana, for although she had initiated the break, he had reached a similar point in the relationship. Dana had, fortuitously it seemed, merely been the one to pull the plug the previous day. This was entirely different. He'd been fine initially, but as the previous evening progressed, he'd gradually become more and more infatuated until now, with every nerve on edge, all he could think about was how not to mess things up.

As it was, he needn't have worried; it was Rachel's remark, delivered as they inched slowly along Georgia Street in the Vancouver morning traffic en route to the Tsawwassen ferry terminal, which brought things to a head.

"I thought you might drop by for a nightcap last night," Rachel said, staring fixedly ahead.

"I did."

"You did? I don't remember you coming; in fact, I don't remember anything after getting into bed. I was either exhausted or drugged. You didn't drug me, did you?" Rachel turned and looked directly at Hayden as he drove, a mock serious expression plastered all over her face.

"No, the door was locked, and I couldn't get in."

"You couldn't? I left it unlocked. I distinctly remember turning the deadbolt."

"It locks automatically. The dead bolt is extra. You'd have to jam the door open; there's no way to leave it unlocked. If you fell asleep before I got there, though, it's probably a good thing it wasn't left ajar. You never know who might have tried to get in."

"But you came?"

"I did, but perhaps it's as well it was locked."

"Why? Are you involved with someone?"

"No," Hayden paused, "well not anymore anyway."

"Oh, I thought you were having an affair."

Hayden glanced sharply at Rachel. It seemed she was never going to let this affair business go, but once again, she sat staring straight ahead. *All or nothing,* he thought before answering. "I was, but it's ended."

"Can I ask who?"

"Better not, but trust me, it's over." Hayden glanced at Rachel again as he spoke. When no response was forthcoming, he spoke again. "Look, I'm probably going to botch this delivery, but I really enjoyed our evening and I like you a lot. I'd like to go out again, and while I have been seeing someone, it's really over. I would have told you this last night, but I didn't want to disturb you by banging on the door when I found it locked." Hayden waited. Everything he'd said was true; he just hadn't admitted how few hours had passed since his affair had ended.

The silence seemed to go on forever before Rachel finally spoke. "I hate to dwell on this, but the office rumour was that it was someone on staff. If that's true and we do go out again, I'm going to be spending all my time looking at everyone who works for the premier and wondering who is smirking behind my back."

"How about if I assured you that whatever rumour you heard was wrong and that it wasn't anyone who worked for the premier?"

"Well that would certainly make me feel better. Is it true?"

"Yes," Hayden replied, mentally assuring himself that as the premier wasn't a member of her own staff, technically, he hadn't lied.

"Okay, then," Rachel replied, her smile returning, "I'd love to go out again."

Hayden relaxed, things were looking up.

#

Sitting in the dining area of the nineteen-thousand-tonne ferry, Hayden pointed to the enormous container ship passing alongside. Travelling from Tsawwassen on the Vancouver mainland to Swartz Bay on Vancouver Island and carrying twenty-one hundred passengers and four hundred and seventy vehicles, the MV *Spirit of Vancouver Island* was the largest vessel in the BC Ferry fleet. Despite its size, the passing ship dwarfed it.

"Aren't you glad we took the late morning ferry back?" Hayden said. "You don't get close up views like this every day."

"What's her name?" Rachel asked as the stern of the giant ship slid silently past the windows.

Hayden looked startled. "I thought we'd agreed to forget about that," he said.

"We did. I meant the ship."

"Oh. Sorry." Hayden replied sheepishly, turning as he spoke for a better look at the passing vessel. "It's the MV *Ubekamanzi*."

"What a strange name. I wonder where it's headed?"

"Through the Panama Canal and then somewhere across the Atlantic, I would imagine. We could look it up if you'd really like to find out."

"No, just a little curious about all that cargo and what's in the containers? Not enough to disrupt breakfast, though, and I'd rather hear more about you. There seems to be quite a bit I don't know."

CHAPTER 50

Andre

Standing quietly in the relative calm of the bridge of the Zulu named MV *Ubekamanzi*, or "Dragonfly", as some of the English crew still called her, Captain Andre Malherbe was glad to be underway. With a brief blast of the ship's whistle to acknowledge the passing ferry, he turned his mind to the strategically placed pale-blue container below. Despite his earlier anxiety, the loading had been uneventful, and as long as the next stage went as planned, his part in Philip's hurriedly concocted plan would be over in sixteen days. Even though they were family, this whole thing was crazy. Had it not been for his mother's pleading and her sworn assurance that his uncle had done nothing illegal, he wouldn't have touched this scheme with a ten-foot pole. Once he had them out of that container and into the cabin he had set aside, he wanted to know what this was all about. And, as he had told Philip the previous evening, if he didn't like the answer, he was turning them over to the authorities. He wasn't going to jeopardize his career for some illegal bullshit, family or no family.

CHAPTER 51

Vivian et al

By Tuesday of the week following the Mohles' missed dinner engagement, there was still no sign of them. An undercover RCMP patrol car periodically passing their Kitsilano home reported no sign of activity during either the day or night. Still concerned for their safety, the RCMP did not attempt to enter the house for fear of revealing the continued surveillance.

All this changed on the Wednesday morning when Vivian failed to arrive at work for the second day in a row. In all the years she had worked at the salon, Vivian always arrived on time. With appointments backed up, the manager's call to check on her whereabouts on the Tuesday morning went directly to voicemail. When there was no sign of her the following day, another call was made to her home with the same result.

It was only then that one of the stylists offered to call Vivian's sister, Lori, who she had once met. That call too yielded no pertinent information other than Lori saying that she knew nothing about Vivian needing to attend an unexpected family emergency. She suggested the salon assume Vivian would not be in that day and offered to try to contact her, promising that either she or Vivian would call the salon as soon as Vivian was located to let them know when she would return to work.

Lori's further attempts to reach Vivian or Neil on their mobile phones and home phone all failed. In frustration, she finally called

Neil's office. Grateful to hear from Lori, Neil's assistant told her of Vivian's call the previous Thursday, saying Neil would be back at work the following week, and that, despite her own several attempts to reach him on his mobile or home phone, she had heard nothing further.

Now very anxious, Lori drove to her sister's two-storey house where she found their burnt-orange convertible parked in the garage, the front door unlocked and their pampered cat inside and desperately waiting for food. Her anxiety level now through the roof, Lori used the house phone to call 911 and alerted the RCMP to her missing sister and her husband.

Within eight minutes of the 911 call, notification of the enquiry into the apparent disappearance of Neil and Vivian Mohle had reached Inspector Jack Bowie. Deciding that, with growing public awareness, it was no longer in either the police or the Mohles' best interests to keep the investigation under wraps, a full-scale missing persons alert was launched that same day into the couple's disappearance. No mention was made in any internal or external police communication of the earlier threat to the Mohles' lives.

#

Both major Vancouver newspapers carried the same front-page story the following day and, outside of a slight variation in the banner headlines about a "Missing Vancouver Banker," the basic details were the same. Included within both stories was also the identical colour photograph of Neil and Vivian Mohle, casually dressed and smiling directly at the photographer. Details were sparse, and besides confirming that the pair had missed an important business dinner engagement immediately before disappearing, the RCMP provided little other information.

Not surprisingly, the effect of the local newspaper article and its digital global versions on the various parties either knowingly or unknowingly connected to the disappearance varied significantly.

#

Alone at his computer in the ECB building in Toronto, Chris Broughton stared at the picture of Neil and Vivian Mohle on his computer screen. It seemed like only yesterday that they'd been discussing Neil's Monger deal. Knowing Neil, Chris figured he was probably languishing in the sun somewhere and would call in later with the excuse that he forgot to tell anyone where he was going. A faint recollection of Neil's question about an international criminal also flickered briefly alight before being immediately extinguished. What was it Neil had said at the time? Something about it being a name his wife picked up in her hairstyling salon. Deciding he had nothing to contribute, Chris shut down the news and returned to his work. It was his last day at ECB and he had a lot to do; after all, it was why he'd come in early in the first place.

#

Always an early riser, Damian Slater, still dressed only in tartan boxer shorts and a freshly laundered white t-shirt, picked up his neatly rolled newspaper from the front doorstep. The fact that others in the upscale neighbourhood might object to his choice of public attire never once entered his mind. Removing a blue elastic band, he unrolled the paper, his eyes focusing on the front-page photograph, where he stared at Vivian's face for several seconds before glancing briefly at Neil's and then the headline. The order of his unspoken reactions was typically Damian. *That's our banker . . . nice wife. Hope this doesn't affect our LNG deal. The bank probably has a backup. I'll get James to look into it.* By the time he reached for his mobile phone to call James, he was already reading the next article.

#

James Lee woke to the sound of a ringing telephone. Briefly nonplussed, he groped around the top of the bedside table to find his glasses and to check the time. His first coherent thought was that it was still dark outside; the second, made after successfully locating and putting on his glasses, was that it was only 5:15 in the morning. By then the telephone had stopped ringing and lay quietly on a nearby dresser, a small glowing red light alerting him to a waiting message. Getting out of bed, James picked up the phone while glancing at Kitty's unmoving body as he left the room. One naked leg thrust out from beneath the duvet while the rest of her, head included, stayed buried deep inside its warmth.

Walking into the living room, James listened to Damian's message.

> *Seems our LNG banker and his wife are missing. It's front-page news. Get our finance department to check with the bank who his replacement is so that our LNG financing isn't delayed. I'm sure they must have a backup. Let me know. Thanks.*

There was an audible click as Damian had ended the call.

James stood shaking his head. Typical Damian, didn't give a shit about the banker, just the deal. It was only after James had turned on his laptop that the full realization of Damian's message hit home. The company's LNG banker was Neil Mohle and his wife, Vivian, was Kitty's hairstylist friend. No longer trying to be as quiet as possible, he went to wake his wife.

#

Her head still buried under the thick duvet, Kitty Lee felt James's hand on her leg before she heard his voice. Reflexively she kicked out in frustration, this was far too early. Even with her head beneath the duvet, she could tell by lifting the edge ever so slightly that it was still dark outside. James's hand left her leg, and seconds later, the duvet was pulled back from her face.

"Sorry to wake you," he said. "Damian called. Apparently, Vivian and Neil Mohle are missing and it's headline news. I was going to check the news and thought you'd want to know."

Kitty sat up in bed and nodded, not trusting herself to speak as the shock of the news surged through her body and her sleep-addled brain. Her head bowed, the duvet now crumpled around her waist, Kitty watched through her hanging hair as, with a last lingering look, James walked from the bedroom, speaking as he went.

"I've turned on my laptop to check the local news. There's a B.C. provincial segment on the main CBC webpage. Coffee will be here when you're up."

Still sitting slumped over, Kitty grabbed the duvet and pulled it back up to her chin. Had Vivian taken her warning and run? Or had something happened to her and Neil? Sick to her stomach and with no one with whom she could share her racing thoughts, she slid from the bed and, standing alongside, pulled on her black floral silk housecoat and walked slowly to the living room. She wasn't sure what she would do if her father had harmed them because of something she had said. Composing herself, she looked at James sitting in front of his small laptop and reached for her waiting coffee. "What does it say?" she asked.

#

John Ng woke at exactly 5:30 a.m., as he did every morning, to the gentle chirping of his mobile phone alarm. The muted bird sounds were the only thing that didn't seem to wake his wife. Early mornings didn't suit Bobbie's lifestyle, and he could do without her morning bitchiness. Moreover, he enjoyed his half-hour workout on the rowing machine while he watched the early financial market report. Stopping in the kitchen to start the coffee maker, he made a quick visit to the guest bathroom before turning on the TV in the den, the sound muted, and sitting on the rowing machine, all within ten minutes of first arising. The 5:30 a.m. national news had concluded, and John knew that after the brief regional news headlines, the financial market report would follow. He eased back on the rowing machine, slow and steady to start and then faster as he warmed up.

With no sound, it was the picture of Neil and Vivian Mohle that captured John's attention. Taken from the society pages of the pre-eminent Vancouver gossip magazine, he had sent the same one to Vegas Kolnick, along with the money for the hit. Dropping the rowing handle, he grabbed the remote and restored the sound just in time to catch the word "missing", followed by "police are investigating" before the newscaster announced a commercial break that would be followed by the financial market news.

His workout forgotten, John headed for the shower. He needed to check with Vegas and then get to the office and report to Dong Lai. All things being equal, Dong would get John's report to Quon before he heard it from anyone else; Komodo liked to stay ahead of the news.

#

Vegas stared at the telephone willing it to stop ringing, and the call display to change from John Ng to "missed call". He didn't want to speak to Ng today and get into an argument about a job half done, at least not until he'd spoken to the twins. He'd not heard from them since they'd borrowed his boat and, as far as he knew, they'd still not seen any sign of Neil Mohle. Deciding that a face-to-face meeting was necessary, he went in search of Drew. Despite his own size and reputation, he'd rather not visit those two crazy fuckers alone.

#

Woken by the banging on Drew Jamieson's bedroom door, Scrubber Barker emerged from his own room at the far end of the hall.

"Jeez, Vegas, do you have any idea what time it is?"

"Yeah, sorry, man, but this can't wait. Where the hell is Drew? His door's locked."

"Toronto. His parents were in some accident. He left yesterday. You weren't around at the time, but I thought you knew. He said he may be gone for a couple of weeks."

"Shit." Without another word, Vegas turned and walked away.

Scrubber stood watching as Vegas banged his way out of the house, slamming doors as he went. There was no point in trying to speak to Vegas when he was this agitated. Scrubber was sure he'd hear all about it whenever Vegas returned from wherever his apparently bad mood was taking him. As soon as the house was quiet again, Scrubber shrugged and returned to bed.

#

The Evans twins were watching TV when Vegas arrived, neither one exhibiting the slightest reaction to the sound of his motorcycle as he parked in their drive. Their apparent indifference to any possible interruption continued until several minutes later when there was a sharp knock on their open front door.

"Can one of you tell me what the hell's going on?" Vegas said, his frustration boiling over as he walked through the door and directly into the living room of their North Vancouver house. "It's taken me over two hours to travel here on the goddamn ferry to see you two. If I hadn't come on my bike, I'd still be sitting in the bloody lineup. You've been paid. The news says both Mohle and his wife are missing, and as far as I know, you only found the wife. John Ng's trying to reach me. I need to tell him something, and preferably not that the job's half done."

"Tell him we're on it," Griffin replied. "We'll deliver a large shrub to his house in the next couple of days and place it somewhere suitable. When the second one arrives, he'll know the job is finished."

"A shrub? What the hell is that all about?"

"It's our new communication method. We dreamed it up ourselves. Fits in with our landscaping business."

"You have a landscaping business?"

"We do now." Both twins grinned stupidly at Vegas, but made no further comment.

"What about my boat?" Vegas asked, realizing the first topic was going nowhere. "Did you clean it?"

"It's good, but you should probably go fishing," Griffin answered. "Make a mess on the deck and then clean up. Fish blood and guts will hide anything we missed."

Before Vegas could answer, Garrett spoke. "Hey, can you two keep quiet? I want to watch this."

Both Vegas and Griffin looked at Garrett, who leaned forward in his chair while continuing to stare at the television and some political newscast about LNG.

"Why? What the fuck do you care about LNG?" Griffin asked.

"Not the LNG, idiot, the premier. Now that's one good-looking piece of ass," Garrett answered.

#

While the said "good-looking piece of ass" would not have appreciated the delivery of the description, Garrett's observation was precisely the effect Dana Holmes hoped her appearance would have on certain of her constituents. Polished but suggestive, she had thought as she dressed that morning. Normally desperate to be judged on her ability alone, she was not above using all means at her disposal to advance her political agenda when the need arose and, based on the hecklers at the scheduled LNG project press briefing this morning in downtown Victoria outside the legislature building, she could do with all the help she could get.

To make matters worse, neither Rachel Burton nor Hayden Jones were around for support. They were off on another business trip together. Only this time to Kitimat of all places. Why had she let Hayden talk her into agreeing? Surprised at her own thoughts, she glanced down at her notes and the closing paragraph of her speech. She needed to finish up and get out of here. Not only were they not here, their absence was distracting. Looking across the sea of faces and the unwavering lenses of the TV cameras mounted behind the reporters, Dana forced herself to finish the prepared remarks, smiled brightly at the cameras and turned to hurry away.

"Madame Premier?"

Dana turned to look. She knew that voice, a senior CBC reporter and an old political ally.

"Any comment on the missing banker and his wife?"

Dana looked startled. "What banker?" she asked, immediately regretting the question.

"Front page news this morning. Name of Neil Mohle. Both he and his wife are missing."

Dana flinched as if she'd been struck. "I haven't seen the news yet," she replied, recovering quickly, "but I'm sure the appropriate authorities are looking in to it."

Resuming her previous path, she hurried away before any further questions could be asked. Neil Mohle! The banker who'd disappeared after meeting with Hayden and Rachel the previous week. She wondered what had happened for the story to be in the news. She needed to speak to Charles Crofut and find out what was happening. If the solicitor general didn't know, who would?

#

After several attempts to reach Charles Crofut, Dana finally stopped trying. There was no reply from his direct line, and she'd left two messages already. She looked down at the morning paper spread out on her desk, the colour picture of Neil and Vivian Mohle in the centre of the front page. Reluctantly, she looked for Hayden's mobile number and called.

#

"I still can't believe the premier agreed to me going away on this business trip with you," Rachel said. "It's barely a week since we went to Vancouver together." She stood at the side of the bed looking at Hayden, a sheet held up to her chin hanging almost to her toes. "Who did you tell her you were going to see? And what did you tell her you needed me to do?"

Hayden smiled without answering. While the sheet covered the front of Rachel's body, her naked back reflected perfectly in the Kitimat hotel's tinted windows.

"What are you grinning at?"

Hayden assumed a serious expression, but still didn't speak as he stared past Rachel and at her reflection.

"Well?"

"I was thinking," he said, still not looking directly at Rachel.

"What?" Then, realizing that Hayden had not once looked directly at her, Rachel turned to see what he was staring at and noticed her own reflection.

"You brat. You could have told me," she said, frowning while simultaneously reaching behind herself to gather the sheet.

Before Hayden could answer, his mobile vibrated violently, skidding across the small bedside table. Reaching over, he picked it up, looked at the screen and answered.

"Jones."

"Have you seen the papers?"

"Hi, Dana. No, not yet." Hayden looked at Rachel and held his finger to his lips. "What's up?"

"Your banker and his wife have disappeared."

"My banker? You mean the Mohles."

"Yes, the Mohles. It seems they've been missing for a week. From the timeline in the article, it looks like you and Rachel may have been the last people to see them."

"Why does this worry you? Were we mentioned?"

"Well, either they've been murdered or someone's going to link Mohle to Woodstock's LNG deal, and both possibilities are bad for us. If it leaks out that we knew they were targets and we didn't or couldn't stop it... that will cause a stink. If nobody discovers they were targeted, but they connect him to the LNG deal, there's sure to be negative press or conspiracy theories. The environmentalists would love that."

"Do you want me to come back?"

"No, I don't think so at this point. Just watch the news in case something new turns up. I'll call again if I need anything. I may need Rachel to come in, though. We have to prepare some form of press release, just in case. I'd rather stay ahead of this one if we can. Will you tell her or should I?"

"It might be better if you did?" Hayden replied, looking directly at Rachel who still hadn't moved from her earlier position.

"You owe me, Jones," Dana answered. "How many other former mistresses of yours would be so accommodating? I assume you've kept your word, and she doesn't know about us."

"Yes, I have, and no, nothing at all."

"Does she know I know about her?"

"Not yet."

"Okay, I'll keep it to myself for now, but as I said, you owe me."

"Thanks. I'm trying not to screw this one up."

Dana laughed. "Excuse the pun," she said as she disconnected the call.

"What was that about?" Rachel asked. "I couldn't follow the conversation from your side."

"The Mohles are still missing, and now it's on the news. Dana said she might need you to come in to help with a standby press release. She'll probably call you." Hayden had no sooner finished the sentence than Rachel's mobile phone rang.

CHAPTER 52

Jack

Several days after the news about the Mohles disappearance appeared on the news, the RCMP group responsible for the Mohle case assembled in Inspector Jack Bowie's office.

"Okay, who wants to go first," he asked, looking around at the group.

"I will," said Sergeant Kate Harrington. "It was our internal notice that got the 911 missing persons call referred back to this group. That, unfortunately, is about the only thing we seem to have got right. As you all know by now," she said, looking around the room, "the Mohles gave us the slip the night of their planned dinner with whom we suspect was the contracted killer. Based on subsequent events, we are now convinced this was intentional. Our CSIS contact confirmed at the time that on the night of the dinner, he delivered the witness protection offer and seemed to be making progress until Vivian Mohle received a call on her mobile phone. Everything went to hell in a handbasket right after that, and the Mohles disappeared. No one has seen them since."

"What did we find at their house?" Jack asked.

"Nothing that would clarify their disappearance," a senior RCMP investigator answered. "Maybe I should go over everything we've uncovered since that night? There's not much, but I can take questions as we go along, if that's alright?"

"Go ahead."

Looking down at the papers in his hand, the investigator started speaking. "As Sergeant Harrington has already said, neither the Mohles nor the party they were supposed to meet turned up for their 8:30 p.m. reservation. By 9 p.m., as they had still not arrived, their table was given to another group of diners. The maître d' said he was surprised they didn't turn up as Neil Mohle was always punctual when he had a reservation. Interestingly, the Evans twins, two of our more notorious local biker gang members, were eating in the same restaurant at the time. A coincidence that we are still looking into, but which right now doesn't appear to be directly related to the Mohles sudden disappearance."

"I wouldn't bet on it," Jack growled.

The investigator looked up briefly from his papers at Jack's face and then quickly looked down again and continued, "Inspector Bowie is right. Our undercover source has identified the twins as being involved in the contract in some way, but they neither asked for the Mohles table when they arrived nor changed their behaviour after the Mohles 'no show'. We'll keep watching, but right now, we have no basis for apprehending them.

"The following morning, two phone calls were made from Neil Mohle's cell phone, both of which were routed through Bowen Island's repeater, off West Vancouver. This means the calls could have been made anywhere from the Sunshine Coast to Point Grey on Vancouver's west side. We have also since learned from the recipients of these calls that they were made by Vivian Mohle, not Neil. No one has heard from either of the Mohles since."

"What about her phone records?" one of the assembled group asked.

"One incoming call from a downtown payphone at the time of their meeting with that CSIS officer, Jones. Nothing after that."

"Go on," Kate urged.

"Yes, Sarge. Mrs. Mohle's sister, Lori, was the first person to visit the Mohles' house several days after their disappearance. As far as we know, she didn't touch anything besides the front door until we got there. Despite the house having a security system, the front door was unlocked; which is how Lori got inside. Their cat was also in the house and looked like it hadn't been fed for several days. Lori felt this was really unusual, as they doted on the cat and would never intentionally have left it without food.

"Subsequent investigation showed their bank accounts untouched and their credit cards unused. There are relatively small credit balances in the accounts, and in total, they owed several hundred thousand dollars in loans, most of it by way of their house mortgage. Sounds like a lot, but it's pretty well covered by their assets. We also discovered that they had made a trip to Bermuda earlier this year and opened a bank account with a thirty-thousand dollar deposit."

"Now that's interesting. I thought these two were supposed to be clean?" Jack said.

"We thought so too," Kate replied. "That was the first we'd heard of a possible Bermuda connection although an offshore bank account in and of itself doesn't mean they were up to no good, maybe just planning for the future. In that same vein, the local financial community thinks he's clean and just enjoyed hanging out with the city's high-rollers, often eating at the best restaurants and attending local celebrity roasts. Apparently, he was such a regular at these upscale restaurants that he was a favoured customer. His ECB colleagues believe he was only able to get away with that lifestyle without upsetting their conservative bosses because he generated so much business for the bank."

"That's another strange thing," the senior investigator interjected. "ECB has made absolutely no comment on his disappearance or even encouraged us to do our best to find him. It's almost as if they expected something like this to happen and are hoping it will go away without damaging their reputation. In my experience, that's a very odd way for a Canadian bank to behave."

"Okay, let's break this down," Jack said. "Kate, you run with the gang links. That's where we're going to get the most political heat. Assign teams to each of the personal and business connections, and let's see if we can wrap this up sooner rather than later. I'll handle the solicitor general, but the earlier I have something I can tell him, the better. Right, people. Let's get on with it."

CHAPTER 53

Neil

"How are you holding up?" Captain Andre Malherbe asked, his back toward Neil as he locked the cabin door from the inside. Adjoining his own cabin, a large NO ENTRY sign on the outside of the door kept any unwanted visitors at bay.

"Okay, I guess," Neil replied. "At the risk of sounding ungrateful, it's been almost ten days since I first got into that container and I still don't know what's happened to Vivian. To be honest and while I understand your reasons, your refusal to contact Philip is not helping."

As Neil finished speaking, Andre turned around and stood quietly, in his perfectly pressed captain's uniform, and looked directly at him. Sitting at the cabin's small desk, dressed only in boxer shorts, his washed but still damp clothes hanging on any available hooks around the cabin, Neil, at that moment, felt decidedly inferior to his nephew.

"It's far too risky," Andre replied. "Philip and I agreed there would be no contact until we reached Freeport."

"But what about Vivian?"

"From what you've told me, I'm sure there must have been a good reason she couldn't get back into the container before Philip had to load. My guess is they'll probably both meet you in the Bahamas, and it's only another six days. Seeing how inventive Philip was in getting you both into that container in the first place, I'm sure he can come up with another plan for your wife."

Neil nodded without speaking. Vivian's sudden disappearance had unnerved him, and despite acknowledging the enormous risk his nephew was taking by secreting him aboard, he remained desperate to find out what had happened to her.

"How are the meals?" Andre asked, breaking Neil's train of thought.

"Better than expected." Neil smiled despite his mood. "Packets of dinner out of a bucket . . . I can't believe I just said that."

"Only the best for our guests," Andre replied. "I'll try and bring you some ice cream from our kitchen later. The whole crew knows how much I like the stuff, so no mystery if I have an extra bowl or two during the voyage. If all goes well, you can probably stay in this cabin for another couple of days until it's time for us to go through the Panama Canal.

"As I said before, anytime we are close to shore, our risk of random customs inspections increases exponentially, so be prepared to get back inside the container at short notice. I can't run the risk of you being seen by any members of our crew either, so I plan to pre-emptively lock you back in anytime I think the risk is getting too great. We've done well so far, and I'll try to keep the lock-up times as short as possible, but you need to be ready when I give the word. I'd also prefer to move you at night, so during this next leg of the voyage, your spells in the container may be a bit longer than you'd like. I assume your original supply of food and water essentials that Philip has set up is still intact, in case anything goes wrong. Any questions?"

Neil shook his head. "No, but I'd better take my laundry down and keep the place tidy, just in case I have to leave in a hurry."

Andre smiled. "You sound like my mother," he said. "I must admit I'll be glad when this is over. I still don't really understand why you didn't just take the police protection. The plan that you, Philip and my mother have hatched is pretty high-risk, if you ask me. And with your wife going AWOL, it's already way off track."

"It seemed a simple decision at the time," Neil replied. "If you weren't sure who was threatening to kill you, or why, who would you trust? A government agency, highly reputable I admit, but filled with people you didn't know or your own family?"

"If you put it that way, I suppose the latter, as long as I thought they had the ability to pull off the disappearing act in the first place."

"I guess we'll find out," Neil said. "At the time, we were making decisions on instinct and didn't know who to trust. Right now, I'm trying hard not to start second-guessing myself. My main regret is having pulled all of you into this mess, so the best I can do is follow your instructions and let you get back to your normal lives as quickly as possible. I assume Philip also told you there is an account in Bermuda with thirty thousand dollars in it, which we were planning to use after I retired. I've signed all the paperwork, which Philip will get to you somehow. You can draw it out whenever you like to compensate you for your help and the risk you're taking."

Andre's face flushed. "And you can shove it up your arse," he replied. "I'm not doing this for money; and if the truth be told, I'm not really doing it for you. I'm doing it against my better judgement only because my mother literally begged me to help. In six days, I'm dropping you off and then planning to forget that it ever happened. All I can do in the interim, absent worrying myself silly, is try my best not to let us get caught." His outburst over but his face still flushed, Andre stood staring down at Neil, who hadn't moved a muscle during the brief tirade.

Neil waited until his nephew's face had resumed its normal colour before he spoke. "Okay, as I've said several times before, I'm sorry I got you into this mess. Forget the money, but just know that it's there if you ever want or need it. I'll not touch it; as far as I'm concerned, it's yours."

"Okay, enough said on that topic," Andre replied. "I'll see you later. Relax as best you can, but be ready to move at a moment's notice. I'll lock the door behind me as usual so no one can come in unexpectedly although with the sign outside, they really shouldn't even try."

Neil sat quietly, his head hanging down, until he heard Andre leave and the door lock behind him. Then, leaning his head back, he sighed deeply. Perhaps Andre was right; maybe he should have taken the RCMP offer of protection. That way, he and Vivian would still be together and none of his family would be involved in an escapade, which if it failed, could potentially cost them their careers, if not their lives. How he hated this plan! Although not claustrophobic, being shut inside a moving container was not high on his list of enjoyable activities. Perhaps that was why Vivian was not here? Perhaps she had intentionally waited until it was too late for her to get back inside? She especially had hated every mile of the brief journey to the Deltaport terminal.

#

Neil looked around the cabin one last time. Six days had passed since the awkward conversation with Andre about the money in Bermuda and today was the last one here. He'd grown accustomed to the isolation, his only contact with the outside world being the brief conversations with his nephew in between his regular onboard activities of captaining the giant container ship.

The tension between them had mounted as each day took them closer to their final destination, and every conversation was like walking on eggshells. There was little doubt now how much Andre hated being placed in this situation and how relieved he would be when it was all over.

They had been lucky too. The only unscheduled customs inspection had occurred shortly before they entered the Panama Canal, and to Andre's credit, he had insisted Neil return to the container the previous night, "just in case". After a claustrophobic full day stuck inside, Neil couldn't wait to get out the following evening, grateful for once that Vivian wasn't here; she'd struggled enough on their brief journey from Philip's office. Now as they approached Freeport, it was time to go back inside again.

Neil turned at the sound of the door being unlocked and watched, with some satisfaction, as his nephew's face registered surprise, then appreciation.

The Banker's Box

"Hell, man, it's spotless," Andre said. "If it wasn't for those folded towels on the desk, you'd never know anyone had been in here."

"It's the least I could do," Neil replied. "I've put all the garbage in the bag you gave me, and it's in the locker out of sight. I assume you'll move it later, along with the towels. They're wet and dirty. I dried the shower with them after I was done. The emergency food pail is in the same locker as the garbage. I'm not sure how you'll explain why it's been used."

"I'm going to move it to my cabin once we've returned you to the container. I plan to keep it there for the whole voyage, and longer if necessary. I'll eventually return it to the stores letting them know I've opened it and have been testing the meals. They'll think I'm a bit nuts, but nobody's going to question me. Okay, let's get you back in your box. It's dark outside and the route is clear." Andre smiled. "Gives whole new meaning to a Bankers Box, doesn't it?"

"I guess," Neil replied, with far less enthusiasm. He was beginning to hate that container and Andre's description had done nothing to alleviate his dislike of the big steel box.

CHAPTER 54

Philip

Philip Mohle watched as the huge gantry crane plucked the pale-blue container from the ship before gently depositing it on the dockside. Moments later, like some giant insect, a straddle-carrier scuttled over and pulled the container up between its legs before moving quickly away.

He was not looking forward to the reunion with his brother. Quite honestly, he was more worried about Neil's reaction to the news that Vivian had disappeared than he was about getting him out of the Freeport dockyard. They would both have to have all their wits about them to slip past the dock security and then out of the Bahamas. If Neil reacted badly after hearing about Vivian, all his preparations may have been in vain.

Arriving in Grand Bahama several days earlier, Philip booked two rooms at the colourful Pelican Bay Hotel, one for himself and one for a South African visitor by the name of Mark van Aswegan. Both passport numbers he supplied, along with the reservation requests, were legitimate. Two passports had arrived, by courier from his sister, several days earlier. What strings she pulled to renew Neil's outdated South African passport without him personally making the application, he didn't know, but renew it she had. The second passport, complete with an identical photograph of Neil but in the name of Mark van Aswegan, she had assured him would pass any inspection. The real owner would not be reporting the theft of his passport for at least thirty days, by which time it would have served its purpose. All Philip now had to do was get his brother out of the container, out of the dockyard and then out of the country. Without warning, the gravity of what he had done so far and what he now planned to do kicked in, and his hands started shaking. Why he thought he could pull this off, he'd never know; the whole idea was insane.

The vibration of Philip's mobile phone interrupted his thoughts. Pulling it from his pocket, he answered, "Philip."

"Where are you?" Andre Malherbe asked.

"On the dock, watching you unload."

"Cargo is off already," Andre replied.

"I know; I saw it. Any problems?"

"None. All good. We got lucky."

"I'd buy you a beer, but it's probably best we don't meet."

"Agreed. You can owe me one."

"Thanks, and don't forget the Bermuda account."

"*Ag, man;* forget the bloody account. As I told your brother, I'm not interested," replied Andre.

"Fair enough. It's your call; we won't touch it. Go well, nephew, and thanks again. I'll see you around."

"Stay well. I'll let my mom know we talked." There was an audible click as Andre disconnected the call.

Dropping his mobile back in his shirt pocket, Philip walked along the dock toward the stacked containers, his hands in his pockets to stop the shaking.

CHAPTER 55

Jack

A month had passed since the Mohles' disappeared, and the intensity of the RCMP investigation had yet to wane. As each new detail emerged and the formerly private life of one of Vancouver's more colourful bankers was spread over the daily newspapers, the pressure on the RCMP for answers grew. With the press on one side and the solicitor general on the other, Inspector Jack Bowie was not enjoying the attention the case was attracting. The only good news, as far as both he and the solicitor general were concerned, was that there had not been a single enquiry or suggestion of the threat on the Mohles' lives. Plenty said on what may have been the reason for their disappearance, even the suggestion of witness protection, but that was it—pure speculation that he'd been able to fob off with ease at several press briefings regarding the case. However, the sad truth was that not a single clue had developed into a significant lead.

Jack looked up from the open folder on his desk at Sergeant Kate Harrington seated on the opposite side. "Still nothing, I take it?" he said.

"Nothing substantial," she replied. "You'll see what I mean from the summary page. I'll talk you through the key investigation areas if you like. It may be quicker than getting bogged down in the details, unless there's something specific you find interesting."

"Sure. Go ahead."

"Well, first off the family: We've interviewed Vivian Mohle's sister, Lori, who lives locally. The hair salon called her after Vivian didn't turn up as scheduled. After trying unsuccessfully to contact either her sister or Neil Mohle and finding their house unlocked, empty and the hungry cat inside, she made the 911 call. She's no wiser than we are and can think of no one who would want to harm either of them. She describes them as a devoted and very sociable couple. She has confirmed with her parents in China that they too have heard nothing.

"Neil Mohle has an adult daughter from a previous marriage, and a brother, Philip Mohle, who he sees quite regularly. The brother and daughter both live in London, and we've been in telephone contact with both of them. Philip says he and Neil also have a sister, whom Neil hasn't seen in ages. Philip believes they had a falling out years ago. She lives in South Africa. The daughter, Sonja Gous, has not seen her father for almost a year, but maintains that has everything to do with distance and nothing to do with any family issues. According to her, she likes her stepmother, despite Vivian being quite a bit younger than her father. Philip was travelling when we initially tried to reach him, but returned our call on his arrival back at his London home. He had apparently seen his brother a couple of days before Neil's disappearance while he was in Vancouver on business. According to Philip, Neil visited his company's Vancouver office, looked around at the activities there and then left. This seemingly was a normal routine to try to get together however briefly when Philip had business in Canada. He is as mystified by events as we are. He said Neil seemed quite normal and cheerful that day. Both the daughter and brother have asked to be kept informed as our investigation progresses and promised to get in touch if they hear anything at all."

"That's it for immediate family?"

"That's it. Neil Mohle's parents are deceased. The ex-wife also lives in London, but she and Neil have had little contact for several years. She was unable to provide any information, except their relationship is amicable and her ex-husband dressed somewhat stylishly."

"That's the one constant in this thing," Jack said. "It keeps coming up. The staid banker with a flashy streak. I wonder if we're missing something? What else have you got?"

"Very little. He has some extended family, but they too are all in various overseas locations with no regular contact. Same thing with the wife; save for the one unmarried sister in Vancouver, the rest of her family live in mainland China. Unfortunately, as each new lead surfaces and is tracked down, it just gradually peters out."

"Anything new from the bank?"

"No. We dug deeper this time around and even reviewed Neil Mohle's internal correspondence. Nothing remotely suspicious. The closest thing we found to an unusual item was a recent enquiry he made through the bank's security group about a local company called Monger Capital. Apparently, Monger's shareholders include several holding companies whose own shareholders are unidentified. It appears Mohle wanted to confirm Monger was above board, and it all came back clean. The bank's internal security officer, who did the checking, has since left the bank for another outside position, but we got a hold of all his old correspondence and there were no red flags at all."

"Anything from your informants?" Jack asked.

"We've pressed most of the low level Chinese mob that we can, and there is nothing out there at all. If the contract originated with the Chinese, it came from the top of the local hierarchy and well under our radar. We've also heard nothing further from our internal biker source, but will keep pressing. Maintaining his cover is every bit as important to us as trying to track down this banker."

"Agreed. What about picking up the Evans twins?"

"I'd rather wait until we hear from our source. Those two are tough nuts to crack, and with nothing to go on apart from their being at the same restaurant where the Mohles had a dinner reservation; if we move too early, we'll spook them for sure and get nothing. They've used Oscar Bott as their legal counsel before, and assuming they'd use him again, we'll really get the run around for our trouble. The man is dodgy, but he certainly knows the law. I'd much rather wait before we go that route."

"Fine, let's wait. The only good news so far seems to be that what started out as a possible juicy financial story in the press has morphed into a standard missing person's case. At least all the heat we're now getting is internal. Just the occasional report on quiet news weekends in the papers. Have you talked to Jones from CSIS to see if he's heard anything?" Jack asked. "What is he doing out here anyway? Or have they still not shared that with us?"

"I've spoken to him a few times just to let him know where we are in our investigation and see if it triggered anything in his memory about their meeting with the Mohles. Nothing has worked so far. He's been tight-lipped about his own activities besides making the general comment that he sees no direct correlation between his investigation and our own. I almost believed him for a while, but he was a little too interested in what we had learned about Monger Capital from the bank for my money. To be fair, though, he seemed to lose interest pretty quickly when I said the bank report was clean. If I had to guess, I'd say he's looking into money laundering or some such thing."

"Okay, leave the report with me, and I'll go through it in detail," Jack replied. "I'm not sure what good it will do, but you never know. Tread carefully, but see if we can get a message to our undercover biker that we need the name of who in the Chinese organization ordered the hit. Without that, we're flying blind."

As Kate left the his office, Jack leaned his six-foot five-inch frame back in his chair, the report dwarfed in his large hands, and began reading. After a while, he reached out for a notepad and pen and started listing bullet points. Several hours and three cups of lousy coffee later, he surveyed his notes from the RCMP investigation into the Mohles' disappearance:

- *In the absence of any positive news, the family seem to be losing hope that the pair are still alive.*
- *The brother and daughter, who appear to have the closest relationship with the couple, say they lead low-key lives and have no known enemies.*

- *All family members agree that despite his outward appearance, Neil Mohle is very conservative and lacks the ability to stage a phony vanishing act alone.*

- *Despite Mohle's many years of service, ECB representatives refused any official comment on his disappearance. This apparent lack of concern troubles investigators although no substantive reason for the bank's apparent disinterest has been established. Belief is that this is probably a public relations issue rather than anything sinister.*

- *Unofficial comments from several of Mohle's colleagues indicate he is generally well regarded by his peers. Most common observation is his propensity for socializing with controversial types in the Vancouver financial community. Most are also ECB clients, and his colleagues assume that he is likely a useful business contact for them.*

- *While he seems to know everyone in the city's financial community, Mohle appears to have no inherent street smarts and might merely have found himself in the wrong place at the wrong time.*

- *Mohle often introduced affluent customers to new acquaintances at social functions. Suggestion made that someone may have lost money through one of these introductions and borne a grudge.*

- *Just prior to his disappearance, Mohle had been subpoenaed as a prosecution witness in the trial of one of his clients who was charged with stealing company trust funds. He is not viewed as having had any part in the crime.*

- *Despite Neil Mohle's occasionally controversial connections and behaviour, no criminal activities by the Mohles have been uncovered during the investigation.*

- *There are currently three unsubstantiated rumours circulating in the Vancouver financial community: The Mohles were placed in a witness protection program (because he knew too much, but no one knows about what); They've been killed (but no one knows why); They're alive but in hiding (but no one knows from what). The rumours are standard speculation covering every possible aspect of a disappearance.*

- *Current classification is a "suspicious missing-person" case. There is no evidence of forcible kidnapping.*

- *Mohle doesn't look like a banker. With a younger attractive wife, they could easily hide as "just another pair of snowbirds" by blending into an affluent resort community environment in the USA.*

- *Very little information has been obtained on the wife. What might we be missing? Are we barking up the wrong tree?*

Dropping his pen on the desk, Jack sighed deeply. As was often the case with these investigations, they would have to start over. Back to square one and re-examine each of the leads, see what if anything they had missed and this time also follow the wife. Perhaps it was a separate trail; perhaps it would lead somewhere.

CHAPTER 56

James et al

James Lee was content. He didn't understand why, but the Mohles' disappearance had really bothered Kitty. Now, at last, almost a month later, she was finally settling back into her pampered daily routine. Their brief but satisfying lovemaking this morning was proof of that. Work too was going well. His relationship with Damian was, if anything, better than before the arrival of the family money. Whether it was his newfound confidence the wealth provided or some change in Damian, he didn't know or, for that matter, didn't care. Life was good. Neil Mohle's replacement at the bank had assured them he had the Woodstock LNG deal in hand, and with that potential glitch out of the way, all was smooth sailing within the company.

Very occasionally, his thoughts turned to the Mohles and he wondered what might have happened to them. He'd heard the rumours, of course, but who knew what to believe these days? Satisfied that, for the moment at least, all was well in his world, he went in search of Dan Fortin. The board was scheduled to meet in several days time, and there were a few items he needed included on the agenda.

The Banker's Box

#

With James away at work, Kitty Lee was well into her daily routine. It had taken several weeks, but finally she had her anxiety under control. Her calls to her father during this time, often intercepted by Dong, had not helped. Both men had assured her they were not involved in the Mohles' disappearance, but their smooth protestations smacked of well-rehearsed excuses and she had not been convinced. Finally, she had stopped calling, and with time and the absence of any further bad news, she had convinced herself that the Mohles had indeed taken her warning seriously and intentionally disappeared. Now, in a numb, almost mindless state, she had forced herself to resume her daily routine, hoping that with time the numbness too would pass. If only she hadn't turned on that stupid bitch in the hair salon, none of this would have happened. Her father was very careful with anyone in his employ, so she had to assume John Ng was smart. How he could have married that empty-headed moron, she just didn't understand.

#

Unbeknownst to Kitty, at that precise moment, John Ng was wondering exactly that same thing as he sat seething behind his desk in the downtown offices of Monger Capital although, in his case, he knew the answer. Bobbie's sexual appetite was, in John's experience, without parallel. Unfortunately, so too was her growing drug habit, the fallout from the latter now starting to eclipse the benefits of the former. Not only was she using all the drugs he supplied, but she was supplementing his carefully controlled supply from elsewhere. The result of her recent behaviour, together with the call he had taken moments earlier, was that, unlike James Lee, nothing seemed to be going right in his world. Bobbie was almost off the rails, Dong was all over his ass about Neil Mohle and Vegas Kolnick was avoiding his calls.

It was Dong's most recent call that pushed him into deciding on the risky and unusual step of taking matters into his own hands. Dong's less than subtle reminder that this whole business had started with his wife upsetting Quon's daughter was enough of a threat for him to recognize the importance of straightening things out without delay. That reminder had also confirmed what he long suspected and which Dong had earlier denied: Kitty Lee was indeed Quon's daughter. He couldn't wait and rely on others; his head was squarely on the chopping block. He would contact the Evans twins himself. One of his people would know how to reach them; perhaps a direct threat that either they finish the job or return all the money he paid would get things moving. Screw Vegas. If he couldn't handle his crew, John would do it for him.

#

Griffin Evans was always a little less volatile than his brother, and yet as he looked up from polishing his already gleaming motorcycle at Willy Sands standing alongside, his greeting was far from friendly.

"What the fuck do you want?"

"Whoa, who bit you in the ass? Where's your brother?"

"Why?"

"I had a bit of product to spare and thought you boys might like some in return for the favour you did me the other day?"

Griffin mellowed slightly at the explanation. "Thanks. We'll take it, but it's probably not a good time to talk to Garrett right now. He's still pissed after a call we had with some Chinese mob boss. Hey, you deal with them sometimes, don't you?"

"Yeah. Don't like it much though. Supplying dope to rival gangs is not one of my favourite activities. High risk and I'm always on edge for some trouble."

"Ever deal with some guy called John Ng?"

"No, but according to his wife, he's way up the ladder from the thugs I deal with."

"You know his wife?"

"Long story. She's a heavy user. Her husband supplies her, but keeps things tight. When she wanted more, she went to the Asian street people she knew, but because of who her husband is, they wanted nothing to do with it. They finally gave her my name after she threatened them with some shit or other. I've been supplying her at premium prices for almost a year."

"You'd better come inside. Garrett will want to hear this. We need to talk."

"Why? What's happening? I didn't mean to mess with you boys."

"You're not messing with us. Maybe you can help. Come inside, and we'll fill you in."

#

Willy Sands wiped his sweaty palms on the leather steering wheel of his bright red Camaro as he drove over the Iron Worker's Memorial Bridge from the North Shore to the east side of Vancouver. Terrified of the potential fallout from the twins "request", but recognizing that he had little option but to comply, he tried to focus on the details of the plan as he drove. The odds were that somewhere in the resulting police investigation, his name would surface and he'd better be ready with his alibi. Machiavellian in its simplicity but totally disregarding any possible collateral damage, the plan was to include a single fentanyl-laced heroin pill in his next drug delivery to Bobbie Ng. By randomizing the timing of this potentially lethal overdose, they would obscure any direct connection to him, leaving her death the result of her own experimentation with this lethal substance. Any subsequent testing of his "product" would fail to reveal any traces of fentanyl in any of the other pills, removing any suspicion from him as the source—a situation where he was less worried about any police investigation than he was of retribution from Bobbie's husband or his cronies. That someone else may inadvertently take the tampered pill was discussed and quickly dismissed as not being of any concern; collateral damage was always a risk in his business. The twins needed to send a message to John Ng, and assuming all went as planned, this was the easiest method of delivery.

#

By the time Vegas Kolnick received word that John Ng had gone behind his back and contacted the twins directly, it was already too late to prevent the resultant fallout, not that he would have tried in any event. As far as Vegas was concerned, Ng's breach of criminal protocol warranted whatever crap descended on his head. He'd never even had a chance to pass on the message about the shrub and the job being half done. He'd speak to them later to find out exactly what had been said, but he wouldn't rush. He'd also need to give the club a heads up. If John Ng tried to throw his weight around, things could get ugly in a hurry.

#

Scrubber Barker was poring over the club accounts at his desk in the Outpost when he heard the front door open.

"Vegas?" he called without leaving his desk.

"No, it's Drew."

Scrubber returned the accounts in their plain white binder to his bottom right-hand drawer, locked it, then stood up and walked into the living room. "Hey, man. Good to see you back. How are your folks?"

"Pretty banged up but okay, thanks," Drew replied. "Multi-car pile-up on the 401. My mom has a broken arm, and they both still have some cuts and scrapes, but they'll be all right. I'm glad I went back, though. They were both pretty shaken up. What's new here?"

"Nothing much. Vegas has been stomping around looking ugly, but without saying anything. I'm sure we'll hear about it sooner or later."

"No doubt. Well, I need a shower. I'm going to dump my things and clean up. You want to grab a beer when I'm done?"

"Sure. Give me a shout. I'll be in the office. Maybe Vegas will be back by then as well."

#

Locking the bathroom door before turning on the shower, Drew turned on his mobile and dialled Dolly's Massage Service. Rarely were there any waiting messages, and not checking for several days was not unusual for him. The more random his schedule remained, the less likelihood anyone would suspect anything.

Moments later a disembodied voice said, "You have one new message."

Surprised, Drew punched in the requisite numbers and listened carefully to Nolan Kulla's message left several days earlier: Kate Harrington needed the name of the Chinese mob boss. Frowning, he recalled asking Vegas once before about his Chinese contact, but immediately changed the topic when Vegas became instantly alert, and the moment had passed. Bringing it up again was going to be tricky. Replacing the mobile in his jeans pocket, he hung them behind the door and stepped into the welcome warmth of the shower.

CHAPTER 57

Hayden

Hayden Jones looked over his report for the umpteenth time. He knew these investigations often dragged, and there was enough circumstantial evidence to keep this one going. Why then did he feel so guilty? There was a brief knock on his door, and Rachel walked into his office. *She's one reason*, he thought, *and Dana is the other.*

"Hi. You busy?" Rachel asked. "Donna said I should come straight in."

Hayden looked up, understanding immediately the reason for Donna's action. Rachel looked gorgeous, her clothing setting off her hair and eye colour to perfection.

"Just finishing a report, but it can wait," he replied, smiling broadly.

"What's wrong? Why are you grinning like that?"

"Smitten," he replied. "I feel like some teenager who gets to date the prom queen. You look amazing."

Rachel blushed uncomfortably, quite sure Donna could hear what Hayden was saying. "Thanks. Dana's looking for you, though. Can you come through and see her as soon as you're done? She's working on another LNG press release and wants you to look it over before it goes out."

"Okay. Be right there. Give me about fifteen minutes."

As Rachel left, Hayden looked down at his report to the director general of CSIS one last time. It was all there. All except Dana's possible knowledge of the funding source behind the Monger donation and his own intimate involvement with both Dana and Rachel. He'd probably be forgiven for the latter, but they'd likely crucify him over the former, particularly if it transpired Dana was involved in some political impropriety. He'd got himself into this one, and if his suspicions about Monger proved accurate, he'd have to find some way to get himself out without ruining his career in the process.

#

"What do you think?" Dana asked.

"Honestly?"

"Of course. That's why I wanted you to look at it."

"I think it's premature," Hayden replied. "It's good, but I'd sit on it a while longer. There have been no recent police reports. The press are getting bored, and the rumours are settling down. Any official statement from you, even remotely connected to the Mohles' disappearance, is bound to stir things up. I'd wait and keep fine-tuning the statement as and if anything develops. If we get lucky, there may be no need for a statement at all."

"What do you mean 'if we get lucky'?"

"Well, maybe they'll turn up, or maybe the police will discover the reason for their disappearance and it will have nothing at all to do with the LNG project."

"All of that's true, but you must admit that the threat on their lives is bound to be front and centre in any explanation for their disappearance or their death, for that matter. I can't afford to have my constituents think we were aware of the threat and did nothing to keep the Mohles safe."

"But won't commenting on their disappearance in an LNG press release, even if it's only as Woodstock's banker for the LNG project, imply there might be some connection between the two?" Hayden asked.

"Maybe, but why should that be of any concern to us? The only connection we know of is that Neil Mohle was the group's banker. That shouldn't worry anyone. I'm more interested in burying a statement about our concern for the Mohles in a bunch of other information to try to diffuse the heat, while simultaneously getting ahead of the press if the threat on their lives ever gets out. Even a hint that the police are doing everything in their power to find them will be better than having made no comment at all if they turn up dead somewhere."

Hayden looked at the press release again. Not a single mention of Monger Capital's interest in the LNG transaction. As much as he'd like to direct some attention their way and see what the press might dig up about them, mentioning it might also uncover their political contribution and focus unwanted attention on what Dana might know about it—a problem for which he still had no solution.

"What does Hugh Ruff think?"

"Why would I ask Hugh?"

Immediately recognizing his error in introducing the party's chief strategist into the conversation, Hayden tried to cover his tracks. "Sorry, wrong guy. I meant your press secretary?"

"He drafted this . . . are you paying attention? Or is your mind elsewhere?" Dana looked out of her office to where Rachel was sitting as she spoke.

"Right. Of course. Stupid mistake. Why don't you expand it further then," Hayden said bristling at the implication and irritated at his own stupidity in allowing his personal life to interfere with his investigation.

"What do you mean?"

"Well maybe include some reference to the new investor into the project. That might give the press something fresh to focus their attention on. It's probably better to have them speculating on Monger Capital rather than the Mohles."

"Actually that's not such a bad idea. I'll talk to Hugh. We'd better be sure they're squeaky clean before we offer the press a new source of speculation. Thanks Jones. How's your own investigation going by the way? We seem to have you well and truly embroiled in our business."

"It's okay, but slow I'm afraid. Still just gathering information. You may have me around for a while longer if you can bear it."

"That's fine with me. I don't know what you're up to, and despite my curiosity, it's probably better that I don't know although perhaps you wouldn't tell me anyway."

Dana stopped speaking and looked pensively out of her office door at Rachel before continuing. "Don't ever tell Rachel about us, Jones. No matter what you think. I know you're smart, but when it comes to women, you're about as intuitive as a brick. Trust me on this one; she'll never forgive you. Not because you had an affair, but simply because it's me." Before Hayden could offer any response, Dana picked up her telephone and spoke. "Rachel, get me Hugh Ruff, will you... I'll stay on the line."

#

Heading back to his office after his somewhat abrupt dismissal, Hayden had to agree with Dana's assessment. He really didn't understand women. Not that he wasn't attracted to them, or them to him, for that matter. He just didn't seem to know what made them tick. Relationships had always seemed to take so much effort until Rachel. Somehow things with her were different. Not effortless, but uncomplicated, a kind of comfortable familiarity. Assuming Dana was right, he'd better be careful about any reference to their brief affair.

CHAPTER 58

Neil

Neil Mohle saw his sister standing in the corner of the arrivals area long before she picked him out from the people exiting Cape Town International Airport. Angling his way across the crowd, he continued walking until he had almost passed her, then spoke.

"Hi, Connie."

Connie Malherbe looked momentarily taken aback by the greeting and then shrieked, "Neil! I almost didn't recognize you." Throwing her arms around him, she hugged him tightly. "No moustache and that ginger crew cut. You look different, and you're so thin."

"Not eating too well," Neil replied. "It's been a long trip."

"Ja, I'm sure. Let's get out of here. You must be sick of the crowds. How was the flight? Did you have any problems clearing customs in Johannesburg? Come, my car's not too far, and we can chat while we drive. If we hurry, we can miss most of the afternoon traffic. It gets crazy later on, and the taxi's drive like lunatics." Continuing to ask questions without waiting for any replies, Connie grabbed Neil's arm and steered him through the flow of people towards the airport parking.

Neil smiled; despite the years that had passed, his sister hadn't changed. Thin as a rake and several inches taller than him, she still exuded the same nervous energy he recalled so well. "Jo'burg was fine," he said. "I still don't how you organized it, and I've got a million questions, but I cleared customs as Mark van Aswegan without a problem, and the torn remnants of his passport are scattered in various garbage cans between the international and domestic terminals. No one could put that thing together ever again. I used my own renewed South African passport that you sent when I checked in for the domestic flight from Johannesburg to Cape Town. Without any arrival or departure stamps, as far as any cursory check is concerned, I've never left the country. Also, if anyone is checking from offshore, there's no record of my departure from Canada or my arrival anywhere else."

"Good. All went as planned then."

"It did, and I owe you. Have you heard any news of Vivian?"

"No, sorry, Neil. Nothing. Here's my car." Connie opened the hatch on the large white SUV and continued speaking. "Just put your stuff in the back. It'll take us about an hour to get to the house in Newlands. Jannie will meet us there, and we'll all head out to the farm tomorrow. After that there's no rush, and we can discuss what you want to do now that you are here and safe."

"Thanks. How is he taking all this? After all, he was a senior member of the SA police service before the government changed. He can't be very happy about you arranging a false passport for his brother-in law?"

"He's fine. How did you think I got the passports anyway? It's not something I could have done on my own. Actually, I didn't even know where to start. He did the whole thing himself."

"Really? I would never have believed that if I hadn't heard it from you. He must have changed since I last saw him?"

"Lots of things have changed since you were here, and there's still a lot of resentment on both sides. People like Jannie, who were suddenly cast aside, continue to find it hard to adjust. I think he quite enjoyed the exercise of seeing whose arm he could twist to get help with the passports and thumb his nose at the existing hierarchy at the same time. You can thank him yourself. He'll probably be quite happy to get into all the details with you. He's quite proud of himself; seemed to have more fun being a crook than a cop."

As the SUV sped toward the city, Neil looked out of the passenger window at the seemingly endless squatter camps lining the highway, a constant reminder to anyone arriving in the city of the enormous challenges facing the country's government. "Is there any solution to all this," Neil asked, pointing to the shacks.

"Probably not," Connie replied. "The poverty feeds the crime. The criminals constantly destroy what little infrastructure exists, and the absence of infrastructure worsens the plight of those already in dire circumstances. The problem just keeps growing while slowly destroying everything in its path."

"Why doesn't the government do something?"

"It tries, but between the inability to satisfy so many people quickly enough and the corruption within their own ranks, it's a losing battle I'm afraid."

"So what do people like you and Jannie do besides for possibly leaving the country?"

"Enjoy it while we can. Sad but true. Anyway, it's a conversation that we are sure to have many times over now that you are here, so let's talk about something else. Like how did you get into this mess? And what's it all about?"

#

Jan and Connie Malherbe's house, in the upscale and leafy suburb of Newlands, had been in the Mohle family for some time. Originally owned by Neil and Connie's parents, it was located a short walk from the Forester's Arms, a well-known and ever-popular university student watering hole. Surrounded by an eight-foot wall, which, although lower at the time, had formerly served to stop the odd inebriated student from falling into the beautifully manicured garden, it was now also topped with rolled razor wire, along with several feet of electric fencing— enough of a deterrent to discourage even the most ardent of the ever-present criminal element. Not that the house's perimeter security was unique. As Connie pulled into the drive, Neil noticed that almost every house in the neighbourhood had similar security provisions, presumably supported by the usual slew of electronic surveillance cameras and sensors in the interior.

Welcome to Africa, he thought.

\#

Several hours and a very good bottle of wine later, Neil leaned back in his chair while holding his wine glass by the stem as he rested it lightly on his knee. "Well, that's about all I know," he said. "The next piece was when Connie picked me up at the airport, and we came straight here."

"Man, I still don't understand why you didn't just take the police offer of protection," Jannie said. "Not that we mind helping. Hell, I even enjoyed sticking it to the government after what they did to me, the bastards." He smiled. "And it will be fun having you at the farm to help with all the work we've got going there. But, this thing with Vivian going missing worries me, man. As a former cop, I have to tell you, the way she suddenly disappeared doesn't sound good."

"I know," Neil replied. "Hopefully, Philip will have some news when he calls. In hindsight, I agree with you about taking the witness protection offer. It's just that it all happened so fast, and we got spooked and ran. We knew if we could get here without using our passports, no one would ever find us. Philip planned to tell the police, or anyone else who asked, that Connie and I were estranged and hadn't been in contact for years. Hell, even if they considered South Africa, they'd never find us, except through you. How else would they know where to look? It's a big country with over fifty-five million people. As a last defense, I was confident that if you were ever questioned, you wouldn't say anything about our whereabouts until you knew what was going on. As things now stand, thanks to you both and Mark van Aswegan's passport, there's no record of me arriving here at all."

"Okay, you two," Connie interjected, "it's time for bed. Let's drink a toast to Vivian's safe return and the beginning of Neil's new life. Early tomorrow, we'll head out to Stellenbosch and the farm and get Neil settled in. You boys can make whatever plans you want after that and when we know both he and Vivian are safe."

CHAPTER 59

Quon

Quon Jin Hu hated loose ends, and Neil Mohle was certainly a loose end. Although, that said, with the woman gone, Quon was reasonably content. The Canadian press seemed to be getting tired of a missing person story with no ending, and the direct link to Kitty had been eliminated. If Jun Ng now delivered as he promised, any possible risk from the banker would soon be over. Quon knew that using outside contractors to take care of the problem had been a mistake, but excluding that decision, he trusted Ng's judgement. Jun was effective in his double role, and Monger Capital had served them well as a legitimate business front. What's more, thanks to some creative accounting practices, it was also a very effective money laundering operation. Any news tying Jun Ng or Monger Capital to the disappearance of the Mohles could bring unwelcome attention and ruin a business model that had taken years to establish. When all this was over, he would talk to Jun about his wife. Her behaviour was the cause of this problem, and she was a risk they could ill afford.

CHAPTER 60

Bobbie

Bobbie Ng shook out the remaining pills in the light yellow container. Only seven of Willy's original twenty-four remained. She knew she had dropped one down the side of the seat in her car, but she couldn't believe she had gone through all the others already. It was time for her to get some more; she couldn't afford to run out. Deciding to wait before taking another, she placed the container in her handbag and headed to the garage. It was almost noon and time for her meeting with John and their architect to go over the new house plans. She knew she had better be on her best behaviour; John wouldn't forgive her if she embarrassed him in his own downtown office.

Thirty-five minutes later, Bobbie, her short skirt riding up her thighs, climbed inelegantly from her low-slung BMW sports car in the below-ground parking garage of John's office tower, bumping her head on the door frame as she stood. Irritated, she glared at the car as if it was at fault before noticing a single small pill lying on the floor mat, just below the brake pedal. Her need for another fix over-riding her earlier resolve, she picked it up, quickly popped it into her mouth and reached between the seats for her ever-present water bottle. After a few swallows, she replaced the bottle and, smiling for the first time that morning, closed and locked the car before walking to the parking garage elevator.

In the time it took the elevator to reach the office tower lobby, Willy's fentanyl-laced pill, mixed with Bobbie's usual dose of heroin, had amplified the potency of both drugs and Bobbie was already experiencing the early effects of an oncoming and extremely powerful high. Changing elevators in the lobby, Bobbie joined the coffee-carrying crowd in its packed interior before finally exiting on the floor that Monger Capital shared with several other corporate tenants. By then, thanks to the elevator having stopped on several floors to disgorge passengers, the depressant effects of both drugs were taking hold, and Bobbie was barely able to stay awake. Walking unsteadily to Monger's reception, she asked for directions to the nearest washroom where she locked herself in the vacant corner stall. Slumping down onto the already open toilet seat, she sat unmoving, her head hanging between her knees, the contents of her handbag slowly spilling to the floor as her fingers gradually lost their ability to maintain their grasp.

It was almost an hour later when Bobbie's lifeless body was discovered by one of the building cleaners as she mopped her way around the washroom, her curiosity aroused by the items scattered on the floor of the locked stall and the continued silence of the occupant.

Emergency paramedics called to the building to attend the unidentified and unresponsive female, checked Bobbie's handbag for any medications and established her identity during their initial examination. The pale-yellow container with seven as yet unidentified tablets found during the same search was subsequently delivered by the Vancouver municipal police to the Canadian government's Drug Analysis Service. Upon identification of the tablets as heroin, Bobbie's death was immediately referred to the Vancouver Police Department's Drug Unit for further investigation.

CHAPTER 61

John

John Ng was still seething over his wife missing the meeting with their architect when the first in a series of Vancouver police constables arrived at his office door. His shock on receiving the news of Bobbie's death was, as later noted by the attending constable, as genuine a reaction as he'd ever seen. While John had long since accepted Bobbie's recreational drug use, he genuinely believed she had it under reasonable control. That his own action, in periodically cutting off her supply in an attempt to maintain control over her occasionally erratic behaviour, would push her into finding alternative sources of potentially more dangerous drugs had never crossed his mind.

John's shock at Bobbie's death was followed shortly by the unpleasant realization that it would soon be front-page news. Quon Jin Hu did not tolerate unwanted attention around any of his businesses, and the drug overdose death of the wife of one of his top corporate lieutenants in the company's washroom would not be well received. His earlier shock now replaced with fear for his own position, John feigned feeling ill, and after assuring the police of his complete cooperation during their investigation and a brief comment to his assistant that he would be at home if needed, he left the office for the remainder of the day.

#

In the days that followed, the mandatory autopsy carried out on Bobbie's body identified the presence of both heroin and fentanyl in her system. This finding resulted in a re-examination of the contents of the pale-yellow container, which confirmed nothing was missed in the initial examination and there was no fentanyl in any of the remaining tablets.

The continued frequency of fentanyl-induced deaths in Vancouver and the obvious affluence of the drug's most recent victim resulted in the Vancouver Police Drug Unit obtaining a search warrant for the Ng home. The warrant's objective was to locate any further fentanyl and, if found, to try to identify its source.

Arriving unannounced at the Ng home, the police found it locked and unoccupied. Given John Ng's offered cooperation in their investigation and prior to entering, the police officer in charge called John's mobile number, which immediately defaulted to his voicemail. The disembodied voice requested that either a message be left or that John be contacted at his office at the telephone number that followed. On calling Monger Capital, the police were advised that John was travelling, having left Canada the day following his wife's death to attend an urgent meeting in China. On questioning his assistant, she said that she had no other details as she had received merely a brief voicemail telling her of his planned departure and her only contact number at this time was his mobile. Like the police, she too was surprised at the suddenness of the trip, particularly as there had been no further contact from John.

#

While the police were speaking to John Ng's assistant at Monger Capital, he was already sitting in Quon's opulent Shanghai offices, carefully drafting a proposed press release to be issued by Monger that same morning. In it, Monger announced the embezzlement of certain sums of money by one of its senior employees, as well as various agreements illegally entered into on behalf of the company by that same employee. Although the staff member in question was not identified, they did go on to say that at an emergency meeting of the Monger Capital Board of Directors in Vancouver, Mr. P.K. Chin had been appointed as interim president and CEO and would take up his position with immediate effect. All parties impacted by the employee's actions would be contacted without delay, and the company's board of directors pledged that it would use its best efforts to find an acceptable resolution for all those affected. The press release concluded with the statement that no client of Monger Capital was expected to lose any money resulting from the illegal actions of the said employee.

John read the statement over again and decided that he was finally satisfied with the result. His carefully established legitimate career was over, but he thought, smiling ruefully, as was often said in circumstances such as these, *at least I've got my health*. He looked over at Dong working quietly at an adjoining desk. "It's done," he said. "Do you want to take a look?"

"Let us take it to Komodo," Dong replied. "He will decide." He stood and, taking the offered press release from John, walked directly to Quon's closed office door and knocked.

#

John had called Dong Lai immediately after learning of Bobbie's death. Listening without interruption, Dong had waited until John finished speaking before asking several questions and then providing a series of instructions. Shortly after the call, John returned home where he removed any unmarked containers from Bobbie's bathroom cabinets and flushed their contents down the toilet before briefly leaving the house to dispose of the containers, along with a small bag of household garbage, in a commercial dumpster at a nearby shopping mall. Returning to the house and without stopping to rest or sleep, he had then carefully examined every conceivable hiding place for Bobbie's drug supplies. Not that he really needed to conduct a search, as he later reported, they both knew she took drugs, so there was really no need to hide anything. Still, he had done as asked, and after a thorough search, he was confident there was nothing else to find.

John's second call to Dong went directly to the speakerphone on Quon Jin Hu's office desk. Despite periodic heated interjections by Quon, John finally managed to report that having completed all of Dong's earlier instructions, he would depart for China the next day once he had cleaned and tidied his entire house.

Leaving at midday the following day, John looked back at the house as the limousine pulled out of the drive. Picture perfect, the inside was spotless, the outside too. Not a blade of grass out of place. Even the new evergreen shrub alongside the front path was flowering. He wondered why he hadn't noticed it before? Maybe Bobbie had someone plant it although that would have been very unusual; gardening was definitely not her thing. It looked unbalanced; maybe he should get a matching shrub for the other side. Suddenly realizing the futility of his thoughts, he flopped back in his seat where he remained motionless for the remainder of the ride to Vancouver International Airport.

A little before three that afternoon, John boarded a Korean Air flight to South Korea. After an eleven-hour journey in a comfortable fully reclining first-class seat, he landed at Incheon International Airport where he switched to Asiana Airlines for a relatively short two-hour flight to Shanghai, China.

Landing at Pudong International Airport at 8:55 p.m. local time, John cleared customs without incident before taking a local bus to downtown Shanghai, where he entered the building housing the offices of Quon Jin Hu and, for all intents and purposes, simply disappeared off the face of the earth.

#

Failing to establish contact with John Ng and disturbed by his absence from the country, the Vancouver Police Drug Unit wasted no further time in executing their search warrant at the Ng house. When a thorough search of the premises revealed no evidence of drugs or drug paraphernalia, the team called for help from their Canine Unit.

The oldest municipal police dog unit in Canada, the Vancouver Police Canine Unit's fifteen dog teams, work twenty-four hours a day, seven days a week. Highly mobile and trained in a variety of disciplines, their primary purpose is to attend the scene of a crime that is in progress or that has just occurred. On this occasion, the call was answered by *Snoop,* the unit's beagle narcotics dog, and his handler who arrived in their specifically designed SUV, fitted with an air-conditioned kennel and heat alarm. Despite Snoop's enthusiastic efforts and occasional frenzied sniffing, no evidence of any drugs was discovered; the house was clean.

CHAPTER 62

Quon

Quon looked up from his desk as Dong Lai and Jun Ng entered. His anger had long since subsided. Ng had fulfilled an important role for many years and, outside of the current problem caused by his wife's death, was still useful to the organization. What was more, it was he who had subsequently suggested how this whole matter might be manipulated to Quon's advantage. He had to give the man full marks for thinking on his feet. After hours of further discussion, the plan, with several enhancements made to satisfy Quon's long-term goals, was about to be implemented. Ng would never be able to return to Canada, but he could easily "disappear" within Quon's business interests in China where his financial talents could continue to be put to good use. The Canadian authorities were unlikely to waste much time looking for him in connection with an accidental drug overdose by his wife, and if Monger Capital did not press charges for the "corporate embezzlement" about to be announced, there would be no police investigation into that matter either.

"Sit," Quon said. "Let me see what you have written."

CHAPTER 63

John et al

Monger Capital issued their press release at 6 a.m., Pacific Standard Time, the morning after the search of the Ng home, and its impact was immediate. The company's office was inundated with calls, all of which were diverted to a predetermined voicemail, which repeated the contents of the press release and advised any who wished for further detail to contact Mr. P.K. Chin through his e-mail at the address which was then provided. Callers were assured that their e-mail would be directed to the appropriate person within the organization to deal with their specific enquiry within twenty-four hours. Although they too were unaware that there had been no actual embezzlement of funds or illegal contracts made, in the absence of any serious complaints, the Monger staff quickly handled the enquiries and normal business was restored before the markets closed that same day.

#

Damian Slater, up early as usual, was one of the first to read the news. "Fuck," he said, flinging the TV remote across the room. He stepped carefully over the broken plastic on his way to the bathroom for his morning shower. They'd need an emergency board meeting to put some form of damage control in place. Picking up his mobile as he walked, he scanned through his contacts until he found the number he wanted and pressed "Call".

\#

Dan Fortin looked at the display on his mobile: *what in hell's name could Damian want at this time of the morning?* Answering, he listened without interruption, then, smiling broadly at Damian's obvious discomfort, he disconnected the call and went in search of his laptop to send out the Woodstock Marine meeting request.

\#

Copied on Dan Fortin's e-mail, James Lee was still reading about the requirement for an urgent board meeting when his home telephone rang. Answering with his usual, "James Lee," he heard Quon Jin Hu's voice.

"How are you, my boy?" Quon asked.

"Fine, thank you," replied James cautiously. "Did you wish to speak to Kitty?"

"No. I'm not sure if you've heard the news, but I wanted to speak to you about the unfortunate events at Monger Capital concerning its president, Jun Ng."

"I'm reading it now," James replied. "Mr. Ng is on the board of Woodstock Marine as well. It is very unfortunate."

"Well, maybe not so unfortunate. Perhaps there is an opportunity for you in all of this. Mr. P.K. Chin has been appointed to take over from Jun Ng and will shortly be making certain proposals, including one to your company. I would like you to ingratiate yourself with Mr. Chin at the earliest opportunity, but otherwise do nothing."

"Do nothing? What do you mean?"

"Whatever is proposed by Mr. Chin, have no strong opinion, neither for nor against. Just go along with whatever your company decides. That shouldn't be too hard, and that way you will be insulated, whatever the outcome."

"That's it? How do you know this anyway?"

Quon laughed, making an ugly gating sound, before replying. "Not to worry. I have fingers in many pies. Just do as I ask and trust it will be for your benefit."

Before James could say anything further, Quon disconnected the call. Perplexed, James looked down at his computer and read Dan's e-mail again.

#

Hugh Ruff's mind was racing as he scanned the financial headlines. So much for a quiet morning. Preoccupied, he sipped on his hot, freshly-poured, morning coffee, burning his tongue in the process. He had to find out more about this business with Monger Capital and John Ng. Monger was the source of the large party donation, which had influenced his subsequent manoeuvring to get them a slice of the lucrative LNG pie. The press would be all over this Ng business and any sign of unusual patronage was going to need careful handling. He didn't relish the thought of telling Dana, but knew he'd better do so before she read the news herself. What was more, he'd better have some form of solution. One thing was for sure, Dana was going to be furious.

#

Oblivious to the impending storm, Dana twisted and turned as she stood in the bathroom and examined her naked body. She looked good, and while she missed the attention provided by her affair with Hayden Jones, she was once again free to focus on her role as premier without personal distractions. Things were going well, and at moments like this, she really enjoyed the freedom and control of being single. She pressed her palms against her sides and ran her hands over her hips. *Too bad, Jones,* she thought. *Look what you're missing.* Smiling to herself, Dana walked over to her bedroom closet and started dressing. There was a lot to do today.

#

Hayden was still languishing in bed watching Rachel as she dressed hurriedly. "What's the rush?" he asked.

Rachel fidgeted uncomfortably. "I can't really talk about it. Hugh Ruff wants to meet with Dana first thing this morning, and I need to print out some material he's sent over before that meeting."

"Okay, lunch today?" Hayden asked.

"Should be alright. Not counting this unexpected meeting, I don't think the day's too busy. Got to go. Love you."

As Rachel hurried out of Hayden's apartment, she wondered if he noticed her instinctive endearment. It was the first time either of them had said such a thing. Well, she didn't have time to stop and see how he reacted, but she imagined there'd probably be a need to bring it up later. Right now, she had to print out all the information Dana needed for her meeting about Monger Capital and John Ng.

#

Finally dragging himself from the bed, Hayden walked over to the window and looked down at Victoria Harbour below. Things with Rachel were getting serious, and he had several decisions to make, including whether or not to reveal his true occupation. His investigation was dragging again, and either something needed to break or he was going to have to start beating the bushes to see if he could flush anything out. Absent that, he might as well pack up and go home. Rachel's mention of Hugh Ruff reminded him that he should check his e-mail to see if anyone at CSIS headquarters had discovered any more about Monger Capital's shareholders. Turning on his computer, he wandered away to brush his teeth while it started up. Returning minutes later, the CBC morning news page had loaded and with it a report on Monger Capital and John Ng.

CHAPTER 64

Dana et al

The finger pointing went on for several days after the Monger Capital press release before things finally settled down.

First out of the blocks, in an attempt to get ahead of any negative political press, was an announcement from the Office of the Premier of B.C. Short on details and less than entirely accurate, it outlined the government's shock at discovering that Monger Capital was the same company introduced to them by Woodstock LNG as a future minority partner in their Kitimat gas deal. What the announcement failed to say was that Dana and Hugh had agreed between themselves that Monger's donation would be "discovered" long after the initial press interest had died down and then quietly dealt with in whatever manner was most appropriate at the time.

Second to speak out and, in the light of the government announcement, entirely too little, too late was an interview given by Damian Slater. Hampered by the government's blatant misstatement that he had introduced Monger to them and trapped by having purposely elevated his own role in developing the Monger relationship to his own board, he was, without ruining his own credibility, unable to deny the government's version of the facts. Not at his best when ambushed outside his office by the press, he lashed out at them, insisting there was nothing to suggest Monger Capital had done anything wrong despite whatever inference they may have drawn from the earlier announcement by "that bloody woman". Feigning not to remember how his relationship with Monger or John Ng had developed, he stopped talking and merely walked away when asked how he planned to deal with John Ng's role on the Woodstock Marine Board of Directors.

The third and last statement on the matter, which was later viewed as the epitome of fine corporate behaviour, was that made by Mr. P.K. Chin on taking up his new position. In his initial interview with a Vancouver daily newspaper, he confirmed that any of Monger Capital's investors affected by John Ng's actions had already been contacted and any account irregularities rectified from the company's own funds. In addition, he was able to confirm that all contracts entered into by Mr. Ng on behalf of Monger Capital would be honoured with only one exception that still had to be resolved. Mr. Ng had been terminated *in absentia*, and the company would not be pursuing any legal action against him, preferring to put the matter behind them and move on with the business of managing their clients' funds without the distraction of criminal proceedings. That there were, in reality, no affected investors and that some creative accounting would need to take place to maintain the illusion and satisfy the company's external auditors would never be known. Manipulating financial records was considered nothing but a minor inconvenience when cleaning matters up to Quon Jin Hu's satisfaction.

#

Hugh Ruff breathed a sigh of relief on reading P.K. Chin's interview in the morning paper. In the absence of any contact from Monger about their donation, he presumed it was above board and not part of John Ng's reported illegal dealings. With a bit of luck and no further public attention, he should be able to quietly deal with its ultimate exposure in whatever way was necessary to keep Dana happy and out of political trouble.

#

Damian Slater was every bit as relieved as Hugh Ruff. Without any recent contact from Monger, he assumed that Woodstock's deal with the company remained intact; God knows, they needed the funds. While Damian hadn't bothered to inform the press, the Woodstock Marine board had quietly suspended John Ng pending resolution of the charges levelled against him. Although, for reasons he seemed unable to clearly articulate, Damian had abstained from voting on the resolution; if the truth were told, he was happy with the decision. It was easier to run things without any interference from Monger. He knew at some point he'd have to meet with this Chin person about Monger's representation on the board, but until then, it was business as usual, as far as he was concerned.

Damian also made several attempts to reach Hugh Ruff regarding the government announcement, all without success, and his increasingly irate voicemail messages on Hugh's telephone remained unanswered. Finally recognizing the futility of pursuing this avenue of attack, he had decided to bide his time and seek retribution later, and when it was least expected.

As a result, he was almost in a good mood when he received P.K. Chin's request for a meeting to discuss Monger Capital's continued representation on the Woodstock Marine board and the ship purchase agreement executed by John Ng on behalf of the company.

#

With John Ng's disappearance from Canada and the statements by the government, Damian Slater and P.K. Chin—none of whom had any desire to extend the life of the story—Monger Capital and any association the company may have had with Bobbie Ng's death soon ceased being front-page news.

The Vancouver Police Department search of John Ng's home yielded no further clues as to the source of Bobbie's drug supply and his whereabouts. Following the use of his passport, his movements after leaving

Vancouver were traced to Pudong International Airport, in Shanghai, where Chinese authorities confirmed his arrival by aircraft, but had no record of his location thereafter. He had passed through customs and then simply vanished among the country's other one and a half billion inhabitants. According to the local police liaison, unless John Ng wanted to be found, the trail would likely end right there.

At the offices of Monger Capital, a flurry of carefully crafted board resolutions quickly allowed the company to resume normal operations under the steady hand of the new president and CEO, local Vancouver resident, Mr. P.K. Chin. Moreover, with yet another trusted employee in place at Monger Capital, Quon Jin Hu's orchestration of the plan, so carefully conjured up by Dong Lai and John Ng, entered its final phase.

#

Like Bobbie Ng's death, the disappearance of Neil and Vivian Mohle had also moved well into the inside pages of the local Vancouver newspapers. In the absence of any further information from Drew Jamieson on the identity of the Chinese mob boss responsible for the contract on the lives of the Mohles, the RCMP investigation had slowed considerably and received little public attention; the latter point, if Inspector Jack Bowie were to be asked, suited him just fine. Retracing their steps, investigators remained convinced that the Evans twins were involved due to their apparently coincidental restaurant timing, but had no actionable evidence. Questioning of several low-ranking Chinese gang informants yielded nothing, confirming that the order had come from high-up the gang's criminal hierarchy. Review of Neil Mohle's bank correspondence and e-mails showed little of interest other than his recent correspondence with the bank's security group regarding an LNG deal. Christopher Broughton, the security officer concerned, had since left the bank and had not been questioned; however, a review of his internal ECB e-mail records indicated nothing untoward. The Mohle family were unable to provide anything further of value but remained concerned, regularly contacting the RCMP for updates on their investigation.

Only peripherally involved in the Mohle investigation, Hayden Jones was happy to stay off the RCMP radar. Although intrigued by the circumstances surrounding the Mohles' disappearance, his real interest lay with the Vancouver police investigation into the death of the wife of the president of Monger Capital. Monger was on Dana's special donors list and, as he had learned, had not yet been vetted by Hugh Ruff. What he'd really like to know was who was behind them and what other names were on that list.

CHAPTER 65

Damian

If P.K. Chin had been a duck, not one of his feathers would have been ruffled. Impeccably groomed, the slight bespectacled person standing in the Woodstock Marine reception was not what Damian had expected.

"Mr. Chin?" Damian held out his hand in greeting as he spoke.

"Mr. Slater."

P.K. Chin's hand feels as soft as any woman's, Damian thought shaking the offered hand.

"I suggest we meet in the main boardroom," Damian said, pointing as he spoke. "It's through the door to your left."

Neither man said anything as they settled themselves at one end of the long pale wood table surrounded by high-backed black leather chairs. Then, after a momentary silence, Damian spoke again. "Well, how can I help? I assume from your message you'd like to discuss taking John Ng's place on the Woodstock Marine board. I'm afraid that might not be quite that easy," he added, with a smug half smile. "The board would want to know a lot more about you before they made that decision."

"But didn't you appoint John Ng because of the ship purchase deal?" P.K. Chin asked.

"Yes, but that was different," Damian replied, assuming he knew where Chin was going with his question.

"Different how?"

"Well . . . we had an understanding," Damian said.

"Quite," Chin agreed. "And that's what I'd like to discuss. I assume that you came to this arrangement with Mr. Ng for your own, or his, purposes."

"What are you implying?" Damian snarled, completely taken aback by the abrupt change in direction of the conversation.

"Nothing," Chin replied. "Just that we at Monger cannot understand the reason for the necessity of the board seat and would prefer if you immediately terminated Mr. Ng's position."

"What reason could we possibly give for doing that?" Damian asked, confused by both the tone and focus the conversation was now taking. "It's not yet been proven that he's done anything wrong, and he's still missing. He'd sue the pants off us for wrongful termination if he suddenly reappears and establishes that he's not been involved in any wrongdoing."

"Ah, but he has," Chin replied. "The contract which he signed for the purchase of the ships was done without proper company authorization. Unless you agree to cancel it, we shall be testing its validity in court."

"You can't do that," Damian's voice rose. "We've already structured our LNG bid based on the fixed ship prices. We'd lose a fortune if our consortium doesn't get the LNG contract and you don't purchase the ships as we agreed."

"As you agreed with John Ng," Chin corrected.

"Alright then," Damian snapped. "As I agreed with John Ng."

"So," P.K. Chin continued, still unruffled, "let me offer a possible solution."

Damian listened impatiently for several minutes to Chin's protracted delivery before replying. "I can't see that working," he said. "As I mentioned before, unwinding the ship purchase arrangement could result in a significant loss for us if the LNG deal doesn't go ahead. We'd end up with spot market ships that we might not be able to contract out. Right now, you people, Monger Capital that is, have agreed to assume that risk in return for a discounted purchase price while we lock in our own downside risk. I assume you did this because you believe you can package them in some form of company structure and then get rid of both the ships and the associated risk through an IPO while simultaneously making a substantial profit."

"You mean John Ng agreed," Chin once again corrected.

"Right, right," Damian muttered. "John Ng has agreed."

"Perhaps then we could try and work together," Chin suggested. "Maybe you could find a way to have me serve on your board as a replacement for Mr. Ng, and in return Monger Capital would ratify the existing agreement that you have made with him. That way we would have insight into the progress of the LNG deal, and you would avoid a lengthy legal battle. A reasonably elegant solution, I believe."

Damian nodded. There was nothing else he could think of, but to agree. His side deal with John Ng had not been mentioned, perhaps Chin was unaware of it. Time would tell, but for now, he had nothing to lose.

#

While it was not the easiest meeting Damian had ever attended, P.K. Chin's confidence in his ability to convince the Woodstock Marine board of the wisdom of accepting the negotiated arrangement was not misplaced. Aided by an impeccable and entirely legitimate résumé provided by Chin, which included post-graduate degrees in engineering and mathematics, the offered solution was ultimately accepted. Following an accelerated and successful vetting process, Chin was welcomed onto the Woodstock Marine Board of Directors less than a week after his first meeting with Damian. Unfortunately for Damian, it was also readily apparent that his own standing with the board was simultaneously diminished both by Ng's disappearance after his wife's overdose induced death and the bullying attitude he had adopted in his earlier efforts to get Ng appointed. The announcement by the B.C. government suggesting that Woodstock had been responsible for introducing Monger Capital to them as a partner in the Kitimat

LNG deal served only to exacerbate the growing tension. Unable to defend himself without revealing Hugh Ruff as his original source and directly contradicting the premier's statement, Damian resorted to a more personal attack indicating he "didn't plan to be pushed around by that bloody incompetent woman", a sentiment which did little to endear him to the two existing, and exceptionally competent, women on Woodstock Marine's own board.

CHAPTER 66

Quon

After reading P.K. Chin's report of his meeting with Damian Slater, Quon Jin Hu was content. With the proposed new arrangement between Slater and Chin, Quon's left hand recaptured what his right hand had given up.

It would have been easy enough to suggest that Chin merely replace John Ng on the Woodstock Marine board and admit that there was nothing wrong with the original ship purchase contract, but that way nothing was gained. Chin's "negotiation" allowed Monger to further distance itself from John Ng and potentially gain some goodwill from the board by ratifying Ng's "illegal" agreement.

Furthermore, Chin was so confident that Slater would be successful in making the necessary arrangements he hadn't even felt it necessary to play their trump card. Whatever the outcome of the ship purchase deal, Quon was satisfied. Any agreement that facilitated the laundering of the proceeds from his illegal operations was welcome, and if he could make a legal profit in the process, so much the better.

CHAPTER 67

John

With the various related but uncoordinated investigations all at a relative standstill, there was little in the news to upset the routine activities at Woodstock Marine and Monger Capital, a state which continued uninterrupted for several months.

Meanwhile, at the Office of the Premier of B.C. and in the absence of any negative press, Hugh Ruff's advice to Premier Dana Holmes regarding Monger's political donation continued to be: "Say nothing and let's see what unfolds. Unless they're part of the successful bid on the LNG project tender, the issue may well be moot."

It was against this peaceful backdrop that the next development at the home of John and Bobbie Ng exploded onto the daily news.

#

RCMP Corporal Josh Small and his dog *Nyx* looked at the cars lining the edge of the baseball diamond. The recreational ball game had ended, and he and two uniformed Vancouver police officers had just reached their waiting patrol car late on the Saturday afternoon.

"Thanks for the offer of a ride, guys," Josh said. "It was either leave early with the RCMP group who got called out or hitch a ride home. Not everyone wants a dog in their car, no matter how well behaved."

The Banker's Box

"No problem, given some of the characters who usually end up in the back of our squad car. And, we like your dog."

All three men laughed, and Nyx, seemingly sensing the playful mood, gave a few cursory wags of his tail.

"We've one quick stop to make, though. It's on the way and won't take more than ten or fifteen minutes. We're required to make a periodic check on a house that's part of an old drug overdose investigation. The woman died, and the husband disappeared. It's all locked up, but we walk around once in a while to make sure it's undisturbed."

"How long has this been going on?" Josh asked.

"Ever since the first search warrant was served some months back. Hop in; we'll fill you in on the whole story as we drive."

Pulling up outside the Ng home a short while later, Josh asked to sit on the front lawn with his dog rather than wait in the cramped squad car while the officers checked the house. Entering the grounds, Josh walked across the lawn to a nearby bench as the two police officers checked the front door and then proceeded around the house. Deciding Nyx could walk around unrestrained in the safety of the yard, Josh removed the dog's leash and watched as she wandered aimlessly away sniffing the occasional interesting patch of grass as she went. Reaching the newly planted shrub John Ng had noticed on his departure, Nyx sniffed furiously at its base before sitting down directly facing the shrub, unmoving and alert. Beckoning the Vancouver police officers immediately when they returned, Josh asked to speak to whoever was in charge of the drug investigation.

After a long silent stare at the relatively unknown RCMP corporal and his dog, one of the officers spoke. "Why? What's up?"

"There's a body buried out here," Josh replied. "Nyx is a cadaver dog."

#

During the time it took for the Vancouver police forensic team to excavate the shrub and sift through the surrounding soil, it became readily apparent that the "body" discovered by Nyx was, in fact, a collection of finely ground bones loosely mixed with plant fertilizer. Subsequent investigation confirmed the bone fragments were human remains, while later DNA testing revealed they were not, as was originally surmised, those of John Ng.

Already frustrated in their investigation into the death of Bobbie Ng by her husband's disappearance, the Vancouver police made no announcement regarding the discovery of human remains at the Ng home. A press briefing was held, however, in which the police once again confirmed their interest in making contact with John Ng, the former president of Monger Capital, and requested that anyone with any information on his whereabouts contact them through the police hotline.

CHAPTER 68

Quon

Quon Jin Hu rose from the chair behind his desk and, walking to the corner of his large office, picked up the brass headed golf putter leaning against the wall before taking several practice swings at an imaginary ball on the carpet in front of his feet.

"We need the original of the agreement between Jun Ng and this Damian Slater person," he said.

"I will get it immediately," Dong Lai replied.

"Tell me again what the agreement promised."

"Damian Slater gets paid a one percent finder's fee if Monger Capital goes ahead with the ship purchase deal."

"How much is that?"

"The four ships will cost about a billion dollars in total. Slater would be paid roughly ten million dollars."

"Ten million! And what did we get for that?"

"He supported our request for a seat on the Woodstock Marine board."

"Ah, yes. But if there is no ship purchase required, he gets nothing and we still keep the board seat, right?"

"Right," replied Dong.

Quon smiled. "When you have the agreement, tell Ng to come and see me, not before. In the meantime, we need to deal with this renewed interest in Jun Ng's whereabouts and its impact on Monger."

"Yes, Komodo." Without another word, Dong turned and left the room, leaving Quon still practising his putting with his imaginary ball.

#

John Ng was not unduly concerned at Dong's request that he go and see Quon. In reality, he had initially been more concerned as to why Dong insisted he hand over the Slater finder's fee agreement. However, once Dong pointed out that with his "disappearance" the agreement needed to be in the hands of others, the request made sense. Besides, he didn't want to rock the boat. Things had steadily improved since his arrival in China and Monger Capital had dropped from the British Columbia news headlines. A role had been found for him within the office, and he was feeling almost at home. He wondered what Quon wanted? He usually only dealt through Dong Lai.

#

"Come in, come in," Quon said in response to the knock on his office door. "Ah, Jun," he said as John Ng entered. "How are you settling in?"

"Fine, thank you."

"Good. Sit." Quon stood and picked up the putter that was now lying on his desk and commenced putting an imaginary ball around his office, talking as he followed the path of the ball.

"Did Dong get the agreement?" he asked.

"Yes. He said it was necessary because I have now disappeared."

"Quite. We may have to consider other options with Monger unless the attention your wife's death has brought stops," Quon said, walking behind John still following his imaginary putts.

"I believe it has already stopped," John replied as Quon reappeared in front of him, but continued to navigate around his office with his imaginary game.

"Unfortunately, that is not so," Quon replied. "I heard from Mr. Chin this morning that the police have renewed their efforts to find you, and Monger is once again in the news."

"What! Why? I know no reason why they would do this. Her death was a simple overdose. I promise, Komodo, I have no idea what this is about."

"I'm sure that's true," Quon replied, once again moving out of John Ng's sight. "The trouble is, it has brought renewed attention to you and, in so doing, brought further unwanted attention on Monger Capital."

"What can I do to fix this?" John asked.

"All I can think of at the moment is that we need to stage some sort of accident so that you are no longer the focus of their interest."

"An accident?" John asked looking at Quon, who briefly reappeared from behind him, then disappeared once again still following his imaginary ball. "What sort of accident?"

"Perhaps a car accident," Quon said as he swung the putter with all his strength and listened to the resulting crack as John Ng's neck broke under the crushing impact of the heavy brass putter head. "Dong," he called loudly. "There is work to be done in here."

CHAPTER 69

Dan

The day following John Ng's meeting with Quon Jin Hu, his body was found with a broken neck apparently suffered in a single vehicle accident on a deserted road on the outskirts of Shanghai.

Two days later, an envelope arrived on the desk of Dan Fortin addressed to the "Corporate Secretary, Monger Capital". There was no covering letter, and the envelope contained nothing more than a certified copy of the two-page agreement between Monger Capital and Damian Slater, signed on behalf of Monger by its president, John Ng. Damian's signature followed immediately below in his usual ostentatious purple ink.

Instinctively rising from behind his desk, Dan walked directly to Damian's large corner office, with the agreement clutched firmly in his hand. Separated by several other executive offices and fifty feet away, Dan was half-way there and almost directly outside James Lee's door when he stopped. *Maybe advising Damian wasn't the right move,* he thought.

"Hey, Dan, looking for me?" James Lee's voice echoed through his open door.

"Hi, James. Nope, just having second thoughts." As he finished speaking, Dan turned and headed back to his own office, re-reading the document as he walked. The agreement was a clear conflict. There was no point in advising Damian, who obviously already knew of its existence and presumably would try to pressure Dan to keep it concealed. Who knew what means he would use? Whoever had sent it had now purposely put Dan in a difficult position. Failure to deal with it properly could mean exposure later if the sender went public about its existence and confirmed having delivered a copy to Woodstock's company secretary. As far as Dan was concerned, he really only had two choices. Either report what had happened to the chairman or to the head of the board's corporate governance committee. Making his choice, he reached for the telephone. The agreement was best placed in the hands of someone who was a stickler for ethical behaviour; he wasn't going to leave himself exposed in order to protect Damian. After all, what had Damian ever done for him? It was payback time. Whatever the chair of the corporate governance committee decided would be good enough for him; she was definitely the right person to call.

#

Immediately after reading the agreement forwarded to her by Dan Fortin, the corporate governance committee chair convened a meeting of her committee. The independent directors serving on the committee were unanimous in their condemnation of the agreement, which not only showed Damian as being severely conflicted in Woodstock's dealings with Monger, but also generously rewarded him in the event the Woodstock LNG bid failed and the four LNG tankers were sold to Monger Capital.

Dan Fortin, as corporate secretary and the only executive of the company in attendance, drafted the necessary resolution carrying the committee's recommendation. This was forwarded to the chairman of Woodstock Marine, along with a request for a meeting of the full board as early as feasible to discuss what was now being referred to as "the Slater agreement".

By the time the board met, the outcome had all but been decided. Several private discussions had already been held among the directors, and whether it was the nature of Damian's side deal with John Ng, his historical stance on women in positions of authority or just his generally unpleasant manner, the knives were out. Damian had to go, and the agreement provided the perfect means. The biggest concern among the directors seemed only a question of who would replace him.

As corporate executions go, Damian's was swift. Having been asked to leave the full board meeting as soon as it was called to order, he had waited outside the room during the discussions. Recalled less than a half-hour later, Damian was asked whether he had any mitigating information regarding his arrangement with John Ng and Monger Capital. After a blustery response, covering the company's success under his leadership, but completely ignoring the issue under discussion, he suddenly switched tracks and attacked those he deemed responsible for his current predicament, including the members of the corporate governance committee.

In the silence that followed his outburst, the chairman once again requested he leave the room while the board voted on the resolution before them. As the door closed behind Damian, the chairman asked, "Any further discussion?"

No one spoke, and after a moment's silence, the chairman continued, "Okay, there is a resolution before us; all those in favour?"

All the directors in attendance raised their hands.

"Against?"

There was no response and no movement from any of the directors present.

"Dan, will you minute that accordingly, please?"

"Okay," the chairman said, once again addressing the members of the board, "I will deal with Damian after this meeting concludes. Before you leave, I would like to discuss how we go about making the announcement and how we go about finding Damian's successor. Dan, we'll continue 'in camera'. Will you leave us now and ask Damian to wait for me in his office? Oh, and please don't say anything about what has just transpired. If Damian enquires, you can tell him we have not yet concluded our business and have asked you to leave while we continue the meeting in private."

Dan Fortin nodded, then rose and left the room without a word.

CHAPTER 70

James

James Lee first learned of what was happening when the company chairman summoned him to Damian's office. Not one to waste time on social niceties when there was business to conduct, the chairman got straight to the point.

"There've been a few developments, James, and Damian has left the company." Before James could utter a word, the shock of the statement still evident on his face, the chairman continued, "We will be conducting an expeditious search for his successor, but as you know these things take time. In the meantime, the board has recommended that you be appointed on an interim basis to fill the role. How do you feel about the challenge?"

James stood quietly, his racing mind still trying to cope with the information that Damian had left the company. What was going on? Had he had some sort of better offer? It was hard to imagine a much better job than the one he had at Woodstock Marine.

"Well?" the chairman asked.

"Sorry, I'm still trying to come to grips the fact that Damian has left."

"Look, you know you're highly thought of here, and you'd have to be naïve to have not realized you were being groomed for more senior roles. This has come a bit suddenly and a bit early in your career. Nonetheless, it's a great time to display your abilities. You and several other executives will be offered the chance to apply for the president's position on a permanent basis. How you perform in this interim role will certainly affect how your application is viewed if you were to apply. So, what do you think?"

"I think it would be a great opportunity. Thank you for considering me. When would you like me to start?"

"Immediately. We have a few tricky issues to tackle right away, so you might as well jump in the deep end. Sit down, and we'll get started. You can work out the logistics for everything else once we are done. I'll leave that up to you."

#

"Guess who the president of Woodstock Marine is?" James said as he walked into the condominium that evening.

"I assume it's not Damian," Kitty replied. "Otherwise you wouldn't ask. Where has he gone? Hopefully somewhere far away; he's a lecherous prick."

"Really? You seemed to like him."

"I seem to like everybody I think is good for your career. What I actually think is another matter entirely. So, where has he gone? And who's the new president?"

"He's been fired, or forced to resign anyway, and we have a new interim president while they conduct a search for someone permanent."

"Can you apply?"

"For what?"

"The permanent job. Why are you dragging this out?"

"Yes, I can apply, and I will. I'm also the interim president."

"You are?"

"I am."

"That's brilliant. Congratulations." Kitty moved closer and kissed James full on the lips. "Maybe we should celebrate, and then you can tell me what happened to Damian."

"Why don't I tell you while we celebrate?"

"Because I don't fancy discussing Damian while we're having sex, you dummy."

"Oh."

CHAPTER 71

Neil

Life in Stellenbosch agreed with Neil. He'd forgotten how much he loved this crazy country. Jan and Connie were the perfect undemanding and non-judgmental hosts, and aside from frequent flashes of guilt and anxiety about Vivian's whereabouts, he was settling in well. The person entering the country as Mark van Aswegan had long since disappeared, and no one in South Africa was looking for Neil Mohle. The farm work kept him busy, and there were very few people around who might wonder who he was, let alone have any reason to connect him with the infrequent doses of Canadian news on the local channels. Africa provided enough drama of its own to keep everyone fully occupied with his or her own troubles.

Philip called occasionally, always from different phones and always to the farm landline, with public updates on the search, as well as anything he learned from his direct contact with the police. Nervous at first at this seemingly dangerous strategy, Neil eventually came to realize that Philip's periodic enquiries to the police served as an effective double bluff and actually drew attention away from the possibility of any family involvement in his disappearance. Furthermore, the police were their only real source of information in finding Vivian. Still unaware as to the reason for the contract on their lives, Neil spent endless evening hours poring over events leading up to the warning from Kitty Lee and their sudden decision to flee. Most puzzling of all was Vivian's disappearance. She was only supposed to be gone for a minute or two. Why had she run away? He knew she was claustrophobic in the container, but it was only for a limited time and they were together. In his darker moments, he wondered whether perhaps she'd somehow been involved in the threat all along. Maybe she wasn't even a target, and it was only him? Until he had news of her whereabouts, he wasn't going to take any chances. He'd stay below the radar and keep replaying events repeatedly in his own mind while making detailed notes. Maybe they'd come in handy someday. If nothing else, they kept him from going insane with worry and reduced his frustration at not being actively involved the search. The best he'd been able to do had been to convince Philip to consider hiring a private detective to help find both of them. At this point, he was confident enough in his own disappearance to feel safe that they wouldn't track him down, but that any enquiries might lead to finding Vivian.

CHAPTER 72

Drew

"You sure like this place," Vegas Kolnick said as he and Drew Jamieson parked their gleaming Harley-Davidson motorcycles outside the Qualicum beachfront pub. "I don't think we've ever gone by without you wanting to stop for a beer."

Drew laughed, but felt his heart rate increase. "Not sure that's true," he replied. "But what's not to like? Ocean view, beer and good service. It's definitely one of my favourites. I like the ocean; I thought you liked it too."

"I do. It just seems to be getting a bit routine with you."

Drew's heart rate continued to increase. "Want to try somewhere else?" he asked. *Vegas certainly didn't miss much,* he thought.

"Nah, this is good for now. Maybe next time."

#

Nolan Kulla watched as the two bikers entered the pub. He'd not been expecting Drew, and the gathering of his Shady group was in full swing, with both beer and provocative conversation flowing freely.

"Hey, Nolan," someone called across the length of several small tables they had pushed together to accommodate the dozen or so members who had dropped in on this particular Thursday. "Tell us again how big that salmon was that you lost last weekend."

"I didn't lose it," Nolan replied. "It was my idiot brother here." He paused and pointed to another member of the group sitting several chairs away. "Missed it with the bloody net." Seeing Drew stand up on the other side of the room, he continued, "I need a senior bladder moment. I'll tell you the rest when I get back." Pushing back his chair, he left the table and taking a different route arrived at the men's washroom moments after the door had closed behind Drew.

Entering the cramped confines of the small washroom, he stepped up to the only other urinal alongside Drew and unzipped his pants. "Didn't expect to see you," he said.

"I need to get a message back to Kate Harrington. Tell them Vegas Kolnick is hyper-alert, and I need to be more careful. I know the Evans twins are involved in the Mohle contract, but little else. No idea on the head Chinese honcho, but I'll call if I find out. For now it's a case of 'don't call me, I'll call you' until the heat is off. Got to go. Give me a couple of minutes before you leave." Without another word, Drew turned and quickly rinsed his hands under the tap on the nearby small basin before wiping them dry on his jeans as he left the washroom.

Nolan glanced over at Drew's table as he returned to his own. The two bikers were hunched over their beers in deep conversation and neither looked up as he made his way back to his group. "Sorry," he said as he sat down. "Aging sucks. Now, where was I with that fish?"

#

Sergeant Kate Harrington received a telephone call from Nolan Kulla with Drew Jamieson's message shortly after pulling up outside the salon where Vivian Mohle had worked. With no actionable evidence against the Evans twins and no lead on who might be the head of the Chinese gang, the Mohle investigation was on the back burner, revisited only when time allowed. Along with a review of all their earlier leads, the RCMP had also shifted their focus to the banker's wife, as directed by

Inspector Jack Bowie. Still, Kate had to admit she really thought Drew would have eventually come through with a name. Shaking her head, she stepped from the car and walked into the salon, her police uniform decidedly at odds with the stylish clothing of most of the clientele.

\#

"Are you sure? It's been quite a while," Kate said.

"I am. I told the police officer who interviewed me at the time."

"What did you tell them?"

"Just what I told you. Everybody loved Vivian. Apart from that one incident, there was never anything even remotely off."

"An incident? That's exactly what you told them at the time?"

"Yes. Well not about the incident, just that everybody loved her. The incident was such a small thing, I didn't think it was important."

"So you didn't mention the incident before?"

"No, and I probably wouldn't even have remembered it now; it was so unimportant. But then she died, and they were all over the news."

"What do you mean she died?" Kate asked.

"The customer, the one who got mad with Vivian."

"And she died?"

"Yes."

Kate took a deep breath as the conversation continued in circles. "Can you remember her name?"

"Of course I can. She's been all over the news . . . Bobbie Ng. Her husband's some hotshot investment type, and now he's dead too. That's why I remembered the incident in the salon."

"He's dead too?"

"Yes. Yesterday in a car accident in China. Don't you watch the news?"

Kate Harrington's mind was racing as the salon attendant babbled on. Could this finally be the break they needed? She'd seen the news, of course, but not made any connection to the banker and his wife. Cutting the interview short, she left her contact details with Vivian Mohle's former co-worker and hurried back to her car. She needed to speak to the local Vancouver police, and find out if there was anything on the Ng deaths that hadn't been in the news and might connect them to her case. Hoping against hope that the usual inter-divisional police politics wouldn't come into play, she picked up her police radio and started making calls.

#

"Thanks for seeing me at such short notice. I had a feeling my enquiry might get bogged down in red tape."

"No problem, Sergeant," said the Vancouver police detective sitting across the table from Kate Harrington in the downtown coffee shop. "We probably owe you one on this case already."

"You do?" Kate was beginning to feel that she was a step behind everybody in this investigation. First the woman in the salon and now the detective opposite her. "Why is that?"

"Well, your guess was right. We do have some information in the case that we've withheld from the public, but it was one of your people who turned it up. As long as you can assure me it goes no further until we're ready, I'm happy to share it with you. That sound fair?"

"Sure," Kate replied, not knowing what she was agreeing to, but seeing no harm at this stage. Release of information to the public would be out of her hands anyway if the top brass got involved, no matter what she'd promised. "So how did one of our guys get involved?"

"Beer league baseball," the detective replied smiling broadly. "And letting his dog pee on our crime site."

As Kate listened to the story, and despite the seriousness of both investigations, she too couldn't help smiling at the nature of the accidental discovery. *These were the kind of breaks you sometimes need to solve cases,* she thought. "So you've no match on the DNA?" Kate asked as the story concluded.

"None, but we're still looking. We know the bone fragments are from a female, but that's it."

"Any chance you could try and match one of our missing persons cases? It's a long shot, but we have an Asian female missing with a very tenuous connection to the Ng's. Our case is cold, and quite frankly besides this and a couple of shady underworld characters, we've little else to follow."

"Sure. As I said, we owe you one. It was your man and his dog who dug this up; excuse the pun. Send us the sample, and we'll go from there."

"Okay, if I send it without an identifying name? Our case is still pretty sensitive."

"Doesn't bother me. We will want to know if there's a match, though. There may be something there that ties all this stuff together."

"Deal."

#

Kate's earlier enthusiasm had long since dissipated as she gathered a few appropriate items from Vivian Mohle's personal effects to conduct the necessary DNA test. As a result, when the lab report finally arrived on her desk five days later, her expectations were almost zero. Her scream as she checked the result caused several officers to reach for their holstered weapons and Inspector Jack Bowie to rush from his office in what was later described by one irreverent office comedian as looking "shaken not stirred".

CHAPTER 73

Vivian et al

Within days of the identification of the remains at the Ng home as belonging to Vivian Mohle and the subsequent notification of her death to her sister Lori, the news had leaked to the press. Once again, Bobbie and John Ng were front-page news; only this time, so was their association with the Mohles and, peripherally, the men's association through the Kitimat deal with Woodstock LNG and Monger Capital.

#

Hayden Jones, who up to this point had maintained a careful distance from the RCMP investigation, used the news to press them into looking closer into Monger Capital, despite his skepticism that anything would be uncovered that his own CSIS colleagues had not already found.

#

P.K. Chin, operating under the ever watchful, albeit distant, eye of Dong Lai implemented Quon Jin Hu's strategic vision for Monger Capital, while simultaneously engendering himself to the Woodstock Marine board and senior executives in general and James Lee in particular. Nothing it seemed was too much trouble for the impeccably attired and polite investment banker in his efforts to erase the stain on Monger and Woodstock created by the "illegal" dealings of the late John Ng. Even the provincial government were not immune to his charm. So effective was he in his efforts that, shortly after his meeting with Hugh Ruff and satisfying him of both the legitimacy of Monger Capital and their "no-strings attached" political donation made at the time of John Ng's leadership, the B.C. Government issued a public statement on the matter. In it, they blamed any negative press on the actions of John Ng, fuelled by the creative speculation of the opposition party. The provincial government also expressed their enthusiasm for Woodstock Marine and Monger Capital's continued involvement in the Chinese consortium bid for the LNG project in Kitimat under the new leadership of James Lee at Woodstock and P.K. Chin at Monger.

What many may have missed, but what was certainly not lost on P.K. Chin, was that his positioning of James Lee alongside himself in his dealings with the provincial government had effectively secured James a front-runner position for the long-term presidency of Woodstock Marine.

#

Returning to her office shortly after the press briefing to make the announcement, Dana Holmes stood alongside Hugh Ruff and looked down from her office window at the gradually dispersing crowd on the legislature lawn below. "Tell me again how that Chin fellow phrased his comment about John Ng."

"I don't think I can do it justice as I've forgotten his exact words. The intent was crystal-clear, though. Essentially, he said that no matter what comment we made about John Ng and who might be to blame for any perceived negative implications from Monger's donation, they would back our story. He gave us carte blanche to say what we liked. Our comments since then, outlining that whatever Ng may have planned had become moot with his death and that the Monger donation was now specifically earmarked for environmental impact studies, were very well received by the voting public. From everything Chin said, it's my guess that we've secured another long-term supporter."

#

The reaction to the news of John Ng's death and the discovery of Vivian Mohle's remains caused barely a ripple in the routine at the house on Airlie Road. Having shared little of the previous events with either Scrubber Barker or Drew Jamieson, Vegas Kolnick now became the proverbial clam. Not long after receiving the news, however, with a brief comment about heading over to Vancouver to check his boat, he roared out of the driveway on his motorcycle and later boarded the 10:30 a.m. ferry to Horseshoe Bay in West Vancouver. With almost two hours before the ferry would reach its destination, he stood in the breakfast lineup and, fifteen minutes later, was seated alone, armed with the traditional full breakfast and a large black cup of coffee.

Arriving at the home of the Evans twins, he was clear on what needed doing. Firstly, those idiots had to shut down their "landscaping" activities. While he understood their twisted thinking in leaving a trail back to the instigator of the contract in case they were ever implicated, the method was so specific that anytime it was used and discovered in the future, it would automatically link the crimes. Far better to stop it now and let it be picked up by some future copycat killer that had no link to them. The twins would understand that. Secondly, he would terminate the deal to look for the banker. John Ng was dead, and he'd had no dealings with anyone else. The twins could keep the money, and that would shut them up. Other than Drew, he hadn't mentioned the twins' involvement to anyone else. He had also done as they suggested and, after purposely leaving fish residue all over the deck, used the resultant mess to have his boat cleaned by a commercial outfit right in the marina. There was nothing left to link his boat, or him, to the crime. Unless there was some unprovoked attack on one of the motorcycle club members, as far as he was concerned, this contract was over.

#

"Shit, I'm glad he's gone," Garrett said. "I'm never sure what's up when Vegas is that quiet. He's goddamn dangerous when he's pissed."

"Yup. It's a good thing he didn't ask how we found the woman," Griffin said. "Do you think we need to do something about Willy?"

"Nah. He's in too deep. He's not going to say anything; after all, it looks like the tampered pill idea worked. The Ng woman is dead, and when I last spoke to Willy, no one had even suggested he might be involved. Apparently, he's still a supplier of choice to that mob because they can trust his product. Man, that's funny."

As Garrett finished speaking, both twins laughed uproariously before standing and walking towards the front door as if connected by one brain.

"I think this calls for a beer," Griffin said, his arm draped around his brother's shoulders as they squeezed through the door side-by-side. "I'll drive."

#

"What did Damian Slater want?" David Gibson asked. "That's the second time he's come to our offices rather than calling us down to his."

"He's looking for a job," Michael Burt replied. "Said he wants to get back into investment banking."

"What about Woodstock?"

"Seems they've parted ways for good although the details he offered were pretty vague."

"Do you think it had something to do with that Monger Capital business?"

"Could be. Despite looking for work, he's still pretty arrogant and certainly less than open about what's happened."

"What are you going to do? Are you interested in having him aboard?"

"First instinct . . . hell, no. Then I remind myself that he's highly intelligent and very well connected. He could be good for business."

"What did you tell him?"

"I said I'd think about it and discuss it with the rest of the partners."

"How did he take that?"

"Fine, I think. He said we'd be bloody idiots to miss an opportunity to employ someone of his calibre."

"Well, at least you know he's not afraid to speak his mind."

Michael was still laughing long after David had turned and walked back to his own office.

CHAPTER 74

Hayden

Immediately after the identification of Vivian Mohle's remains, the story of her disappearance and a possible connection to the Ng's deaths once again made headline news. Yet, despite the connection and the unusually cooperative liaison between the RCMP and Vancouver police teams, neither group managed to generate any major leads for themselves or for the other. With no breaking news and both investigations again grinding to an unsatisfactory halt, the public interest and media speculation waned, and the once prominent news story gradually dwindled into an occasional inside-page news article and then finally nothing.

A less advertised by-product of the initial media frenzy was a dramatic, albeit temporary, change in the daily behaviour of the various parties associated with these crimes. Illegal activities were suspended and procedures altered. They knew time was their friend, and as long as nobody slipped up, the police would ultimately have other serious matters with which to occupy themselves, and activities could return to normal.

Neither of these events were helpful to Hayden Jones. Accustomed to working alone with extended periods of inactivity, he envisioned his role as more of a bird-watcher than a made-for-TV super spy. Endless patience and behavioural observation were the trademarks of his past successes. Then, when the time was right, a major sweep by the strong-arm people and it was all over, bar the shouting. Unfortunately, while Monger Capital was his best lead into possible illegal money laundering in British Columbia, the arrival of P.K. Chin as its new president had, by all accounts, also resulted in a major overhaul of company operations. Any chance Hayden might have had of some corporate slip-up had certainly been reduced at this time. Monger had even disappeared from Hugh Ruff's special donor list. To make matters worse, Hayden's investigation into both of the other two names on the list, which Rachel had finally disclosed after Hugh removed them from the list, had not proved even remotely interesting. If he were to be honest about it, only two good things had come out of his investigation thus far and neither related to his work, an unexpected affair with the premier of the province and a now serious relationship with her executive assistant.

Despite the lack of progress in his investigation, the e-mail from the DG that awaited him on his arrival at his desk that morning came as a shock. One of only two overnight e-mails in his inbox, it was short and to the point. Either produce something actionable or the DG was going to pull the plug despite their interest in Monger Capital.

Hayden stared blankly at his computer screen. It had been a long time since he'd been involved in an investigation and achieved so little; and he certainly wasn't accustomed to failing. On top of it all, his personal entanglements would, if they ever became known, always end up being suggested as the reason why he'd screwed up. He needed a break in his enquiries—a major break.

Finally looking at the second message, Hayden grimaced; the day was getting worse. Like the first message, it too was brief; only this one was from his assistant Donna Gray. She was ill and would not be in. There was a box for him next to her desk. A courier had dropped it off the previous evening; aside from that, he was on his own. She would try to come in the following day if she was feeling a bit better.

Deciding he wasn't even going to think about work again until after another coffee, he left his office and headed for Rachel's. Maybe she'd like one as well. The box forgotten, he decided to try to catch her before

Dana arrived. They could go together to pick them up. He'd enjoy that; he was getting used to having her around.

#

Returning to his office, Hayden stared at the box on his desk. There was nothing remarkable about it, and yet despite the urgency with which he had ripped away the plastic outer wrapping, he was reluctant to open it. Grainy brown, with a separate lid and handhold slots on the sides, it was identical to millions of others in worldwide office use for file storage. A standard Bankers Box, it was still identified by the company name of the original 1917 manufacturer.

His reluctance came from the brief typed letter inside a plain white envelope, which was taped to the outside of the lid and which he had read several times since tearing away the wrapping.

Dear Hayden:

I send this to you with mixed emotions. What you do with it will ultimately determine whether I continue to live out my remaining years in this place in relative anonymity or will, once again, need to disappear. I have chosen to send these documents to you, as, based on our last meeting, I assume you must have some connection to the police or at least access to those with suitable authority to deal with these matters.

Since our meeting, I have watched with interest and, I admit some trepidation, as events have unfolded. However, the most recent discovery has now also forced me to accept that Vivian is gone forever while those responsible for her death remain, not only unscathed by events but, more than likely, also enriched by their actions. It was this latter realization that finally prompted me to send you the enclosed material.

I leave it to your good judgement how best to proceed although I have little doubt that once your curiosity is piqued, you will be unable to resist further investigation. Stay well my friend. You will not hear from me again.

Neil

Hayden read the letter for the third time; the box still unopened on his desk. Could this really be from Neil Mohle? There was no accompanying invoice; no sender information. In fact, no information on the box at all. Discounting the envelope addressed to *"Hayden Jones Esq. Private & Strictly Confidential"*, there was nothing to identify how it had arrived or from where it had come. Where the hell was Donna when he needed her? Surely, there was some sender information somewhere? Unable to contain himself and still without opening the box, he looked up Donna's home number and called.

"Why are you checking up on me? Don't you believe I'm sick?" Despite being unwell, Donna's greeting was as spirited as ever.

"No, I mean, yes, of course I do. I'm not checking up on you," Hayden replied. "How did you know it was me anyway?"

"What kind of question is that? Haven't you heard of call display? If you're not checking up on me, why are you calling?"

"It's about this box."

"Oh, the box. Yeah, that is a bit weird. What do you want to know?"

"Where did it come from? And who's the sender?"

"Well, that's the weird bit. This delivery person came in just before we closed yesterday looking for you, and when you weren't in, just handed me the box and asked that I give it to you. I wanted to know who it was from and all he said was 'no message, just give him the box', and then he walked out. What's in it?"

'I don't know. I haven't looked yet."

"What?! Why not?"

"No reason. Look, I've got to go. Sorry to have disturbed you." With that, Hayden disconnected the call before Donna could ask another question. He'd apologize tomorrow. Right now, all he wanted to know was what was in the box.

#

His office door closed and locked, Hayden looked at the files he'd removed from the box and laid out on the surface of his desk. There were forty in all, neatly labelled and each one containing at least several handwritten pages. Packed in alphabetical order, Neil Mohle had reconstructed his entire ECB client portfolio from memory, detailing his notes with everything he recalled about each particular client or transaction. What was also obvious after a quick examination of the contents was that he had abandoned any pretense of confidentiality. The files contained not only business deal details, but also any personal information known or rumoured about the specific client and their transactions. Taped to the inside of the lid was a neatly printed index of the contents, along with another brief note.

> *I've racked my brain, and I still can't think of anything in either my or Vivian's personal lives that would cause anyone to want to harm us. That said there were certainly some unconventional characters among my clients although I have a hard time imagining there was anything in their often scandalous behaviour to warrant a contract on our lives. I guess it all depends on how much money might be at stake or what we might inadvertently have learned.*

> *More than ever, I believe that the reason has to be somewhere in one of these bank deals, the most recent of which you're already somewhat familiar with due to your own involvement on behalf of the B.C. government. If nothing else, public disclosure of a lot of what I have written in these files will certainly shake up an awful lot of lives.*

#

It was several hours later before Hayden unlocked his office door and, without advising anyone of his intentions, left for the day. The contents of the box now securely locked away in one of his own cabinets, Hayden's briefcase contained only one file and his laptop. While Neil's files contained a virtual treasure trove of possible financial irregularities and damaging personal information, it was the one marked "Woodstock LNG—Kitimat" that had captured his attention and which now, still unread, resided securely in his briefcase.

#

Hayden was once again reading Neil's note when Rachel returned to his apartment after leaving the legislature building for the day. Looking up as she entered the front door, he felt a surge of excitement as he watched her kick off her shoes and walk barefoot over to where he was sitting.

The speed with which their relationship was progressing still surprised him, yet for some reason, it felt right. Despite a variety of almost irrational responses to her own bouts of jealousy about his previous affairs, Rachel obviously felt the same way, for it was she, who, as her sleepovers increased in frequency, suggested that she might as well move in with him. Not that he had resisted; he enjoyed her company and the physical attraction was obvious. What eventually would happened, he couldn't guess, but at that very moment, he knew that for him, the relationship was now serious.

"What's up?" Rachel asked, flopping down on the sofa next to him while leaning in for a kiss.

Hayden kissed her lightly on the lips, and then spoke. "Have you ever considered living back east?"

"Not seriously. Toronto's a bit too big city, concrete and sterile for my liking. Why?"

"What about Ottawa?"

"Better, much more character, but I've never spent much time there, except on odd jaunts with the premier. What's going on . . .? Are you moving?"

"No, just thinking out loud. I want to share something with you, but it's not going to make much sense unless I tell you the whole story. Then again, if I do, it's absolutely confidential and you cannot tell anyone else; my whole career depends on it."

"Is this bad? Are you in some kind of trouble?"

"No, all good. But I need to know, for example, if we were married, could you live in Ottawa?"

"Married? Is this some sort of proposal?"

Hayden smiled. With his thoughts firmly focused on the Mohle letter and wanting to share its contents with Rachel, he'd spoken spontaneously but honestly. "Yes, it is," he replied impulsively, now caught up in the moment. "It sort of came out badly, but yes, it is. Will you marry me?"

Rachel's stunned expression hid any opportunity Hayden may have had of knowing what reply to expect before she spoke. "And if I say yes, I have to go and live in Ottawa?" she asked.

"Well periodically, but with occasional breaks."

"Have you got a new job?"

"Not exactly."

"So you want me to answer both questions at the same time?" Rachel said, her mock serious expression giving Hayden the first glimmer of hope that she might actually accept his proposal.

"Ideally, yes. I don't know what I'd do if you said yes, but that you couldn't live in Ottawa. My work is there."

"Okay, now I'm totally confused. I thought you worked here. But if you promise me there is nothing bad in what you are going to tell me, then yes, I'll marry you, and if necessary, I'll live in Ottawa."

Reaching out, Hayden pulled Rachel to him and squeezed her tightly. "It's a long story, but here goes," he said.

#

"That's everything," Hayden said. "A summary of my whole life from birth to now. No errors or omissions." Still cuddled in the corner of the sofa where they had remained since Rachel's arrival and Hayden's awkward proposal, he had spoken almost uninterrupted for nearly an hour. "Still think you can live with that?"

"I can't believe you're a spy," Rachel replied. "What will I tell my parents you do for a living?"

Hayden laughed. "I'll take that as a yes. Firstly, I'm not really a spy; I'm an investigator. You can tell your parents or anyone who asks that I work for the government. Just another boring bureaucrat. Unless I'm on assignment somewhere; in which case, you just tell them what my role is at the time, like now."

"Does the premier know?"

"Can't say."

"Can't or won't."

"Some things you're going to have to take on trust when I really am not able to speak about them."

"I'm not sure I'm going to like that part," Rachel replied, her mood seeming to change as she spoke and stood up. "I'm hungry. Why don't we fix ourselves something to eat and then you can tell me what's in that file you keep picking up and putting down."

#

Back in his legislature office the following morning and armed with the contents of Neil Mohle's letter, Hayden launched into his investigation with renewed energy. He felt unusually content and focused. It had been a long evening. Rachel's good mood had returned over dinner as they shared personal information and discussed their future together, Neil Mohle's file lying forgotten for the moment on the table in front of them. After their initial euphoria subsided, it was already late, and with a promise to tell her more about the file the following day, they had succumbed to the added intimacy brought about by Hayden's unplanned proposal.

Hayden's first call that morning was to Kate Harrington. After a brief enquiry into how her investigation of the Mohle disappearance was progressing, he broached the real reason for his call. "Have you looked into Monger Capital or any of Neil Mohle's clients?" he asked.

"What's your interest?" Kate replied.

"Maybe similar to yours, I think. We're watching illegal money movements into Canada, and while I have nothing factual to support this theory, I wondered if there might be a tie-in between my investigation and yours; after all, he is a banker, and for some reason, somebody wants him killed."

"Do you have any leads in your investigation?" Kate asked.

"I've received some information from a source whose name I can't share at this time, and mostly it's suspicion at this stage." Hayden grimaced at the lie; it was too early to reveal Neil's file, even to the RCMP. "I'm grasping at straws at this point, and that's why I wondered if you had learned anything interesting about Monger Capital or had received any leads from ECB on any of Neil Mohle's clients? Maybe if we shared what we've learned, one or both of our investigations might benefit."

"Fine, but I think you're going to be disappointed."

"Try me," Hayden replied.

"Okay. We know very little about Monger Capital, save for the recent public news about their president, John Ng's, apparent embezzlement. No charges were brought, and in fact, it seems the company is even better regarded after the appointment of a new president and the way he quickly cleaned up the old mess."

"What about ECB? Anything from them?"

"Nothing. We looked at Mohle's files and interviewed several of his colleagues. No one knows anything. We even looked into an e-mail exchange between Mohle and the bank's security group about Monger Capital investing in an LNG deal. Nothing there either."

"Did you interview them?"

"Yes, several people, but not the actual security manager who responded to Mohle at the time. Guy by the name of Broughton, who has since left the bank. Based on the e-mail exchange, we didn't think it necessary to talk to him."

"Mind if I track him down and ask him some questions?" Hayden asked.

"Be my guest, his first name is Christopher. Now what have you got for me?"

"Well, I heard there might have been some sort of altercation between the woman who died at Monger Capital's offices and Vivian Mohle. It took place at the salon where Vivian worked."

"Yeah, we got that. That's how we decided to check the DNA remains at the Ng house with Vivian Mohle. The altercation seems to have been little more than two irate customer's over a late appointment, though; nothing to write home about."

"If it was nothing, how do you explain finding her remains on the Ng property?"

"I can't. That was a long shot with no real substance. We had a missing female and no leads. The two women had argued fairly recently, and the Vancouver police had the remains of an unknown female. We had nothing to lose by checking."

"Fair enough. I do have one other rumour. Same source, but I have no idea what it's worth. Apparently, Vivian Mohle was seen at the Deltaport container terminal around the date she and Neil disappeared. I guess it's too late for that to be helpful anyway, now that she's dead."

"Now that is interesting. I'll check into it, but I'd really like to talk to your source."

"Sorry," Hayden said. "It's too sensitive at this time. I'll let you know as soon as I can."

"Okay, but I'll hold you to that if this lead comes to anything. Anything else?"

"No, but I'll let you know if I find anything more," Hayden replied. "Appreciate your help." Hanging up the telephone, Hayden sighed with relief. Kate Harrington had been unusually cooperative, and he hadn't enjoyed his own deception.

Excluding that the mystery investor Neil was supposed to meet at the restaurant was "a tall blond-haired man", he'd passed on what little information he could without identifying Neil, including where he'd last seen Vivian. It didn't take a rocket scientist to assume that the location must have some link to the timing of Neil's own disappearance, but for now, he'd leave that to the RCMP. With the exception of the comment about Vivian, Neil's letter offered no further clues or information on his own disappearance.

Hayden knew the RCMP would be mad when he finally told them about Neil's letter, but he'd find some plausible excuse related to his own investigation for keeping it quiet for so long. In the meantime, it appeared that at least Neil was safe, and that's what the RCMP had wanted in the first place. He would use the time to track down Chris Broughton and find out where he obtained his information on this Asian gangster called Komodo. Neil's file made compelling reading regarding his conversation with Broughton and his subsequent conversation with James Lee of Woodstock Marine about his wife's possible family connection to the reclusive billionaire, Quon Jin Hu. After Kitty Lee's sudden warning and Vivian's death, Neil now suspected that despite James's earlier denial, there was far more to the association than he'd previously been told.

CHAPTER 75

Kate

Sergeant Kate Harrington stood in the door of Inspector Jack Bowie's office, her open laptop held in one hand. "I think you ought to take a look at this," she said.

"What have you got?"

"Security video from the Deltaport container terminal the day after the Mohles disappeared."

"And?"

"And, Vivian Mohle, or at least someone we believe is Vivian Mohle, suddenly appears from between one of the banks of containers and then disappears between others. She never reappears."

"Have you checked it out?"

"Officers are already on their way. Although after all this time, we don't expect to find anything. We've reviewed camera footage for the weeks before and after she was spotted, and she never reappears."

"Where did you get the lead? Or was this just a lucky guess?"

"Jones at CSIS gave it to us from an as yet unnamed source."

"Is there anything else on the footage of interest?" Jack asked.

"There's a car, which must have been parked between one of the rows of containers, that leaves shortly after Vivian Mohle vanishes. The cameras cover almost the entire area, but there are a few blind spots. The car is only visible when it comes out from between the containers.

After that, it was easy for us to track its progress right out of the gates. It only appears to have one male occupant, and he shouldn't be too hard to trace. Most likely an employee to have been able to park there without attracting attention. The car is also very distinctive; it's a dark coloured Chev Camaro ZL1. The footage is black and white, and the car is definitely dark but not black, so blue or green or maybe even red. We should find it easily enough with the dockyard records."

"Anything else?"

"Not much, just some people involved in regular loading activity. We'll start with the car and go from there."

"Good work, Kate. Keep me informed. We could do with a break on this case. Oh, and press Jones. I want to know who his source is, spy or no spy."

"Right, sir. We're on it."

As Kate left Jack's office, she wondered how well she would do pressuring Hayden Jones. The people on the covert side of CSIS operations didn't scare easily and could call on a lot of political power for support if ever needed.

CHAPTER 76
Rachel

Excited really didn't do justice for how Rachel felt as she headed back to the apartment. She'd barely been able to contain herself at work, but had somehow managed to keep Hayden's proposal to herself. *At least until I have a ring,* she thought. Right now, it would just be too hard to explain how he had suddenly proposed and why she didn't have an engagement ring; some jealous colleagues might even think she was making it all up. No, she had waited for years for this to happen, and she could wait a little while longer to savour the moment when she announced it to the world.

"Hi, you look happy," Hayden said as she opened the apartment door. "I came back early to make some personal calls."

"Hi, yourself. I am happy. I see you're still looking at that same file. Are you going to tell me what's in it?" Rachel asked.

"Yes, and there's more. I've just been speaking to the former security manager at ECB about a conversation he had with Neil Mohle. Apparently, he used his personal e-mail to check some of the material for Neil, so there was no record of it at the bank. He also reported to Neil by telephone, so again no record, which explains why the police didn't find anything. He made some interesting connections."

"I'm sorry, but I'm lost," Rachel replied. "I thought you were investigating illegal money operations. Can you please start at the beginning?"

"Okay. You get yourself settled, and I'll gather my thoughts. I'll give you the whole story when you're ready. I need a coherent version anyway before I report back to my boss."

\#

"So you developed this whole theory from what you read in that file?" Rachel asked. "Where did you get it from anyway?"

"Sorry, I can't tell you where I got it from, but you're right—I did get most of the information from it, and some from my own suspicions and information I've gathered while working for the premier."

"Do you think she's involved?"

"No, but if my theory is right and there is illegal money behind Monger Capital, it may be a problem for her and Hugh Ruff. I've seen nothing in the government LNG documents to suggest Monger was getting any special treatment."

Rachel suddenly felt sick to her stomach, the premier's handwritten words on the bright yellow sticky note she had shredded etched in her mind:

> *Significant party donor. LNG investment. Ng. Can we help? Nineteen possible projects. Kitimat preferred. HR will call bank. Toronto head office, not local.*

Fiercely loyal to Premier Holmes, she was now faced with revealing what she knew to Hayden without knowing how he might react. The fact that Monger had been on the special donor list was significant, but not necessarily bad, and now the yellow sticky note all made sense. Realizing that her next words could well determine how her future unfolded, she looked directly at Hayden and waited.

"What?" Hayden said, obviously puzzled by her stare and silence.

"I have to tell you something about Dana. She may be more involved than you think."

CHAPTER 77

Dana

"You need to keep me out of this," Dana said.

"I'll do my best," Hayden replied, "but Rachel may be a problem. She has this fixation about that yellow sticky note she shredded for you that mentioned a person named Ng in connection with the LNG deal in Kitimat, and my duty, as she sees it, to be totally above board. Do you have anything else floating around that suggests Monger Capital may have received preferential treatment?"

"We're not stupid, you know. She shouldn't even have seen that note. Besides, it's shredded now, so it's her word against mine. Why does she know so much about your investigation anyway? It sounds as though she knows even more than I do. Are things serious between you?"

"Yes, and I realize it happened somewhat impetuously, but I've asked her to marry me."

"Really, that's interesting, and you're willing to sacrifice my political career to keep your latest fling happy?" Dana felt her anger growing as she spoke.

"It's not that at all," Hayden protested. "I haven't submitted my latest report yet and wanted to discuss this problem before it went in."

"What problem? I don't see a problem. Don't cross me, Jones," Dana said. "This could get ugly. I have friends in some seriously high places. Oh, and close the door as you leave. I have things to do."

CHAPTER 78

Rachel

Hayden looked shaken as he walked past Rachel on his way out of the premier's office without any acknowledgement or even a smile. He'd been different ever since their discussion about the premier's possible knowledge of John Ng and Monger Capital and her insistence that he not avoid the connection. She had even foolishly threatened that if she was ever asked under oath, she would have no option but to mention it, and that would look bad for him.

She really didn't understand why he was so defensive about the premier. Dana was certainly worthy of any admiration he may have for her abilities, but in Rachel's mind that didn't put her above the law. She was still musing when her internal telephone rang.

"Rachel, can you come in for a minute?"

"Certainly, Dana, I'll be right there."

"I've just got off the phone with our staffing group, and I'm afraid I'm going to have to move you to another position," Dana said as Rachel entered her office.

"Why? What have I done wrong?"

"Nothing, nothing at all. Unfortunately, though, there is a problem with your relationship with Hayden Jones and the confidential material that flows through my office. We just can't afford the risk of some inadvertent breach of confidentiality."

"But he doesn't really even work here," Rachel blurted out.

"My point exactly," Dana replied. "That in and of itself is something you shouldn't even know."

"But he only told me because we're going to be married. I wouldn't tell anyone else."

"And I believe you, but unfortunately we not only have to be squeaky clean, we have to be seen doing everything in our power to remain squeaky clean. Someone from staffing will call you within an hour. We'll do the change today. There will be no impact on your salary or benefits, just different responsibilities."

"This is all about the note I saw, isn't it?" Rachel's face reddened as she lashed out.

"What note?" Dana asked innocently.

"The note about Mr. Ng and the LNG deal."

"I'm afraid I don't know what you're talking about."

"The note with your papers that I shredded."

"I'm sorry, Rachel. I really don't know what you're talking about. Are you sure this sudden hostility is not just jealousy because of my affair with Jones? I know it was pretty intense and ended badly for him, but it really is over, you know."

"You had an affair with Hayden?"

"Oh, he hasn't told you? I am sorry. I assumed because you both appear to have shared so many confidentialities, he had told you and that's why you seem so aggressive towards me. My mistake. I'm sure he'll tell you in due course. I'm sorry things haven't worked out here, but maybe a change will be for the best."

Without speaking, Rachel tearfully rose from her chair and hurried from the office.

#

Brushing past Donna's desk without a greeting, a still tearful Rachel burst into Hayden's office. "I've just seen, Dana. We need to talk."

Hayden pointed to the telephone held to his ear without saying a word.

"This can't wait," Rachel said.

Hayden placed his hand over the mouthpiece and spoke quietly. "It's my boss. I can't speak now. I'll call you later."

Rachel stared at Hayden for several seconds her face reddening, then turned and walked quickly to back to her own office, gathered up her things and left the legislature buildings. *It was happening again,* she thought. Just when everything seemed to be going perfectly, suddenly it was all going to hell in an instant. The man she thought was in love with her was screwing her boss, perhaps even while he was doing the same to her. Then, because of it, she gets demoted while the two of them try to cover up some potentially illegal activity to protect their affair and the premier's political ambitions. Well, this time they picked the wrong woman and were they in for a shock.

#

No sooner had she reached their shared apartment than Rachel made her decision. The innocuous circular notice regarding staff vacations from CSIS that lay on Hayden's bedside table had an e-mail address at the top. She had noticed it when Hayden first printed it out to discuss their plans. While she didn't know if it would reach the director general, it was the only one she had and certainly the one she planned to use.

CHAPTER 79

Hayden

Hayden was still at his desk in the legislature building when he received the DG's call.

"I like you, Jones, but you've really done it this time. You'd better get your ass back to Ottawa on the next plane out. We'll work out what to do with you in the interim."

"What?! What the hell is going on? Who's complaining? The RCMP? We've finally had a major break, and as I told you earlier, I'm about to ask Revenue Canada to look into doing an audit on Monger Capital. That should shake something out of the trees," Hayden replied.

"Not the RCMP. There's been an official complaint lodged by some woman against you. It came to our general office e-mail about a half-hour ago. Fortunately, the person who received it brought it straight to me. I've told them to keep it quiet, but I need you back here now. If this goes forward, all hell will break loose."

"Some woman? Who? What's the complaint?"

"Name of Rachel Burton. She says she's the executive assistant to the premier, and that you've taken advantage of both her and the premier making you unfit to carry out your assignment. That of course poses another question entirely: How in God's name does she know what your assignment is? And how the hell did she get our e-mail address?"

"What does she mean, 'taken advantage of her and the premier'?" Hayden stammered.

"What do you think she means? She said you've been screwing them both and are now planning to use her words, 'to defeat the ends of justice'. Unless you can assure me none of this is true and that this is some fruitcake we're dealing with, you'd better be on the next plane to Ottawa. We need to stop this before it goes any further."

"What about the investigation?"

"Forget the investigation. It's over, or your part in it is over anyway. Screwing the leader of the provincial government who may, or may not, be complicit in a money laundering operation that we're investigating is certainly grounds for dismissal, and maybe even jail." The DG paused, then spoke again. "Come on back. Don't bother saying anything to anyone out there, just leave. We'll clean it up later; this one is over."

#

Ignoring his instructions to leave British Columbia without speaking to anyone, Hayden tried calling Rachel, first on her office phone and then on her mobile. Neither call reached her, and he left no messages. On returning to the apartment to collect his things, he found that all her personal items were gone, as if she had never lived there.

Hayden's next call was to Dana Holmes, which she answered after the first ring. "I don't know how," he said immediately on hearing her voice, "but Rachel has found out about our affair and gone ballistic. I know she's prone to behaving somewhat erratically when jealous, but this is way over the top, even for her."

"Well, isn't that too bad," Dana replied. "Perhaps the little bitch ought to think more carefully about threatening me over some note she thinks she saw."

"You mean you told her about us?"

"Yes, so what?"

"So she's just sent an e-mail to my boss detailing our affair and how we were, and I quote, 'trying to subvert the course of justice.'"

"You're kidding."

"I wish I was. I've been recalled to Ottawa immediately. I'm not even supposed to be having this conversation."

"How do we stop this?" Dana blurted.

"Well, I don't know about you, but I'm going to tell the truth. With the exception of Rachel's comments about the yellow sticky note, I don't know that you've done anything wrong, and I plan to say just that. It's about the best I can do. I've tried calling Rachel, but I've not been able to reach her. It's probably best that you and I don't speak again. I hope you can find a way to dodge this particular political bullet. I really enjoyed our time together, and I'm very sorry about how things have turned out."

"Fuck you, Jones" were the last words Hayden ever heard from Premier Dana Holmes as she terminated the call.

CHAPTER 80

Dana

Unlike Hayden, Dana Holmes was an astute political operator and unafraid to cut her losses in pursuit of the bigger prize. Immediately after her call with Hayden, she called Hugh Ruff to plan their further defensive strategy regarding Monger Capital's donation and any possible public perception that it had influenced her decision to award the Kitimat contract to the Chinese consortium that included Woodstock LNG and Monger.

Her second call was to the head of her political staffing group to terminate the employment of Rachel Burton, with a twelve-month severance package conditional upon her signing a very carefully drafted confidentiality agreement.

Her third and last call was to Hayden's boss, the director general of the B.C. division of CSIS, threatening to expose their local activities due to the unprofessional activities of Hayden Jones, who she accused of manipulating both her and her executive assistant, two vulnerable, professional women. Both she and her assistant would be willing to drop this very personal matter, however, provided CSIS ended their current misguided investigation into suspected money laundering in her province and dismissed Jones from his employment. After listening without interruption until she was finished, the DG promised to revert to her within a week.

Despite her bluster, it was several sleepless nights later before Dana received the DG's response. Obviously unwilling to risk the political repercussions of an ugly sexual harassment claim from the premier of British Columbia, the e-mail was terse and to the point. Hayden Jones's employment as a CSIS investigations officer had been terminated and no one new had been assigned to continue the work Jones had been doing in British Columbia. The DG assumed Dana would honour her proposed agreement, and accordingly, there would be no direct CSIS response to Ms. Rachel Burton's e-mail.

Dana couldn't help but smile; the DG obviously knew when to retreat and live to fight another day.

CHAPTER 81

Rachel

After clearing out her things from Hayden's apartment and returning to her own now seemingly sterile environment, Rachel was already regretting her impulsive move. As far back as she could remember, all her relationships seemed to end similarly. Why, she wondered, was it that all her boyfriends seemed intent on having affairs and letting her down?

Still seething about Hayden's affair with the premier, she had not contacted him, nor, she decided, would she be available if he called. Not for a while anyway. Despite her actions she knew she loved him, she just needed time to settle down. If he was still interested when she was ready, then they'd talk. Maybe they'd be able to clear the air—just maybe. Whatever the outcome, she was through being taken for granted. Her mind clear and her confidence restored, Rachel willingly signed the confidentiality notice that accompanied the termination notice and severance package from the premier's office. That done, she went online and scanned the well-stocked inventory of available government administrative jobs. Twelve months of double income would go a long way to easing her emotional pain.

A short time later, Rachel's application for what appeared to be a really interesting position with the BC Gaming Policy and Enforcement

Branch was on its way. The group regulated all gambling in the province—including lotteries and the casinos. Now that looked like fun.

EPILOGUE

Hayden et al

Eight months had passed since Rachel's impulsive e-mail and the ensuing fallout. Alone in his Ottawa home, Hayden looked at the charts and Post-it notes plastered all over his living room walls; the place looked like a war room. *One of the unadvertised detractions of working from home,* he thought.

The innocuous e-mail he had sent was still open on his laptop, nothing in its one brief sentence giving the slightest hint of the voluminous and detailed investigation report attached. *Perhaps you may find the attached report of interest* was all it said. Even less obvious was the list of national media outlets that had received simultaneous copies. Blind copied on the report too was the investigations arm of the Canada Revenue Agency. Hayden had sent it late the previous Friday afternoon. Today was Monday, and so far nothing had happened.

Carefully crafted, the report, written under the byline *Investigative Journalist A. E. Moss*, contained everything he knew, and in some cases speculated, about the Mohles' disappearance and their possible, inadvertent or otherwise, connection to illegal Chinese money laundering operations in British Columbia. He had gone to great pains to disguise his identity, even using an e-mail server secured through a convoluted re-routing system. A system he was assured would hide it from even the most sophisticated of hackers. And, a few items, like his own relationships with Dana Holmes and Rachel Burton were, of necessity, absent.

He wondered what had become of Rachel? She had made no effort to contact him since her abrupt departure, and despite periodic calls and messages to her mobile for several weeks after he left the premier's office, he had not reached her and had no idea where she had gone or what had happened to her. He really missed her. She was the first woman he'd felt about this way. *I should search the online government directories,* he thought. *Maybe I'll find her there. I can't believe how badly I screwed things up.*

Dana was another matter entirely. Visible almost daily in one media outlet or another, she was running at full steam for re-election, a fight it appeared she would win with ease.

#

Unbeknownst to Hayden, the intended repercussions from his report had started the same Friday evening it was sent. Starved for substantive local news and fearing their competition had probably received the same information, dozens of reporters worked independently and tirelessly over most of the weekend confirming information and questioning their own sources. This in turn prompted an unusual flurry of activity at the highest levels within a variety of federal and provincial government departments. Several police services were also subjected to a similar barrage of enquiries with senior officers forced to revisit files and request updates to ensure they were on top of matters before the next question arrived from the hungry press. By the Monday, not only was it clear that the Moss report was not from some offbeat conspiracy theorist, but was well researched and, in many instances, easily confirmed. The journalists' own articles and news reports started flowing early that same Monday morning and, by evening, had become a flood.

#

While neither Dana Holmes nor Hugh Ruff were mentioned by name, there was enough innuendo in the various articles to seriously derail Dana's carefully orchestrated squeaky-clean re-election plans. From an initially perceived sure winner, her party suddenly found itself fighting for its political life. As one pundit put it, "it was no more than that arrogant bunch deserved".

#

Damian Slater read the news with interest. He knew that in the financial world, there was rarely smoke without fire. The reporters had done their work well and obviously had a credible inside source. Once again back working as an investment banker, thanks to Michael Burt and his partners, Damian decided to do some digging of his own. Maybe one of his clients would like to take a run at a hostile takeover of Woodstock Marine. *It might be fun to be re-instated as chairman,* he thought smiling, *and then fire the whole damned board.*

#

Although the RCMP had earlier identified Willy Sands's red Camaro as the vehicle in the container terminal video footage and questioned him at length, he was not in custody. Despite the circumstantial evidence, Sands had both reason to be in the container terminal and no connection with Vivian. A thorough inspection of his car also provided no information other than, as evidenced by its spotless condition, he was obviously a muscle-car enthusiast. Despite a string of juvenile convictions for petty crimes and one minor drug conviction as an adult, his protestation that he had neither seen Vivian nor had any knowledge of her whereabouts was finally accepted, and he had been released without charge—a matter of great relief at the time to both him and the Evans twins.

It was Willy's exotic Camaro, however, that would ultimately prove to be his undoing. After reading Hayden's detailed report and conducting his own further investigation, an enterprising TV journalist obtained a copy of the surveillance video of the last known sighting of Vivian Mohle. As in the original, and clearly identified, was Willy Sands's car leaving the container terminal.

On seeing the video on TV for the first time, a Deltaport container yard supervisor, on vacation at the time of the initial police enquiry, called the RCMP with an anonymous report. No private cars were allowed in that particular area of the terminal, and he wondered whether the RCMP were aware of that fact. After confirming from their earlier investigation reports that this information was not known at the time, Willy was again picked-up for questioning by the RCMP.

The same TV broadcast was also seen by an elderly neighbour of John and Bobbie Ng. "That's it," she said to her husband. "That's the same car I saw going to the Ng's house when he was at work. I'm telling you she was having an affair."

"Isn't that what you already told the Vancouver police?"

"Yes, but I couldn't describe the car, except to say it was red and sort of low and ugly. You know I know nothing about cars."

"Well, how do you know it's the same car? There's no colour in the picture."

"I don't, but it's the same kind of car. I'm going to call and tell them."

"They'll probably laugh at you. It's been months. They'll think you're just being nosey."

"I don't care. I'm going to call anyway. They haven't announced anything, and I'd like to know what's going on in our neighbourhood."

#

Inspector Jack Bowie received a call from the Vancouver police about the probable sighting of Willy Sands's car at the home where Vivian Mohle's remains were found within minutes of it being reported. His call to Kate Harrington, made immediately thereafter, interrupted her questioning of Willy Sands about the location of his car in the Deltaport terminal and the anonymous supervisor's comments, only this time in the presence of his lawyer, Oscar Bott.

"I'm telling you, I don't care what some asshole non-union supervisor thinks the rules are," Willy said in answer to Kate's question. "I often park my car there rather than in the main lot where it could get scratched up by all the macho trucks the employees drive. Ask anyone."

"Don't worry; we will," Kate replied, looking down at her mobile as it vibrated on the table.

"Sorry," she said to the lawyer, "I have to take this. It's my boss."

Kate listened for a while and then turning back to Willy commenced reading him his rights before arresting him on suspicion of involvement into the disappearance and murder of Vivian Mohle.

The last thing Willy did before being handcuffed and led away to a nearby holding cell was to lean over and whisper in his lawyer's ear.

#

"All done?" Jack Bowie asked as Kate entered his office.

"Yes. He's going to have a hard time wriggling out of this. I know it's mostly circumstantial at this point, but he shouldn't be too tough a nut to crack."

"What about the other truck in the picture? Did we look into that?"

"It was a routine delivery. We didn't look beyond that."

"Check into it further, will you. I'm concerned that we've become so focused on Vivian Mohle and this car that we've missed something about the husband. Let's find out who owned that truck and what they were delivering. If it's clean, fine, then just another loose end put to bed."

#

Despite the distance, Neil Mohle stayed reasonably up to date as things unfolded. Identifying Vivian's last known location had been risky, but hopefully, no one would look into a routine container delivery, and even if they did, the container leaving that morning went to the Bahamas.

Then, assuming they even got that far, there would be no evidence of him in either location.

The thirty thousand dollars in his Bermuda bank account might distract them if they ever found it, but as far as he was aware, Andre had never touched it and there was nothing suspicious to lead anyone back to South Africa. As long as he kept his head down and stayed under the radar, he should be safe. After all, who would think of looking in Stellenbosch for a missing Canadian banker?

#

"That must be you they're talking about that the banker was going to meet," Garrett said, pointing to the TV screen. "You're a tall blond man."

"So are you, idiot," Griffin replied as both men burst out laughing.

"Think they'll connect us?" Garrett asked.

"Hell no. Why would they?"

Before Griffin could reply, the doorbell rang. Pausing mid-conversation, he walked over and opened the door to reveal a slightly-built man in his mid-forties.

"Hello, Garrett," the man said.

"Hi, Oscar," Garett said. "What are you doing here?"

"I'm acting for Willy Sands. He's asked me to deliver a message. May I come in?"

#

Two days after his arrest, Willy Sands failed to emerge from his cell at the morning call. On checking, corrections officers found him still in bed, the sliver of glass with which he had cut his wrist still clenched firmly in the other hand. Apparently, neither of the bikers in the two adjoining cells heard any disturbance during the night.

#

Drew Jamieson didn't know Willy Sands and yet his death proved to be the catalyst for the termination of Drew's undercover career. Smiling for the first time in days after the Mohle story first broke, Vegas announced over pancakes at their nearby morning breakfast stop that Willy Sands was dead. Fortuitously, according to Vegas, his death also severed any connection between Willy, the Evans twins and ultimately himself.

Feigning having forgotten something important, Drew returned to the house where he quickly packed a few personal items before heading directly to the ferry terminal where he took the next available vessel to Horseshoe Bay and thereafter continued his journey to RCMP headquarters in Surrey. Leaving his motorcycle and leather protective gear in the police parking lot, he entered the building where he identified himself to the constable on duty as an RCMP undercover officer.

"Enough," was all he said as he finally sat down in front of his immediate supervisor. "I'll give you what I have, but that's it. Reassign me or I'll resign, whichever you prefer. It's been too long, I have enough to start bringing the house down, but I'm done. It's not the violence—I can handle that. It's their casual indifference to killing and death. Those callous bastards are over the edge."

Leaving the building a few hours later, dressed in only jeans and a shirt, Drew walked directly to a nearby barber where after a quick brush cut and shave, he emerged barely recognizable to anyone who knew him before.

#

Insulated to a degree from the initial media blitz, but not from the ensuing attention, were James Lee and P.K. Chin—attention that started later that same week.

"Why?" P.K. Chin asked.

Monger Capital's chief financial officer looked at Chin with some surprise. "It's quite a general enquiry," he replied. "I don't imagine there's anything specific the Canada Revenue Agency are looking for. They probably won't be here very long."

"Good, keep me informed."

"There is one unusual thing, though."

"What's that?"

"They have asked for a large room in which to work. Apparently they will be bringing six auditors."

#

"A courier brought two letters this morning." Kitty's voice echoed from the speakerphone on James Lee's desk.

"What's so important that it couldn't wait?" James asked. Kitty knew his new role as president of Woodstock Marine kept him busy. Surely, she could handle a couple of letters.

"I opened them. They're from the Canada Revenue Agency; we're both being audited. Apparently, they also have questions regarding our trust company."

"Shit," James replied. "I'd better talk to your father. We probably need to have legal counsel. When do they want to see our records?"

"Tomorrow."

"Okay, I'd better go. It's busy here."

"Wait, there's more. Have you seen the news?"

"No, I've been here since six this morning. We're trying to wrap up this deal."

"There's a whole report on TV about the Mohles' disappearance and how Vivian's husband was working on the Woodstock LNG deal. It mentions Monger Capital and some speculation that the 'elusive billionaire Quon Jin Hu' might have an interest in the business. It even says he is rumoured to have family in the city. Where did they get this?" Kitty asked, her quiet sobs now evident over the telephone line.

"No idea, but stay where you are. I'm on my way home, and we can call your father together. This is family business now."

#

Quon Jin Hu didn't need James to call him to let him know what was happening in Canada. P.K. Chin spoke to Dong Lai immediately after hearing of the CRA's planned audit of Monger Capital, and his summary of the day's newscast followed a short time later.

Dong wasted no time in alerting Quon, whose legal and financial teams immediately put plans in place to divert ongoing illegal cash flows through several Vancouver casino holding companies in which Quon was an unidentified silent partner. For the immediate future, Monger would continue its legal operations before ultimately being closed down or sold. Quon had no interest in a legitimate offshore business that did not also serve his illegal empire in some form or another.

When Quon eventually heard from James and Kitty, his advice was simple: *do and say nothing out of the ordinary.* He would provide them with the names of a local lawyer and an accountant who would take over the supervision of all tax enquiries and control the distribution of any information that might be required. What other future actions might be necessary would depend largely on the diligence of the government audit team. If matters unfolded as they had done in several other countries in the past, his team would find ways to tie up the process for years, by which time the evidence of any possible wrongdoing would have disappeared.

"Things," he assured them, "were not likely to get any worse."

#

Sergeant Kate Harrington looked at the e-mail for a second time. Despite its brevity, she had no reason to disbelieve the contents; after all, everything Hayden Jones he had told her so far had turned out to be accurate. *Where had he got this little gem?* she wondered and read it again.

> Hi Kate: This address is untraceable so don't bother trying to track it or reply. My source says that the call to Vivian Mohle, which caused her and Neil Mohle to run, came

from Kitty Lee. Kitty's husband is James Lee of Woodstock Marine. Over to you. Regards, Hayden

Interesting, she thought, *the same names keep coming up time after time.* Not always connected, but always on the periphery. It was time to pay a visit to Kitty Lee.

#

Vegas Kolnick, Scrubber Barker and the Evans twins were all arrested on a variety of suspected crimes the day after Drew Jamieson's report. Despite the best efforts of Oscar Bott, all were held without bail. Notwithstanding their suspicions given Drew's absence, it would be months before they were able to confirm the identity of the informant whose testimony had led to their arrests. By then, though, Drew had once again disappeared under an entirely new identity, his evidence recorded and filmed for posterity.

Among the assets seized from the four men as having been purchased with proceeds of their criminal activities was "the Outpost", the house on Airlie Road. Shortly after its seizure, it was found to have been rented by Larry Barker and reluctantly returned by the RCMP to its numbered company owner, whose registered address was the legal office of Oscar Bott. It's subsequent sale at several times its original purchase price provided adequate funds for the group's long and expensive legal defense.

#

"Well, Jones, what do you think? It looks like this role as an investigative journalist suits you. Want to stay undercover a while longer? There's something fishy about the enforcement of the B.C. gambling regulations, and there are some casinos I'd like you to look into. There are also thirty-nine other possible leads in that box from Neil Mohle."

"Sounds good to me. Did you hear from the B.C. premier? She has to guess I'm behind this."

"Not yet, but I imagine I will at some point."

"What will you say?" Hayden asked.

"Probably suggest that she read my e-mail more carefully. She read what she wanted to believe," the director general replied.

"She won't be happy."

"Nope, I guess not. You know that old adage about never getting into a pissing match with a skunk?"

"Sure—the skunk likes it and you get wet."

The DG smiled and held out her hand. "Nice to meet you," she said. "My name's Skunk."

THE END

About the Author

The author has lived in Bermuda, Canada, and South Africa while enjoying a global career as a banker and corporate executive. An enthusiastic sailor, scuba diver and occasional art collector, B.R. Bentley draws on the experiences from his travels, business career and recreational pursuits to facilitate his writing. *The Banker's Box* is his third novel and is set on the coast of British Columbia, Canada where he now lives with his wife and several family pets.

CPSIA information can be obtained
at www.ICGtesting.com
Printed in the USA
LVHW090959160719
624261LV00001B/24/P

9 781525 548604